Also by Christine Husom

from Indigo Sea Press

Buried in Wolf Lake
Second in the Winnebago County Mystery Series, 2009

An Altar by the River
Third in the Winnebago County Mystery Series, 2010

The Noding Field Mystery
Fourth in the Winnebago County Mystery Series, 2012

A Death in Lionel's Woods
Fifth in the Winnebago County Mystery Series, 2013

indigoseapress.com

Murder In Winnebago County

First in the Winnebago County Mystery Series

Christine Husom

Stiletto Books
Published by Indigo Sea Press
Winston-Salem

Stiletto Books
Indigo Sea Press
302 Ricks Drive
Winston-Salem, NC 27103

First Stiletto Books edition published
December, 2015
Dagger Books, Moon Sailor and all production design are
trademarks of Indigo Sea Press, used under license.

For information regarding bulk purchases of this book, digital
purchase and special discounts, please contact the publisher at
indigoseapress.com

Cover design by Richard Haskin

Manufactured in the United States of America
ISBN 978-1-63066-229-5

Acknowledgments

A very heartfelt thank you to my family and friends for continued love, guidance and support. I am very blessed.

Dedication

Written for my father, Judge Carroll E. Larson, with love.

Prologue

Alvie's need to watch was unexpected and gripped her middle with an intensity that pushed the air right out of her lungs. A middle-aged woman guided Judge Nels Fenneman to a chair at the hospital admitting desk. Alvie forgot about leaving, forgot why she was there in the first place, and dropped onto a burgundy, faux-leather seat in the adjoining waiting room. She shifted so she had a clear view of the judge between the spiky fronds of a silk plant.

The booming voice the judge had used to command the courtroom was gone, replaced by hushed murmurs as he quietly answered the necessary questions. Alvie strained to hear, but his words didn't travel the distance to her ears. Judge Fenneman's wrinkled face was flushed, harsh under the fluorescent lighting, his color deepening to a purplish-crimson with each coughing spasm that interrupted most of his answers.

Alvie had spent much of the past ten years consumed with thoughts of the man. Fenneman was one of the people responsible for her son's death. When Alvie wasn't actively despising him, her hatred seethed just beneath the surface of her consciousness—a living, growing thing with fingers that gripped her throat in the dark of night and lit fires in her head and chest.

The cycle had been the same for years: obsess about what the judge and others had done to Nolan, push it away for a while, obsess, push away, obsess.

The woman with the judge looked vaguely familiar. Alvie studied her a moment and was hit with the realization she was a younger, prettier version of Fenneman. The woman must be his daughter. She had to be. Fenneman was not only still alive, but

1

part of a family. Alvie had never thought of Judge Fenneman as a person before—not really. He was the monster who sat on his elevated bench and ruined people's lives.

Her world had collapsed ten years before when her son died in prison, and no one cared. Had the judge even given it a second thought? She sincerely doubted it. So much for justice.

The judge's daughter wrapped her arm around his shoulders and squeezed gently. Alvie felt ill. Her son would not be there to offer his comforting touch when she was old and sick. The one redemption, the thing that gave her purpose for going on, was the granddaughter Nolan had left for her. Rebecca was Alvie's own little love.

A small brunette nurse approached the admitting desk and assisted the judge into a wheelchair, fussing over him and gently patting his shoulders. She cheerfully told him they would send him home in a few days, as good as new. Alvie grabbed a magazine and bent to hide her face as the trio headed toward her. When they passed, she rose and watched them turn into B-Wing. Her granddaughter had a room on the same wing.

Alvie left the hospital quietly, as usual. The mere thought of making small talk and smiling at strangers made her squeamish. At five foot nine, size eighteen, she was a fairly large woman who favored brown or black clothing, even in the heat of summer. Her dull, steel-colored hair, lifeless eyes the same shade, and flat features—devoid of expression—rarely warranted a second look. Alvie moved through life mostly unnoticed. It was her choice and suited her just fine.

She needed a breath of fresh air to fill her depleted lungs, but had to make do with hot and muggy instead. Her clothes clung to her, heavy with perspiration, by the time she reached her car. Days like that, when humidity hung in the air like fog, Alvie longed for the crisp, dry cold of a Minnesota winter day. She cranked the air conditioning to full blast in her ten-year-old, blue Chevy Impala and headed down the curving drive to the main road. It was after nine o'clock—later than she had planned to stay.

Dusk was settling, and as the streetlight came on, Alvie's gaze was drawn to its reflection spanning across the water of a pond. Funny, she had never even noticed the large drainage area before. Alvie immediately knew there was a reason she had seen the pond that night. She had visited her granddaughter once or twice a day for a week and had not spotted the pond, not once. Until now.

The five miles to her home south of town passed in a blur. Alvie locked herself in and let out a small yelp. She paced and paced, excitement mounting with each step. Ideas bounced to a staccato rhythm in her brain as her heart pounded out its own beat. She walked back and forth late into the night. Eventually, she won control of her thoughts and gathered them into a neat little plan that had logical meaning.

Perhaps the judge would not be going home after all.
Ever.

Chapter 1

I sat back in the black office swivel chair, stretched my arms and legs as far as possible, and glanced around the Spartan room. Cartoons and jokes tacked on the bulletin board offered insights into the personalities of the people I worked with. Most of the cartoons were sick, the sicker the better. How long had some of them been up there, and how many times had I read them? One night shifter posted a joke of the day, and the day's little ditty was, 'What do you get when you cross a parrot with a centipede? A walkie-talkie, of course.' One I could tell my Gramps.

A long row of file-size dividers held every blank form a deputy needed and then some, and took up half the length of one wall. The rest of the wall was dedicated to cubbyhole mail-boxes, one for every employee in the sheriff's department. Mine was in the far left corner, second one down.

A custodian would appear sometime during the night to empty the overflowing wastebaskets by the four computer terminals, collect the abandoned styrofoam coffee cups, and vacuum up the bits and pieces that had settled on the earth-tone commercial carpet.

I smiled at the hands of the standard clock hanging high on the no-color squad room wall. Ten-thirty-five p.m. Only twenty-five minutes to go to the end of my shift. Every other deputy on the evening shift was either patrolling the county or on an assigned call, so I had the room to myself: a nice change.

The night shifters would start rolling in any minute.

It had been a long stretch, working seven evenings in a row. Murphy's Law usually made me put in at least two hours overtime on my last night, trying to play catch up, so I was glad I had finished all my reports and would be done on time for once. My mind left the white walls, laminate-topped tables, and dusty computers, and drifted to plans of how to spend my three days off.

"Winnebago County to Six-oh-eight." The voice on my communication radio brought me back to the sheriff's department.

"Six-oh-eight, County, go ahead," I answered.

"We have a report of an elderly man missing from Oak Lea Memorial Hospital. They are requesting assistance," dispatcher Robin explained.

"Ten-four." I quickly stuffed my copies of the reports in my briefcase and hustled to the sheriff's communication control room, commonly referred to as the "cockpit."

If I was ever assigned duty in the cockpit, I would be in big trouble. The radio panels looked like they belonged in a high tech aircraft. I was in awe that the communication officers kept all the buttons, lights, phones and computer screens separate. The officers wore headsets, so unless they were talking, it wasn't immediately obvious if they were on the radio or telephone. I had learned to wait until I was acknowledged before speaking. Robin's fingers were flying at high speed across her computer keyboard, listing all pertinent data on a complaint.

Jerry, a longtime employee and seasoned for any emergency, was talking into the mouthpiece on his headset to a woman who had found her husband on the bathroom floor, unconscious and not breathing. Jerry had an ambulance en route and was calmly, slowly reading from his manual, step by step of what she should do to initiate cardio-pulmonary resuscitation, or CPR. He adjusted the earphones away from his head for necessary comfort, and I heard the distressed woman's voice all the way across the room squealing into the phone. When the ambulance arrived, Jerry was able to leave the poor woman in their capable hands and exhaled a relieved, audible burst of air.

I walked around to the front of the panel and plopped my elbow on the counter. Jerry and Robin looked at me simultaneously, mildly surprised I had entered their closed communications domain. Sheriff's personnel usually stay clear of the cockpit—it was often too busy a place to socialize.

"An elderly patient lost in the hospital and they called nine-one-one for that? They can't be that short staffed?" I said, sounding obviously crabby about the assignment.

Robin shrugged, her bony shoulders touching her jaw. "No clue, but the nurse that phoned sounded pretty frantic, Corky." She continued typing.

I glanced at my watch. "Can you assign it to Brad? He'll be ten-eight any time now." Sergeant Brad Hughes was my area replacement for the night shift.

Jerry looked at his computer screen and shook his head. "We've got another call pending for him. In fact, two, if you count the barking dog complaint." Every officer's favorite call. Suddenly a trip to the hospital didn't seem so bad—I'd take missing patient over barking dog any day.

Momentarily mesmerized by the blinking buttons on the cockpit panel, I sighed in resignation. "Any particulars on the hospital call?"

"Only that Judge Fenneman wasn't in his room on the ten-thirty round and they've been turning the place upside down looking for him for the last fifteen minutes. Maybe they think we're better at finding people than they are," Robin said with another shrug.

"Okay. Put me en route to Oak Lea Memorial." I half-smiled a goodbye, and they both nodded at me in response.

When I reached the south corridor of the sheriff's department in the Winnebago County Courthouse, I saw rain was still pelting the glass doors. We had gotten over four inches the past week, way above average for the month of July.

The courthouse complex overlooked Bison Lake in the city of

Oak Lea, the seat of Winnebago County in central Minnesota. My ancestors had settled there when the town was little more than a trading post cut out of the Big Woods in the mid-1800s. The last census had listed Oak Lea with a population of 10,502, but four years later, it was closer to 14,000. "Getting kinda crowded for us old timers," my Grandpa Brandt had told me, sitting in his house in the middle of his 1,600 acres three miles west of town.

Picturesque downtown Oak Lea was tucked into rolling green hills on the banks of Bison Lake, which was used for fishing and any water recreation you could name. There were three other lakes within city limits, and every night was a magnified light show when the muted pink tones of the street lamps and the hundred variations of white, blue, green, red, amber, and other colored lights glowed from homes and shops, throwing reflections on the lakes.

As businesses in Oak Lea expanded and moved from downtown to along the state highway, the old brick and stucco buildings of the eight main blocks in the city proper had filled with delis, antique shops, and professional services—pieces of the past recreated for use in the future.

Winnebago County, located forty miles northwest of Minneapolis, was a pleasant mix of small towns, rolling farmland, lakes, and parks. The population of 82,403 spanned every age and economic group. Although predominately divided between German and Scandinavian, most ethnic backgrounds were represented by at least one family. Catholic and Lutheran congregations were the largest, followed by Covenant, Methodist, Presbyterian, Evangelical Free, and Baptist.

In my six years of patrolling Winnebago County roads, I had become thoroughly familiar with the acres of pastures, the fields of corn, wheat, alfalfa, oats, and soybeans. There were two rivers, three hundred lakes, numerous creeks, ponds, marshes, bridges, and seven county parks. I could drive most county roads and list from memory the names on the mailboxes. If I was bored, I even worked to memorize their fire numbers.

I jogged to my squad car, jotted the time in my log book, and drove the two miles to the hospital. With any luck, by the time I got there, the nurses would be tucking the good judge back in bed. I could radio county that no report was needed and be at home in time to catch the last fifteen minutes of "Eric Clapton Unplugged" on MTV. Murphy's Law deserved to be broken.

Oak Lea Memorial Hospital sprawled both inside and outside the city limits, so law enforcement service was shared by the Oak Lea Police Department and the Winnebago County Sheriff's Department. Calls for assistance were assigned to whichever department was available, and jurisdiction was considered equal.

As I steered my squad car along the hospital drive, I noticed a group of people huddled together at the bottom of a hill about one hundred yards from the south side of the hospital. They were standing at the edge of a drainage collection pool. I guessed they were hospital personnel, but it was difficult to see much in the black of night through the rain.

I radioed communications I was "ten-six," slipped on my rain gear, and grabbed my umbrella. I was about to close the car door, but instead I reached in to grab the thirty-five millimeter camera in case my instincts were correct.

Quiet pandemonium was the best way to describe the scene by the pond. People were moving, but no one uttered a word. Like a colony of ants, intent, knowing what to do without being told.

A nearby street lamp was an angel's halo glowing inside the rain, offering little light. Scanning the group, I counted three women in medical scrubs; Dr. Nordstrom, whom I recognized from the emergency room; and another man in jeans and a rain slicker. One of the nurses and the street-clothes guy were shining flashlights onto a figure on the ground. I pulled the magnum light from my duty belt and directed it to the ground for better illumination.

An elderly man stared up at heaven, seeing nothing.

"The judge?" I asked. I hadn't seen Judge Fenneman for several years and didn't immediately recognize him in that condition. The group looked at me collectively. Two of the nurses were crying and the third was shaking almost uncontrollably. Everyone was a muddy mess, especially the poor judge, who had presumably been pulled, lifeless, from the mucky water.

Doc Nordstrom's solemn, dripping-wet face nodded at me.

"Anyone know what happened?" I asked.

I opened my large umbrella and handed it to one of the nurses. The three of them gathered under it in a group hug.

"He wasn't in his bed—he must have ripped out his IV and gotten out the back emergency exit door in B-Wing . . . I suppose he got locked out, and probably couldn't find his way in the rain, and ended up going down the hill. . . . We found him . . . floating . . . face down in the water." The small brunette was the one to speak.

I flashed the water, my light dancing between raindrops across the surface. "How deep is it?"

"Umm." The brunette touched the top of her thigh. "Maybe two and a half, three feet."

"Okay. Let me take some photos, and we'll talk more inside. If you could hold the umbrella over me," I directed the brunette nurse. "Doc, will you hold my light?"

Water had collected in the natural low land, covering an area of perhaps ten feet by twenty feet. Normally half that size, the pond had swelled with all the recent rain. Cattails lined the opposite side. Where we stood, the grass of the hospital lawn disappeared into the water.

We moved as one while I snapped pictures of the corpse, the pond, and the mess of footprints along the edge. Any prints on the wet grass of the hospital grounds had been erased by the downpour. The judge's bare footprints could never be separated from what had become a mass stomping ground in the mud around the pond. So much for preservation of the scene.

As I took the last photo, I caught sight of a large male bulk barreling toward us. Behind him were two paramedics carrying a stretcher. I tried to stretch my five-foot-five-inch height as The Bulk looked down at me from his at least six-foot-four-inch vantage point.

I often admired how easily, almost gracefully, the man carried his three hundred pounds, but also wondered why he didn't take the time to comb his short gray curls or smooth his rumpled clothes. Whether in uniform or not, his disheveled appearance left the impression he didn't care, and I knew that wasn't true. I spotted brown polyester pants where his yellow rain slicker ended just short of his knees. Fashion and preening were not on his list of priorities—not even close.

"Chief Becker, what are you doing here at this time of night?" I asked the head of the Oak Lea Police Department.

"This is my town." He gave me the predictable response he used for just about any professional question he was asked. Not that he needed to remind me. Oak Lea had been *his* town as long as I could remember.

Police Chief Bud Becker was never off duty. He spoke warmly of his family, but being in charge of Oak Lea's finest was clearly the essence of his life. He spent evenings at home listening to his police scanner, not turning it off even when he went to bed. He said routine calls were "white noise" to help him sleep. I wondered if his wife felt the same way.

"I heard the call and phoned the hospital," Chief Becker explained after all. "Got here as the paramedics were on their way down to the pond here."

Becker knelt beside the body and moved his flashlight around, then stood and shook his head at the stomped down mess of footprints around the pond. "Who found him?" he asked the group.

"We did," the middle-aged blonde told him. "Penny pulled

him out." She nodded at the nurse who was shaking so badly.

I probably had the least medical training of anyone in the group, but even I could see Penny was going into shock.

"Sir, perhaps we can move our investigation inside," I suggested to Becker. "These nurses need to get out of the rain."

"Oh . . . right." Chief Becker sounded distracted and shoved his hands in his pockets. "You got pictures?" he asked me.

"Yes, plenty." I patted the camera to be sure it still hung at my side.

The group trucked up the slippery wet, grassy hill. The wind was whipping, and the umbrella did little to protect the three nurses. Doc and I followed with the paramedics and the stretcher carrying the judge. We made a loop around the three blue spruce pine sentinels, standing straight and tall, guarding the main entrance of the building.

You let your guard down tonight, old boys.

Stepping inside, I blinked against the assault of light. I stopped to wipe my boots and drip on the entrance mat for a minute. I sided over to Becker as the paramedics and doctor disappeared around the corner.

The jeans and slicker guy was speaking quietly to the drenched nurses. A passerby could easily mistake them for victims of a capsized boating accident. The man turned to the chief and me, shook Becker's hand, then reached for mine.

"I know Chief Becker, but I've not met you." He was not quite as tall as Becker, maybe an even six feet. His hand caught mine, gripping firmly, while his eyes, dark and stormy as the rainy night, probed mine, telling me he was a force to be reckoned with: a heavy hitter.

"I'm Sergeant Aleckson," I announced, straightening my spine and refusing to blink first.

He looked at the badge on my raincoat. "And what does the 'C' stand for?"

"Corky, er, Corinne."

"Sergeant Corinne Aleckson, I hardly know what to say. This is extremely unfortunate. We've never had a tragedy quite like this here before, but I'm sure we'll get to the bottom of it. I've instructed the nurses to get into some dry scrubs from surgery. They'll be out shortly to talk with you." He let go of my hand, but stayed close to Becker and me.

"And you are?" I asked, blinking a raindrop from my eye.

He raised his hands slightly. "Excuse me. Nicholas Bradshaw, administrator of Oak Lea Memorial."

Oh yes, a heavy hitter. He probably was in bed when the hospital called and pulled on the first thing he found with legs. That explained the jeans.

I nodded and turned to Becker. "Chief, I'm going to phone this in. I don't want to put it over the air so everyone in the county with a police scanner will know what's happened." I escaped a few feet away and pulled out my cell phone.

"Good thinking, Serge."

"Are you going to call Detective Garvey?" I asked. Garvey was the investigator for the Oak Lea Police Department.

Chief Becker ran the cuff of his sleeve around his wet head, messing his hair even more. "No. You took the call. You can handle it."

"Okay. Give me a minute, then we'll start at the patient's room and take it from there," I said while digesting that the chief trusted me with an investigation in *his* town.

"Right."

I reached Jerry in communications, a little surprised he was still working. It was eleven-twenty and his shift ended at eleven, the same time mine was supposed to.

"What's the good word, Corky?" he asked.

"I wish there was one. I didn't want this over the air . . . Judge Fenneman was found drowned in the drainage pond near the hospital."

"My God! The judge killed himself?" Jerry blurted out, and

the first one to ask the question.

"We don't know yet. I'll be interviewing hospital staff and see what we come up with."

"Oh, man. Well, I'll call the sheriff," Jerry said.

"Per policy for unnatural deaths," I agreed.

"Plus, he and the judge were golfing buds."

"Really?" I had been on nights for years before recently going on the evening shift, and I didn't pay much attention to the daytime scuttlebutt. "Thanks, Jerry."

"Good luck Corky."

I'm going to need it, I thought as I made my way back to the police chief and hospital administrator. As I rounded the corner from the lobby, I saw Administrator Bradshaw talking to the three nurses, now clad in dry, turquoise surgical scrubs. The one about my age with the brown ponytail had stopped shaking, but was still visibly distressed. They all were. I overheard Bradshaw instructing them to answer my questions with facts only and not to offer any information or opinions.

My blood immediately hit the boiling point. "Excuse me, Mister Bradshaw, have a minute?" I walked into the nearby staff lounge and waited with my hands crossed over my chest for Bradshaw to join me.

"I can't believe what I just heard. You are interfering with this investigation. Are you attempting to cover something to protect this hospital?" My voice was a stage whisper.

Bradshaw didn't have the courtesy to look contrite. "What are you talking about?"

"Telling the nurses what to say and what not to say," I spit out.

"I did no such thing. I simply told them to stick to the facts. We need to get to the bottom of this and not have everyone speculating about what they think happened," he calmly assured me.

I glared at him. "Are you a lawyer?"

Bradshaw shook his head. "I'm just using common sense."

"Well, keep your common sense to yourself and let me do my job. I am hoping, through questioning, that someone here can provide answers to what may have happened tonight. Just let me do my job," I repeated.

I remembered my rain gear, pulled off my jacket and hat, and hung them on a nearby coat rack. When I turned I caught Bradshaw scrutinizing my body, his expression unreadable. When I was in uniform, I was an officer of the law. But at that moment, Bradshaw was looking at me as a woman, and I found that both irritating and disconcerting. Ugh!

"Please show me Judge Fenneman's room," I said.

He cleared his throat. "Of course."

I doubted getting caught ogling me had embarrassed Bradshaw in the least. He led the way to B-Wing without another word. Chief Becker was waiting for us outside Room 120, where Judge Fenneman had spent his last day on earth.

I pulled out my camera as I scanned the room. Not much was out of place, except on the bed. The sheet and blanket were thrown back, and the IV needle and attached tubing were near the pillow at the head. The bedside stand stood at an angle from the bed, as though it had been pushed out of the way to allow the judge to get out of bed around the guardrail, which was still in the raised position. A significant number of blood drips had pooled on the floor and stained the linoleum where Fenneman had apparently pulled out his IV.

I snapped photos of the entire room, capturing frame after frame of the bed, the nightstand, and the blood, a harsh contrast to the beige floor. The small blood pool by the bed indicated the judge had stood there for a moment, then started walking, leaving one drop about every two feet to the room door.

I followed the drop pattern where it continued—more disguised on the multi-toned, gray corridor carpet—past the unoccupied nurses' desk to the emergency exit door. There were red smudges on the push bar, challenging the stark sterility and disrupting the expected order.

I turned to the group gathered behind me. The three nurses were still joined at the hip. We were on the south side of the hospital. The main entrance was on the west.

"Is this the door you exited?" I asked.

"Yes," the petite brunette spokesperson told me. "I noticed the blood on the door after I had finished checking room one twenty-three there." She averted her eyes to the patient room on the left. "We thought Judge Fenneman must be somewhere in the hospital. We never thought he would go outside, what with it raining cats and dogs. I called to Penny and Linda, and we went out there together."

"Who opened the door?" I asked.

"I think I did," Penny with the oatmeal ponytail answered, and the others nodded.

"I don't want anyone else to touch this push bar until I dust it for prints." Maybe there were a hundred smudged prints on the door, but Judge Fenneman's prints should be on top. I pulled a pen from my pocket and pushed, hard, on the bar to open the door. The most deafening blast sounded, and I nearly dropped my camera when my startled body reacted. I glanced at the second hand of my watch and counted as it cycled twice past the twelve.

After two full minutes of the most blaring alarm I had ever heard, it was finally silent. I turned back to the group. "Did anyone hear this alarm sound between the time the judge was last seen sleeping in his room and the discovery that he was missing?"

The three nurses all shook their heads.

"I'm guessing that given the size of this hospital, and the appalling volume of that alarm, that had it been tripped, someone should have heard it?" Everyone nodded.

"It's a new system, Sergeant—we had it installed about ten days ago. As far as we know, it has been working fine," Bradshaw said.

"We used the code when we went out and didn't even think of why we didn't hear the alarm if the judge went out this door." The small brunette again.

I pushed open the door with my foot. The overhead spotlight revealed more red drops on the cement landing outside the exit. The roof overhang had protected them from being washed away.

"Mr. Bradshaw, you can disarm the alarm?" I asked and he nodded. "I'll get my rain gear and walk down to the pond." I started for the staff room, but Bradshaw caught my arm.

"Sheila, will you gather the sergeant's rain gear from the break room? I'll punch in the code." Bradshaw brushed against me, reached above my head, and pressed a series of numbers to silence the alarm. "All set. You can open the door now without setting off the alarm."

The brunette nurse hurried away and returned a minute later with my outerwear. I donned the apparel and used the same method with the pen to open the door, careful not to damage any remaining prints. I left the group behind and snapped photos of the outside door. Once I left the protection of the overhang, there was no visible trail to follow, but I continued walking toward the pond. The hill from the hospital to the water was a steady decline and dropped probably ten feet. The footprints around the pond were rapidly becoming a washed together mess.

What had happened? I wondered as I made my way back up the hill to the emergency exit. Chief Becker followed my earlier example, using a pen to depress the push bar to let me back in. Housekeeping would have to deal with all the mud the next morning, but it seemed a small matter in the face of the night's tragedy. I stomped off my boots as best I could, then looked into the face of the Winnebago County Sheriff, Dennis Twardy.

His color was terrible, and I felt sad his professional and personal life had to cross like that.

"Sergeant Aleckson," he acknowledged me, "any ideas?"

"Not yet, sir."

The sheriff pinched the top of his nose between his eyes. "Has Clarice been called?"

"Who, sir?" I asked, wondering about protocol.

"Judge Fenneman's daughter."

Of course. I knew her as Mrs. Moy.

"We called her as soon as we found him, Sheriff. She is babysitting her grandchildren and had to find someone to come over before she could leave." Bradshaw again.

"For godsakes, we could have sent someone." The sheriff pounded his fist into his hand. He didn't look well. His normally ruddy complexion darkened to a burgundy tone, and I worried his blood pressure reading was soaring off the charts. Bradshaw rested a hand on the sheriff's shoulder.

Sheriff Twardy had enjoyed exceptional health until his wife's four-year bout with cancer. She had died about a year before. The sheriff was in his late fifties. His body looked fit, but his face bore deep, aging stress creases, and his hair had grayed. Twardy's secretary, a perpetual mother hen, kept a close watch on him, determined to prevent a premature stroke.

"Why don't we go to my office, or better yet, the boardroom?" Bradshaw offered. "Sergeant Aleckson can speak with my staff. Dr. Dahlgren has also been called and should be here any minute."

"Why Doctor Dahlgren?" I asked.

"He is . . . was . . . Judge Fenneman's primary care physician. Hopefully, he can help fill in the gaps." Bradshaw was doing my job better than I was.

As our increasingly large group headed for the boardroom, Paul Moore, the stocky, middle-aged star reporter for the local newspaper, scurried toward us. No one acknowledged him.

Moore pushed his geeky, oversized glasses closer to his eyes and singled out Becker. "Did you find him?"

"Who are you talking about, Moore?" Chief Becker asked.

"The missing patient, the old guy?" He pulled a pen from his breast pocket.

17

"Geez, Paul, you pick that up on your scanner? Must be a slow news week if you come running out here in the rain for that," Becker said in dismissal.

"Yeah, well, I wasn't going to, but I couldn't sleep, anyway, so I figured if they were sending an officer here, maybe something was up, so I thought I'd check it out." Paul sniffed his nose.

Chief Becker put his arm on Paul's shoulder and led him toward the main exit. Becker had several inches and over one hundred pounds on Moore, and looked like a father having a chat with his small son. I couldn't hear what he said, but figured it had to do with assuring Paul he would get the whole story when the time was right. It was common knowledge, even to me, that Becker and Moore had coffee together most mornings. Becker caught up to us as we entered the boardroom.

To say the room was nice would be a gross understatement. It had simple elegance. A long, cherry wood table occupied the majority of the space, while a dozen soft, buff-colored leather office chairs surrounded it. I took one of the side chairs and sank down. It swallowed me in softness and cush. My eyes swept the room, taking in the six-foot-tall ficus tree, the tasteful watercolors, the floor length vertical blinds covering the three windows. The corner lamps promised subdued lighting for more casual meetings.

"I'll brew a pot of coffee," Bradshaw said. "Go ahead, Officers, with your investigation."

I was weary and could not let myself get even a little comfortable. Everything seemed backward, off-kilter somehow. The surreal death scene, the unusual tragedy on such an unlikely spot as hospital property. I sat in a conference room surrounded by people who were shocked with disbelief, each one wishing the outcome could somehow be undone.

It was new territory for me—for all of us.

I pulled a small notepad from my back pocket and leaned forward. Desperation had snaked its way into the hearts and

18

showed on the faces of the people who felt responsible for what had happened on their watch.

Everyone—the sheriff, chief, and hospital personnel—were watching me intently, waiting for me to proceed.

I was the only one with a name badge. The nurses had apparently left them with their uniforms. "Let's begin by introducing ourselves. I'm Sergeant Corinne Aleckson, Winnebago County. This is Sheriff Dennis Twardy and Oak Lea Police Chief Bud Becker." Glances, nods and half-smiles were exchanged.

I looked at the petite brunette nurse. "Your name, please?"

"Oh sorry, um, Sheila Van Buren, RN." She subconsciously reached for the identification that wasn't there.

I nodded at the oatmeal ponytail who had finally stopped sobbing. "P-Penny Smith, RN." Her voice was shaky, and I gave her a small smile of encouragement before glancing at the dishwater blonde with the short perm.

"Linda Pedersen, RN." Her eyes were hazel cereal bowls that dominated her pale face.

"Is that Pedersen with a 'd'?" I asked as I jotted the names in my notebook.

"Yes. P-e-*d*-e-r-s-*e*-n," she clarified.

"Thank you." I noted the time. Midnight. Just. A little over an hour since I'd been dispatched there, and my work had barely begun. "I'm going to record this interview so I don't have to rely on my memory or scribbled notes. Please relax, as best you can, and give me an account of everything you remember about Judge Fenneman from, say, supper on." I set up the recorder Bradshaw had found for me.

Linda Pedersen was the nurse assigned to the judge for the three to eleven shift. Judge Fenneman had been admitted to the hospital for bacterial pneumonia two days previously. Responding well to antibiotics, he was alert and comfortable throughout the evening.

Fenneman requested a sleeping aid around eight p.m. Dr. Dahlgren ordered the medication, and it was administered at eight-thirty p.m. Nurse Pedersen last saw the judge in his room at nine-fifty p.m. He was in bed, listening to his radio with his eyes closed. She checked his vital signs and IV drip. Ever thoughtful, the judge had patted her hand and thanked her. When she checked again on her last round at ten-twenty, he was gone.

"Judge Fenneman's IV needle was apparently pulled out. Isn't there an alarm that goes off when that happens?" I asked, remembering my emergency medical training.

"Only if the flow of IV drip is interrupted," Nurse Sheila explained.

"And it wasn't?"

"No, it was left on the bed, still dripping."

"Ms. Pedersen, how did the judge's spirits seem to you tonight?" I inquired.

She nodded when she spoke. "Just fine, happy even. His daughter and her grandchildren, his great-grandchildren, visited for a while. He was really starting to rally and looking forward to going home so he could check on his garden and keep his usual Wednesday afternoon golf game." Pedersen sniffled and dabbed at her nose.

I glanced at the sheriff. He was glum, his jaw tight, eyes fixed on his hands.

Bradshaw returned with coffee and Dr. Dahlgren. The doctor was around sixty, average height, on the slim side, with a prominent chin and cheekbones. He kept his neat little mustache trimmed just above his top lip. Dahlgren's clear blue eyes looked world-weary, like he'd seen more over the years than he could just about stand.

I stood and shook his hand. "I'm Sergeant Aleckson. Thank you for coming in, Doctor."

Bradshaw handed me a cup of coffee, and I took a sip. It was fresh and brewed to a perfect strength. He'd guessed correctly that I drank my coffee black, and I raised my eyes in approval.

"Thank you."

Bradshaw blinked twice.

Dr. Dahlgren sank into a chair next to Nurse Pedersen. "I can't believe this happened. Nels Fenneman was more than a patient to me, he was like a father. At least I idealized him as someone I'd like to have as a father." He spoke, then took a moment for reflection.

"Doctor Dahlgren, I understand Judge Fenneman was admitted to Oak Lea Memorial on July sixth with pneumonia?" I asked and pushed the tape recorder closer to him.

"I don't have his chart here, but I believe that's the correct date."

I referred to my notes. "And you ordered a sleeping aid for him this evening around eight-thirty?"

"Yes," he confirmed.

"Is this the first time he was given this medication?" I asked.

Dahlgren nodded. "This time around. Nels was feeling better and had slept most of the day without his coughing disturbing him. He knew he couldn't sleep tonight without help."

"You said this time around. Had he had this medication before?"

"Yes. He was admitted just about a year ago for the same condition. He had chronic bronchitis and was prone to pneumonia. I ordered the same drug as a sleeping aid then, and he tolerated it just fine. Said he slept like a baby."

"Doctor, it sounds like you knew Judge Fenneman pretty well." I paused for a minute. "Is there any reason to think his drowning was intentional?"

"Are you saying suicide?" His eyes widened in surprise, and I nodded.

"I would say there is not even a remote possibility of that." Dr. Dahlgren leaned forward, studying my face.

"So what do you think happened?" I asked and glanced

around the table. Every eye was fixed on Dahlgren. Perhaps he would reveal a secret about his patient to help solve the bizarre mystery.

"The only thing I can think of is the condition called 'sundowning' which happens on occasion, particularly to elderly people," he said.

"Sundowning?" I had never heard the term before.

"Yes. A person will wake up and realize he isn't at home, in his own bed. It produces a panic-like response. He will feel a strong compulsion to get home, to the familiar. The patient is in a state of semi-consciousness. I believe that's what happened to the judge." Dahlgren folded his hands and stared at them.

"You mean he was sleepwalking?" I asked.

"No, not quite the same thing." Dahlgren's eyes blinked over and over in rapid succession to remove the gathering moisture. It was a long moment before he continued. "I went to his room and saw the IV needle ripped out and lying on the bed. God, the blood! Nels had no dementia. By my observations, he wasn't depressed. I can only think that perhaps the sedative produced the confusion and panic."

Dahlgren put his head between his hands. "Dear Lord, I wish I could have known. I never would have ordered that med."

Nurse Sheila's eyes watered again. She gently rubbed the doctor's shoulders with her right hand and dabbed her eyes with the left.

Quiet sobbing filled the room.

Chapter 2

I tracked Dr. Nordstrom down in the Emergency Room. He was on duty for the night shift and unable to be part of our conference questioning. Nordstrom didn't have much to add to the account of the night's events. The judge was found shortly before he went on duty, and he reported directly to the death scene at the pond.

I was curious about one thing. "Why didn't you do CPR? I thought it was routine."

"There was a DNR—do not resuscitate—order signed by the patient. The nurses knew his wishes and decided not to initiate resuscitation until he was seen by a physician. And when I got there, he was already showing dependent lividity." Nordstrom threw the chart he was holding on the counter.

"Do you think he did it on purpose? Drowned himself?" I asked.

Dr. Nordstrom rubbed his smooth, tanned chin. I watched his long fingers work for a moment. "The thought crossed my mind, but it doesn't make sense from what I know of Judge Fenneman. I think he probably woke up to go to the bathroom or something. He may not have known where he was and wanted to get home, so he left. It happens sometimes." He crossed his long arms over his chest.

"Sundowning."

Nordstrom nodded. "Yes."

As I made my way back to B-Wing, I saw the judge's daughter, Clarice Moy, talking with Mr. Bradshaw and a few medical personnel. She had been ageless to me before then. That night she looked at least her age, around fifty-five. Her dark brown hair usually provided a nicely shaped, shoulder- length frame for her long face. Instead, it was pulled into a tight ponytail, emphasizing an angular chin, high forehead, and wrinkles I had never noticed on the occasions we spoke, at church or around town. Her pale complexion was blotched with red.

Grief had added another face to its cruel album.

I stuck my notepad in my back pocket. Mrs. Moy spotted me and drew me into her arms, sobbing. My grandma had died a few months before, and I choked up with sorrow, for Mrs. Moy and for me. Another parent, another grandparent. I couldn't stop the tears.

I felt a large, warm hand on my bicep, squeezing gently. I opened my eyes to see Bradshaw's head bend toward Mrs. Moy's face, one hand on her shoulder, the other on my arm. I pulled back as much as his firm grasp would allow and watched him tenderly kiss Mrs. Moy's cheek. It was a bit awkward being included in the embrace, but it didn't last long. We moved apart slightly and formed a small circle.

"Clarice, I don't know what to say," Bradshaw finally managed. Clarice Moy was on the board of directors at the hospital, and it appeared she and Bradshaw were on good terms.

Everyone in town seemed to know and respect Clarice Moy. She and her husband had owned a local real estate business together until six years before, when he ran off with one of their agents. Clarice had acquired the business and continued to manage it successfully on her own. She was bright, thorough, eternally professional at work, and spoke kindly to everyone, even strangers. Nobody could understand why her husband would leave her, but most had written it off as a mid-life crisis.

I knew both of the Moy children. Allan was my brother John Carl's age, a year older than I. He was married and had a lucrative position in Madison, Wisconsin, where he lived. Heather was two years younger and the mother of Mrs. Moy's grandchildren. She and her husband and children lived in Oak Lea. I wondered where Heather was, since her mother was caring for her children.

"I'm still trying to come to grips with what's happened here. I just can't understand it. It's too much of a shock. I need to see his room." Mrs. Moy looked from Bradshaw to me.

I led the way as we walked the short distance together. I un-taped the yellow "Do Not Cross" band, and Mrs. Moy stepped inside.

She gasped a sharp intake of breath and clutched my arm. "There's so much blood. Why?"

"The IV needle is pretty large," Bradshaw explained.

New tears spilled from her eyes. "Nick, why didn't anyone hear the door alarm? It's a brand new system."

"I wish I knew. Maybe, because it is new, it malfunctioned somehow. We've called the alarm company, and they are sending a service representative first thing in the morning. I hope he can give us some answers." Bradshaw's face was pinched, his eyes bloodshot.

I looked at my watch: One-thirty-three, Monday morning. The effects of the coffee were wearing off for all of us.

"Mrs. Moy, the nurses told me you visited your father last evening," I said and steered her back into the corridor.

She brightened a bit. "Yes, I brought the grandchildren. They are the lights of both our lives."

"And how did he seem to you?"

"He was feeling so much better. He teased the kids and promised them a trip to Dairy Queen when he got out of here — probably today." Her shoulders drooped and her lips trembled again.

"I hate to ask you this, but I have to as a matter of formality. Did your father ever talk of wanting to die? I understand depression is common in the elderly," I said as delicately as possible, which wasn't possible.

Mrs. Moy drew in a sharp breath. "Corky, if you're asking if I think he committed suicide, absolutely not. He believed only God should decide when a person died. No, he couldn't have done this on purpose." Bradshaw offered his arm and led her to a bench by a window, where they sat down.

I stepped back into the judge's room and was hit with the same strange feeling I had experienced in there earlier. Something did not feel right. I knew little about medical conditions, and the doctors seemed to concur that the judge had suffered from sundowning. But how had he managed, unheard and unseen, to get around the bed rail, rip out his IV needle, walk directly from his room to the emergency exit unnoticed, and leave through a door that was equipped with an alarm that could wake the dead?

B-Wing consisted of eight private patient rooms forming a circle around a desk area in the center. In addition to Judge Fenneman, there were only two other patients listed on the B-Wing roster that evening—a twenty-two-year-old man recuperating from an automobile accident and a nine-year-old girl with a respiratory disorder.

I knew the man, Bart Rogers. Following his automobile accident three days previously, I was the deputy who had issued him two tickets: one for driving under the influence, and one for criminal damage to property. The preliminary blood test taken by the hospital had shown his blood alcohol level at .225, almost three times the legal limit for intoxication in Minnesota. A sample of his blood was sent to the Bureau of Criminal Apprehension, the BCA, in St. Paul for precise laboratory testing. That would be the evidence the prosecution would use in court.

Bart Rogers would be equally unhappy to see me in the morning, so I decided to question him right now. When he was released from the hospital, he would be transported to the Winnebago County Jail per my arrest report and criminal complaint.

"Mr. Rogers, are you awake?" I asked quietly, entering his room.

The light from the corridor brightened the space. Rogers watched me as I took a seat by his bed. "Actually, Officer Friendly, I am. A real loud blast woke me up a long time ago, and sure as shit, I haven't been able to get back to sleep."

Rogers had a new part in his brown hair where stitches had been sewn to close a four-inch-long gash. His left leg was in a cast to his upper thigh and propped on a mountain of pillows. The bump over his left eye was smaller than it had been three days before, but it had produced a swollen, black eye. Bart stretched his muscular arms over his head and tucked his hands under the pillow. "So, you doing hospital security now or what?"

"Something like that. You said you heard a blast earlier. Can you describe it?" I asked.

"You know, an alarm kind of blast. And too damn loud, especially when your head hurts to hell."

Rogers touched near his stitches, in case I hadn't noticed them. I suppressed the urge to roll my eyes and nodded instead. We both knew it was the bad choice he had made that had landed him there.

"How many times did this alarm go off?" I asked.

"Once, but the damn thing rang about five minutes."

It only seemed that long.

"Did you hear anything before the alarm that seemed unusual to you?" I continued.

Rogers picked at his blanket. "Nah, I was out."

"And after?"

"Yeah, people talking, walking around, sounds like women crying. I asked the nurse what was up, but she said she couldn't talk about it." He shrugged like he didn't care.

"Thank you, Mr. Rogers. I hope you can get back to sleep." I jotted a few notes and rose to leave.

"Yeah, right. I guess I'll be seeing you in court."

Rogers had a record of driving offenses and knew the system. He was lucky his car had slowed to an estimated ten miles an hour after leaving the roadway when it hit the tree. Strangely enough, he had been wearing a seat belt. Rogers probably realized by then he could have easily become another statistic.

The little girl in B-121 was named Rebecca Eisner. I knew of her via the rumor mill. Her father and I had attended our first ten years of school together, until he dropped out. Nolan Eisner was the kind of kid you didn't pay much attention to at first—he was quiet, hanging in the background. When we were in fourth grade, we heard he did some shoplifting. By the time we hit junior high, he was away from school as much as he was there. Oak Lea was a smaller town then, and it was common knowledge that Nolan spent his time away in juvenile detention centers.

In ninth grade, Jason Browne moved to town and Nolan finally had a cohort for his crimes. Jason didn't seem like a bad kid, but he tagged along with Nolan and got into trouble right along with him. They bumped into the big league, the adult criminal justice system, when they robbed a Tom Thumb in a nearby town two years later. Nolan did the dirty deed and Jason drove the getaway car.

The case went unsolved for a month.

The older Tom Thumb store clerk couldn't identify much about the perpetrator, except to say he was tall and skinny. He wore a blue ski mask, hiding his face, and kept a shotgun pointed at the clerk as he gathered money into a brown shopping bag. Too terrified to look out the window when Nolan left, the clerk did not get a vehicle description, much less a license plate number.

Increasingly troubled with the guilt of committing a real crime, Jason confessed everything to our high school principal. They took the information to the sheriff's department together. For his cooperation, Jason was offered a plea bargain and spent only one year in the county jail.

At eighteen years of age, Nolan was prosecuted as an adult for the first time in his career as a criminal. He was tried, convicted on several felony counts, and sentenced to St. Cloud State Prison for five years. It was big news in our small town, and the newspaper covered the details of the trial.

About a week before our high school graduation, Nolan hanged himself in his cell.

His obituary listed his survivors as his wife, mother, and unborn child. It was the first any of us had heard Nolan was married. After the baby's birth, the young mother left the infant girl on Nolan's mother's doorstep, literally. As far as I knew, no one had heard from her since, and the little girl was still with her grandmother.

I pushed the young Eisner girl's door slightly ajar. She clutched a stuffed animal to her chest and appeared to be asleep. There was no reason to disturb her. I would check in on her later in the day when she was awake. I closed the door and leaned against the wall for a moment.

"Sergeant."

I opened my eyes to see Bradshaw studying me.

"You look tired."

I shrugged slightly.

"Chief Becker, Sheriff Twardy, and the evening staff all left a few minutes ago. The sheriff said he'd talk to you later this morning, but to call if you need anything before then," Bradshaw conveyed.

"Thanks."

"Clarice Moy wants to see her father, and I thought you might want to join us. He's been cleaned up, somewhat." I followed them to the exam room.

Judge Fenneman was more recognizable, but still far from clean. The pungent odor of swamp rose from his drying hospital gown. Dirt clung to his eyebrows and scalp and was embedded under his fingernails. Mrs. Moy tentatively touched her father's face and hand, then rested her head on the blanket covering his chest and sobbed once more.

"Doc, we found his glasses." A young intern dressed in scrubs joined us in the crowded room. "Oh, sorry," he said, looking at Mrs. Moy.

I extended my hand and the intern handed me a pair of bifocals.

"They were at the edge of the pond, sort of stuck in the mud. I was lucky my flashlight hit the glass just right, so I spotted them," he explained.

"Thank you." I spoke for the group.

As I started to hand the glasses to Mrs. Moy, I noticed a hair caught in the hinge screw. I pulled the glasses close to my face and held my breath as more swamp smell hit my olfactory. The hair was about five inches long, gray, and coarse. I glanced at the intern. His hair was golden blond and two inches long, at best. The gray hair could belong to any number of people, but it definitely had not come from the judge, who had baby-fine, white, wavy wisps.

I retrieved a plastic tweezers and small baggie from my back pocket, picked the hair from the hinge, and sealed it in the bag. Everyone watched me, but no one questioned my actions. Mrs. Moy accepted the glasses and clutched them to her breast.

"Your father will be sent to Hennepin County for autopsy," Dr. Dahlgren explained.

"No. I don't want him touched . . . cut up like that," Mrs. Moy emphatically stated.

"Clarice, we really should positively determine the cause of death, see if there was some other extenuating factor," Mr. Bradshaw argued.

She was adamant. "No. The coroner can make a ruling without an autopsy."

The medical personnel and Bradshaw looked to me for support. An autopsy was standard procedure in unnatural deaths, and I would have preferred an autopsy reading to a coroner's report, but I believed it was Mrs. Moy's decision.

I excused myself and went back to the emergency exit door in B-Wing. I lifted five sets of readable fingerprints from the push bar, scraped caked blood from both the push bar and the linoleum floor, and gathered the IV needle, tube, and bed sheet from the judge's room. I retrieved plastic and paper evidence bags from my brief case, sealed the items in and labeled them.

Evidence. Of what, I had no clue.

The night crew was halfway through their shift when I carried my armload of equipment and paraphernalia to my squad car. Bradshaw followed, holding an umbrella over me. Heavy drops of rain bounced off the pavement every few inches. When everything was secured in the trunk, I turned and thanked Bradshaw. He offered his hand.

"Thank you, Sergeant. Hopefully, we can answer the remaining questions when the alarm company checks out the system later today."

The rain striking my windshield, and the wipers clearing the drops, was having a hypnotic effect. Slip-slap, slip-slap. By the time I got home ten minutes later, I was obsessed with the need for sleep. After thirteen hours in uniform and tromping around in the rain, I needed a shower, but couldn't face one more task tonight.

I dragged myself through the kitchen and living room, then up the one, two, three, four, five, six, seven, eight, nine, ten, eleven, twelve steps to my loft bedroom. I removed the portable radio from my service belt and put it in its charger, then checked my Glock service weapon and stowed it in my maple bed stand, a routine I never varied. I dropped my service belt on the floor, stripped off my uniform in seconds, and crawled into my antique brass bed in my undies.

My body ached from the tips of my fingers to the tips of my toes. The last thing I remember is stretching to the music of the raindrops dancing on my roof.

Chapter 3

Alvie

Alvie plopped down on her La-Z-Boy and pushed back to elevate her feet. She lit a cigarette and dragged a long, deep inhale. A lightheaded sensation, not unpleasant, forced her eyes closed for a moment. It had been a long time since she'd smoked—going on ten years. She quit right after little Rebecca came to her. She had loved smoking, and that night it seemed like the best way to celebrate her victory.

She could not believe how easy it had been. With only three patients in B-Wing, nurses spent the majority of their time in one of the other two wings, or at the main desk writing on charts and talking to doctors about orders. Figuring out where the nurses would be, and when, was the first part of the plan. She had watched enough *CSI* and *Law and Order* to know she had to be clever and thorough.

It was a treat to be able to use her brain for a change. Cleaning the nursing home day after day was tedious and did not pose much of a mental challenge. Not that she was a genius, but she was smart enough. Alvie knew, deep down, she should have attended a technical school or college, gotten a degree and had a real career. She still could. She'd have to see about that.

The thing that had helped her the most was a trip to the library, where she consulted a *Physician's Desk Reference*. The last time she had been in a library the card catalog system was in little file drawers. This time it was on computers. Rebecca had showed her a few things on the computer at home, but she had no idea how to look anything up on it. Instead, she casually looked around until she found the reference section. There was a *Physician's Desk Reference* at each nurses' station at the nursing home where she worked, but that was too risky. The nurses might wonder why a cleaning lady was reading about drugs.

Alvie did not want to raise questions.

She couldn't believe all the drugs listed in that book. It was a little confusing trying to figure the thing out, but when she came across haloperidol, she recognized the name at once. The doctors had prescribed it for her brother Henry, who suffered from a personality disorder. Before then, she hadn't been all that interested in what he took or how it worked. The doctors had said the medication would "stabilize him," and she couldn't argue with that.

Alvie knew her brother was nuts. He was okay as a little boy, but by the time he was a teenager, the abuse finally got to him, and he snapped. He couldn't put his mind in another place when it happened. Not like she could. It probably wasn't so much the beating, or all the yelling her father did at them when he was drinking. It was the sex stuff their uncle did that was the hardest on both of them.

As big a loser as her father was when he was alive, the worst thing he did was die and leave Alvie and Henry with Uncle—who didn't deserve to have a name.

Alvie figured from his crying those nights that it hurt Henry more than it hurt her. She wanted to run away and take Henry with her, but she was young and really scared. She started hiding Henry the nights Uncle was around. At least she could escape to the pleasant palace of her dreams and concentrate on the beautiful things there. When she was there she couldn't feel or hear—she only saw splendid sights.

After Uncle died, she never went back to that place. Not once.

Henry had spent most of his adult life in state mental hospitals. They seemed to take good care of him and kept him as mentally stable as possible. The doctors tried a lot of different medicines and doses before they settled on haloperidol. Henry complained about the way he felt when he took it. He played little games, like hiding the pill under his tongue so he could spit it out later, or pretending to put it in his mouth while keeping it in his cupped palm, but the nurses were too smart for him. They had a whole hospital full of Henrys and knew all their tricks. They made sure Henry swallowed his pills.

When most of the state hospitals closed in Minnesota, Alvie had to find a new home for Henry. He lived at a group home in Oak Lea. He seemed content there. The group home staff was as good as the hospital staff had been about making certain Henry took his medicine.

Alvie picked up his prescription, along with any hygiene items he needed, at Butler Drug every month. He and Rebecca were the only living relatives Alvie knew about, and it was the least she could do. Alvie had to get stronger as Henry got weaker, and she still loved the little boy he had been once upon a time.

The day before, when she'd picked up Henry's prescription, she had simply removed an even number of ten tablets from the bottle before she delivered them to the group home. What a payoff for her monthly trips to the drugstore for Henry! It became the easiest part of the plan. Yes, she had gotten a phone call from the group home when they discovered there were only twenty tablets instead of thirty in the bottle, but after eight years of faithful delivery without a problem, why would they suspect she'd stolen the pills?

Alvie got a call from the pharmacy, but they had no proof she had taken them. Yes, she was sure she hadn't opened the bottle and spilled any, or given the bottle to someone else to deliver for her. They were quite positive they had not made such a gross error, and were very sorry if they had. They personally delivered ten more tablets to the group home, without charge.

Deciding how to give the drug to the judge was the most difficult problem for Alvie. At first she considered posing as a nurse and giving him a tablet or two to swallow. But it seemed it would be easier, and safer, to crush and dissolve two tablets and add them to his IV bottle.

The first night Rebecca was in the hospital, Alvie watched as one of the nurses punched in a series of numbers on a panel attached to the B-Wing emergency exit door, so she could step outside and have a cigarette without setting off the alarm. The night after the judge was admitted, Alvie was prepared. She bought a pack of cigarettes and watched from her granddaughter's room for the same nurse. When she saw her sometime later, Alvie stepped out of the room and told the nurse she was "dying for a smoke." The nurse, helpful to a fault, asked Alvie to join her for one.

Alvie watched the nurse punch in the code and memorized it by repeating four-six-one-eight-six to herself the entire time she pretended to smoke and listen to the nurse talk about nothing special. She jotted the numbers down on a piece of paper the minute she returned to Rebecca's room. She didn't think she would ever forget those precious numbers, but she couldn't chance it, of course.

That night, everything had fallen into place. Alvie had put together a large, somewhat complex jigsaw puzzle, designed by her for her son and granddaughter. Maybe she was a genius after all. She had crushed two haloperidol tablets at home, poured the contents into an empty pill bottle, and dropped it in her pants pocket. She checked in the mirror and there wasn't a bulge. She kept a box of disposable latex gloves in her bathroom cupboard. Alvie figured she needed at least two pair, so she picked out eight gloves, just to be safe. Always err on the side of caution, one of her teachers had always said. Finally, Alvie knew what he meant. Be careful and plan well.

She got to the hospital at six that evening. About eight-thirty, she heard the nurse tell the judge, in the room next door, that she had a medication to help him sleep. Perfect. A little haloperidol mixed with a sleeping pill would make him putty in her hands.

Alvie waited about twenty minutes, checked to make sure the coast was clear, slipped into the judge's room, and quietly told him she needed to check his IV fluids. She stayed by the head of his bed so he couldn't get a good look at her. But he was groggy anyway. In a matter of seconds, she unscrewed the cover and dumped in the drug. She gave the bottle a few quick swirls to mix it in and replaced the bottle in its holder.

After the nurse completed the patient check just before ten o'clock, Alvie donned another pair of gloves, walked to the emergency exit door, and disarmed the alarm. She put a thin piece of wood in the door jamb so the door would not completely close. It was still raining, sometimes pouring down, so she got a large towel from her granddaughter's room and put it on the protected landing outside the door. She put on the same turquoise hooded raincoat she had worn to the hospital. To protect her white work shoes, she pulled on heavy-duty plastic bags and secured them with rubber bands around her ankles.

When Alvie saw no one was around, she returned to Judge Fenneman's room, shook his arm to wake him, and simply told him to follow her. He didn't even ask why. She helped him sit up and get off the end of the bed. His IV stand started to tip over, but Alvie caught it just in time. She removed the tape holding the needle in place, then pulled it out. She almost stopped what she was doing when the judge dropped his arm to his side and blood spilled from his vein and started dripping to the floor. It took a few seconds for Alvie to regain her composure.

She gently, but firmly grasped the judge's other arm. They walked the twenty or so feet to the door. She pushed it open and the judge grabbed the push bar for support when Alvie let go of his arm.

Fenneman made some small sounds of protest as they tromped through the rain, but they got to the bottom of the hill without real incident. At the water's edge, Alvie gave the old guy a push. It was over in no time.

Alvie jogged up the hill with effort and stopped outside the back door. She slipped off the shoe bags, turned them inside out, and stashed them in her pocket. She wiped the raincoat down to remove most of the moisture and shrugged it off. She held her breath as she pulled the door open slightly. Still no one around. Alvie pulled out the door prop, reset the alarm, and sucked in a calming inhalation. She quickly and quietly made her way to Rebecca's room. Rebecca was sound asleep, the gentle little puffs of her breathing creating the only stir in the otherwise silent room.

Alvie willed her own breathing into pace with her granddaughter's as she hung the coat back in the closet, removed her rubber gloves, and stuck them in the pocket with the bags. She disposed of the wet towel in the linen hamper in the hallway. Finally, she eased her large body on a chair beside the bed and whispered that everything was getting better. At last, Rebecca's father could begin to rest in peace. Final justice for the Justice.

Alvie wondered if she should wait until they discovered the judge was gone or not. When her breathing finally slowed to normal, she reasoned it was best to fly the coop right away. With the raincoat flung over her arm, she walked casually to the main entrance. She was forced to say "goodnight" when the girl at the front desk looked at her. Alvie slipped on her coat and hurried to her car to the separate beats of the raindrops and her pounding heart.

What a night! A glorious, glorious night. She was glad she had bought that pack of cigarettes the day before. She would put them to good use when she got home.

Chapter 4

I was walking around, up and down winding hallways, trying to find the source of the alarm so I could shut it off. It would ring for a few seconds, then stop for a few. Ring, ring, ring, silence. When I finally stepped into near-consciousness, I realized my telephone had taken over my dream and irritated me out of my sleep.

"Yes?" My voice was hoarse.

"Are you still in bed, dear? It's after nine." My mother's voice did nothing to cheer me after so little rest.

"I worked late last night," I croaked, my eyes closed, wanting to hold onto sleep.

"So you probably heard that Judge Fenneman died? Drowned, of all things; I just can't believe it."

"I know."

Falling back asleep would be impossible. I pushed myself into a sitting position, glanced at the blind covering my window, and saw sunlight poking through the slats. The rain had ended sometime in the past few hours.

"It's just so shocking. I mean, how could it have happened? I've got a casserole in the oven to take over to the Moy's before I go to the shop." Good ole Mom, slightly neurotic with a heart of gold.

"I'm sure they'll appreciate it."

"Clarice Moy was so kind to us when your grandma died, I want to help a little now."

"You will. You did the same for her when her mother died," I reminded her.

"Oh, gosh, that's right, her mother, too. It can't be more than two years or so." Mother was silent for a moment. "It's your day off, isn't it, dear? Gramps said you might go fishing."

"That was the plan, but I need to do an interview and file my reports first. I took the call on Judge Fenneman just before shift change and worked until about four this morning. I have to finish up."

I always hesitated talking to my mother about my job. Cop talk made her anxious.

"Oh, you didn't get enough sleep. I worry about you, dear. So how did Judge Fenneman get outside the hospital and drown?"

I heard clanging noises in the background and envisioned her scampering around her old farmhouse pantry. My mother was perpetually doing at least two things at once.

"That's the question of the day. It's a mystery." I gave her a summary of the call and what the doctors surmised had happened.

"How is poor Clarice Moy holding up?" she asked.

"Distraught, but doing pretty well, considering."

"So you met Nicholas Bradshaw. Is he really as handsome as Clarice says?"

Handsome? Had I met Nicholas Bradshaw under different circumstances, I probably would have stopped, dead in my tracks, and stared at him with my jaw resting on my chest. Long, lean, and muscular, somewhere in his thirties, with a tan earned doing some outdoor sport or activity was my guess. His large, warm hands gave just the right touch of comfort and support when needed. Chestnut brown hair, strong chin, straight nose, not too long, high forehead, and brown eyes that held intensity, suggesting he could see into your very soul.

Handsome, Mother?

I hoped my sigh wasn't audible. "He's all right, I guess."

"Corinne, you set your standards way too high. You'll never find a husband that way." She hit the replay button where she had the same message stored and had played for me many times before.

"He's probably married—"

"No, widowed," she interrupted.

"Oh." *Oh? Oh!* Time to toss the ball back to her. "Anyway, Mother, I could say the same thing about your standards. Smoke asks about you all the time."

"You know he's an old friend of your father's and mine. He's just being polite."

"Right, Mom." It was impossible to win that argument with her.

"I'd better get moving so I can be at the shop . . . Oh, no! I'm supposed to open in forty-five minutes. Stop by for lunch if you can. Bye, dear."

"Later, Mom."

My mother owned a dress and accessory shop in Oak Lea, her home away from home. She would be fifty on her next birthday, and with all the worrying she did, she should have had deep creases in her face. Instead, she only had a little crinkle of crow's feet by her eyes and was often mistaken for my sister. We didn't look much alike, but we shared the same coloring and basic figure. Mom had begun to frost her ash blonde hair to "disguise the gray ones that have started to appear," and kept her wavy hair chin length and usually tucked behind her ears.

I had highlighted my own hair for a few years, because it looked better. It was dishwater blonde and a little mousy without the lighter streaks. I did not inherit my mother's natural curls and most often pulled my straight, shoulder-length bob into a ponytail or bun, especially when I was on duty.

My mother was shapely without being matronly. She didn't need to exercise to stay thin because she was in perpetual motion most waking hours. I preferred maintaining a balance between being busy and crashing someplace comfortable to read, watch a good movie or meditate. But it was important for me to stay strong and fit to do my job well, so I worked out in the department's gym, did kickboxing, ran, and took ballet lessons (which I had managed to keep secret from the other Winnebago County deputies).

I stretched, threw back the patchwork quilt my Grandma Brandt had lovingly made, and remembered how I had fallen into bed the previous night, exhausted beyond words. I decided to put on running clothes and go for a short jog before showering. Hopefully, it would clear my mind and jump-start my body. Coffee alone wouldn't do it.

My house sat on the crest of a small hill overlooking acres of cornfields, golden wheat, and a horse pasture, enclosed by yards and yards of white fencing. The back of my property dropped down to a small lake, and when the small woods of maple and birch trees shed their leaves in late fall, the lake was part of my backyard view. I watched it ice over in the winter and thaw in the spring before the trees leafed out once more.

My maternal grandparents had given me twenty acres of land from their 1,600 acre farm. Gramps leased the bulk of his property to a young neighboring farmer who planted corn one year and soybeans the next. I had built a three bedroom, one and a half story home three years before, with my mother acting as my subcontractor. She loved projects, and it kept both of us way too busy for six months: deciding on a plan, finding a reliable builder, plumber, electrician, mason, and everybody else you needed to get the job done.

After walking the tenth of a mile length of driveway, I set my pace at about an eight-minute mile. It was a good thinking speed, and my mind swept over the calls I had been assigned the past few days. Three driving under the influence arrests (including the hospital patient), some minor traffic violation tickets, four or five domestic disputes—with only one landing the offender in jail for fifth degree assault—medical emergencies, vandalism, a house burglary, a small fire in a country tavern, and drug paraphernalia found on a transient were the things that immediately came to mind.

Every call seemed routine compared to Judge Fenneman's bizarre end. I would complete the investigation, file the reports, and most likely defer to expert medical opinion. My training made me question the pat medical answers, and I could not erase the sinking something's-not-right feeling in my gut. What was causing that?

I jogged past my mother's house, about a half mile down the road from my own. It had been her childhood home, and she'd raised my brother, John Carl, and me there, also. Both sets of my grandparents lived on the same road: the Brandts on the east side and the Alecksons on the west side. Overwhelmed with so much family nearby, my brother had fled to Colorado to attend college and stayed there. His acreage awaited his return.

My father's parents were in their seventies and wintered in Arizona. They were thinking of selling their home and renting a condo in town when they returned to Minnesota in the spring. Besides the few months in Oak Lea, they also spent the month of July at a lake resort in northern Minnesota. Maintaining two homes was getting to be a burden for them. Grandma and Grandpa Aleckson had asked me several times if I was interested in selling my newer home and moving into theirs. I loved their old farmhouse and seriously considered it.

My maternal grandparents had retired from farming when I was five years old and built a smaller home on five acres, a quarter mile from the homestead. I was thrilled to move from our small bungalow in town to the rambling two-story one they had given up for us. In addition to living in a home I loved, it meant we could raise animals and ride horses.

My mother's overprotective hovering had put a damper on many of my desired activities, but I still managed to swim in the small, nearby Bebee Lake, climb fences, trees, and hay mounds, and ride my grandpa's mare when Mom was otherwise occupied. My brother, John Carl, was too honest and way too serious to do things behind our mother's back, so he chose to remove himself geographically instead.

After my Grandma Brandt died, Gramps continued to live in his house, largely due to my mother's efforts. She cooked his meals, had his house cleaned, laundered his clothes, and was at his beck and call. I helped when I could, but my schedule was erratic, and I didn't like to make promises I couldn't keep. I rationalized that Mom could handle the extra chores very well, but feared she might explode into spontaneous combustion at any given minute. I also thought she needed a man in her life, but had about given up thinking that would ever happen.

As I trekked back home, I began to feel energized. I preferred hiking through the woods and exploring to running down a road, but a two-mile jaunt was a quick aerobic workout. A long drink of water, a cooling shower, and two cups of very strong coffee, I thought, should bring me completely to life.

I walked along the south side of the hospital grounds. The night before, the site had been sinister, the unrelenting rain pounding on people and the earth. That morning, sunbeams danced playfully across the ripples of the pond water's surface. The dozens of footprints had been reduced to a few depressions in the wetland and no longer resembled feet. The grass where the judge had lain when I arrived at the scene was starting to spring back up as it dried, lifting its blades to the sun.

Rebecca Eisner was propped up in her bed watching television, still clutching what I identified as a stuffed puppy. Scrawny and pale, she looked like she had suffered a lifetime of poor health and appeared younger than nine years old. Her shoulder length blonde hair was nearly colorless, making the blue veins on her temples and cheeks vividly visible in contrast.

"Hello, Rebecca."

She regarded me warily. "Hi," was her small response as she squeezed her puppy closer.

"I'm Corky Aleckson. I went to school with your father," I said as I pulled up a chair beside her bed.

"You did?" She brightened, her pretty little face transformed by the smile.

We talked for a few minutes. I tried to think of something nice to say about her dad, and suddenly realized we had something very basic in common. "I know what it's like to want to know about your dad. My own father died before I was born, just like yours did." I took her bone china hand in mine.

"He did? I thought I was the only one." She held my eyes with hers.

"No, there's you, there's me, and I'm sure there are a lot of others we don't know about. It happens sometimes."

Rebecca looked forlorn, and I wanted to pull her into my arms and hold her.

I paused before changing the subject. "There's another reason I'm here, Rebecca. I'm a sergeant with the Winnebago County Sheriff's Department—"

"A real cop?" she interrupted. "Then where's your gun and your uniform and your badge?"

"I suppose I don't look much like an officer today without my uniform on." I pulled my identification badge from my back pocket and held it up for her. She took her time, reading every word.

"You are very smart to ask whether I am really a cop. Some people might not think of that." She studied me a moment. "My gun is locked in my car. I don't need it here."

"Oh. Wow! A girl cop."

I smiled at her sudden enthusiasm and approval. "Rebecca, I was here last night, checking on some things, and I need to ask you if you heard or saw anything unusual, you know, different than normal?"

She gave me a blank look and shook her head.

"It would have been pretty late. What I mean by unusual is, did you notice another patient walk by your room? Or did you hear any alarm noises? Things that haven't happened before?" I was having difficulty phrasing my questions without giving too much information.

She continued shaking her head. "Uh, uh. But you can ask my grandma if she did." She looked past me to a woman standing in the doorway.

When I turned around, a large woman dressed in black was studying me. How long had she been listening to our conversation, and why was she hovering in the doorway?

"Hello, Mrs. Eisner, isn't it?" I stood and extended my hand.

"It's Ms."

She glanced down at my hand, then finally shook it. Her grasp was firm, her stare severe, piercing.

"Ah, I'm Sergeant Corky Aleckson, Winnebago County. I was in your son's class at school."

"Yes," was all she said, her eyes daggers boring through me.

I was unnerved, anxious to finish my business and get the heck out of Dodge. "Actually, the reason I'm here talking to Rebecca is, I'm doing some follow-up on an incident that happened on this wing last night."

She raised her eyebrows in question. Judge Fenneman's death wasn't a secret, so I gave her the generic version of the story.

Ms. Eisner kept her eyes trained on me. "I was here with Rebecca for a while last night. I'm not sure when I left, but I didn't hear any alarms."

"Okay, thank you, Ms. Eisner, and thank you, Rebecca. You are a special girl, and I know your father would be very proud of you. I hope you feel better real soon." I turned back to her grandmother. "Here's my card if either of you think of anything, or if you have any questions."

Ms. Eisner accepted my business card without a word or change of expression. I slipped out of the room and away from that very peculiar woman. Why did she tell me she hadn't heard any alarms? She must have overheard my question to Rebecca.

I tried to remember her at school functions, but couldn't. I could only picture Nolan alone. If she had attended, she was one in a sea of faces. After meeting her, I could easily believe she had a social phobia. And what had happened to Nolan's father? She'd stressed the "Ms." so maybe she had never married, really none of my business.

I stopped by the judge's room. Freshly cleaned, it shone and smelled of disinfectant, all set for the next patient. A little magic Blood-Be-Gone and, poof, it was—at least the visible sign of it. But for a handful of us, it would be in that room forever. A battleground between a man and the equipment keeping him there. I stepped inside and rested my hand on the bed tray. A chill ran through me.

Not a drop of blood in sight, not an item out of place, yet a tightness gathered in my middle, disturbing, unsettling. Was it how quickly things had reverted to business as usual? A tautly-made bed, polished metal, and shining wood. Stark evidence the world didn't slow down for much of anything.

Mr. Bradshaw's plump, middle-aged, no-nonsense-tolerated receptionist took my name and informed me he was on the phone. I could have a seat if I didn't mind waiting—for how long, she didn't know. I jotted a few details of my conversation with Nolan's daughter and mother. The girl was shy and amiable, and from what I could see, completely normal compared to her very odd grandmother.

"Sergeant," Bradshaw said as he closed the distance to my chair. When I stood, we were so close I caught a hint of masculine soap or aftershave. I felt my pupils widening against my will at the sight of him, gorgeous and exceptionally tidy in his light gray suit.

He raised one eyebrow slightly, smiled, and took my hand in his, confirming I looked as affected as I felt.

"Good morning, Mr. Bradshaw. Thanks for seeing me."

"Undercover today?" His eyes scanned my light blue tank top, jeans, and sandals. He stared at my painted toenails for a second.

"Actually, it's my day off, but I wanted to wrap up this investigation and file my reports," I explained.

"I see. Come into my office. Mrs. Lange, hold all calls, barring an emergency," Bradshaw called over his shoulder.

I sat opposite Bradshaw on the other side of a mammoth dark oak desk, an effective safety barrier between us. "Has the alarm company been here yet?" I asked, opening my memo pad and noting the date and time.

Bradshaw cleared his throat and nodded. "Yes, just after eight o'clock. They ran a series of tests and checks, and found no malfunction whatsoever." He leaned forward and rested his hands, palms up, on his desk.

I jotted that on my paper. "Do you find that strange, Mr. Bradshaw?"

"No, quite the opposite. What I find strange is that Judge Fenneman got out that door without tripping the alarm. I can't understand it." His brows knitted together.

"Nor can I. Frankly, I thought they would find a problem." I considered other possibilities. "Would a staff member have any reason to disarm the alarm in order to go out that door without tripping it? Maintenance personnel, anyone?"

"I did discover we have two nurses on staff who do just that, so they can slip out to have a cigarette."

I jotted that on my memo sheet, waiting for the names.

"But neither of them was on duty last night," Bradshaw explained. He was thorough.

"Okay. Well, thank you for your help. I appreciate your cooperation and concern. And, please call anytime with any new

47

information." I didn't remember giving him my card the previous night, so I handed him one.

Bradshaw stood with me and accepted the card. "Certainly, and of course, contact me with any questions that may arise. I can't adequately express how terrible I feel, how all of us here at Oak Lea Memorial feel."

I nodded and slipped out the door. Twelve hours before I had felt dislike at first sight for this man. So why was I a little sad thinking I probably wouldn't see him again? Common sense betrayed by fickle emotions.

Chapter 5

The sun was bright overhead when I stepped outside. I squinted against it, scanning the parking lot for my squad car. I momentarily forgot I had driven my personal vehicle, a red 1967 Pontiac GTO. My car was a classic, complete with a 400 cubic inch V-8 engine, four-barrel carburetor, three-speed manual transmission, disappearing windshield wipers, leather bucket seats, and hidden headlights.

My father, Carl, had bought it a few days before he received his draft notice for the Selective Service of the United States of America. At nineteen years old, he had been laying concrete blocks for a local company all summer, in addition to helping his father with farm work. He had built both a healthy bank balance and strong muscles. When he reported to the draft office, the enlistment officer asked Carl if he had considered spending his stint in the Marines. The officer said the Marines could use a young man as strong and robust as Carl was. Carl believed it was his duty to say "yes."

Following six months of grueling boot camp, infantry school, and advanced combat training, Carl returned to Oak Lea. He had orders to fly to Da Nang, South Vietnam the next week and was given a short personal leave of absence. My parents decided to marry right away.

Kristen and Carl had grown up on adjoining farms. They were lifelong friends and shared the common bond of each being an only child. They had been born one day apart, and my mother liked to tease Carl—since she was older, she was naturally wiser. As they passed through puberty, their feelings deepened into a growing attraction. They committed, at the ripe old age of sixteen, to marry one day, a plan supported by both sets of parents.

Carl and Kristen exchanged vows in the small county church where they had been baptized and confirmed. A simple sandwich and cake luncheon was served by the ladies guild to the 150 guests in the church basement. The hall was crowded, and the guests' body heat warmed the chilly building that winter afternoon.

My favorite photograph of my parents was captured as they were climbing into the GTO on their way to their honeymoon at the Radisson Hotel in downtown Minneapolis. Their bright eyes and smiles said it all—they were young, excited, and completely enamored with one another. I kept the photo on my bedside stand.

My brother, John Carl, was conceived during their few days together. When he was born nine months later, my father applied for emergency leave and was granted a twenty-eight-day furlough. That's when I began as the sparkle in my mother's eye, as she put it.

Carl died in a Vietnam jungle.

His shrapnel-laden body was sent home for burial a few months before I was born. I had heard the story many times, from many different people, but the impact of it hadn't hit me until a few years before. As I passed my twenty-first birthday as a carefree college student, I speculated on how my mother had managed, at the same age, as a widow with two babies. I felt less resentful of her smothering over-protectiveness and perpetual hovering. Carl was gone, but he had left his progeny in her care, and by God, with His help, she would guard us and keep us safe.

My mother didn't drive the GTO after Carl died. She put it into storage in our garage, almost as a memorial to him, for over twenty years. When Mom was finally convinced I would take loving care of it, I had become the proud owner and brought it back to life.

"You always remind me so much of your father," she had told me.

The years of sitting necessitated a fair amount of mechanical work and replacement of all the belts, but I got my car to run like a top. When I drove it, I felt a connection to my father, the man I only knew through stories.

I hung my Winnebago County parking permit on my rearview mirror bar as I pulled into a permit-only parking lot at the courthouse complex. The sheriff's department offices and common secretarial area were a flurry of activity. There were never enough hours in the day around there. I stopped at the sheriff's open door and knocked on the frame. Sheriff Twardy motioned me in without a word or change of facial expression.

The sheriff's walls were lined with framed diplomas, awards, certificates, and an extensive collection of arm patches from most of the law enforcement agencies around the state of Minnesota. It was my habit to scan the patches to see if I could spot any new ones.

"What have you discovered, Sergeant?" Twardy asked.

"Not a lot, sir. The only thing I learned from my trip to the hospital was the door alarm checked out A-Okay. Without an autopsy, we'll have to stick with the coroner's pronouncement that cause of death was accidental drowning."

I sat down on the edge of a visitor chair. "Since there seems to be no one that actually saw the judge leave the hospital or fall in the pond, the closest thing we have for a reason is what the doctors call 'sundowning.' I guess why no one saw or heard him, or why the alarm didn't sound when he opened the emergency door, will probably always be a mystery."

I followed the sheriff's eyes to my hands and realized I was nearly rubbing the skin off my left hand with my right.

"A helluva mystery, and the coroner's ruling is the best answer, the only answer, we have. Thanks for the effort. I know you're putting in long hours on this." Sheriff Twardy's voice was flat.

I shrugged. "No problem, Sheriff, just doing my job. How are you holding up? Forgive me, but you look awfully tired."

He rubbed his eyes. "I couldn't sleep last night, but I'll be all right. I'll phone Chief Becker. The *Oak Lea Daily News* has been calling both of us for the story. Bradshaw won't let any of his staff talk to Moore. Said he'll issue a statement when we give him the nod. Seems like a decent fellow."

I was coming to the same conclusion. "He's all right. I'll type up my account, put everything on paper so you can read it before I write the final report."

"Sure." Twardy seemed distracted as he reached for the telephone.

It was noon, so I called Mother to tell her I couldn't make lunch. At one-thirty, I handed my findings to the sheriff, then bought a vending machine sandwich and candy bar to scarf for some needed energy.

Detective Elton "Smoke" Dawes was sitting in his cubicle, tipped back in his chair, long legs stretched, resting cowboy boot-clad feet on his desk. His reading glasses were propped on his nose, and he was scanning a criminal complaint. He favored wearing western-style sport coats and bowstring ties. His thick hair, best managed when kept very short, was showing more salt than pepper. In the years I'd known him, he had facial hair about half the time. I preferred the clean shaven look, the way he was at the moment, but Smoke looked good either way. Angular face, long creases for dimples, strong chin, and full lips. What my mother called "rugged good looks."

Smoke had earned his nickname the winter of his junior year in high school, when he was ice fishing on Bison Lake and accidentally burned down his father's fish house. His oil lantern had somehow tipped over and started the fire. Smoke wouldn't tell me the story, but my mother, who was his classmate, said there was a girl with him when it happened, and rumor had it they were doing more than fishing.

"Busy?" I asked and sat down by his desk. He slid his feet over to make room for my lunch. I set it down on a paper-free space.

"Not overly. Same-o, same-o." Smoke's low husky voice matched his nickname and was a melodious treat to my ears. He pulled off his glasses and slid them in his breast pocket. The sky blue eyes that could coax a confession out of almost anyone studied me, his eyebrows narrowed in concern. "Heard you had quite the ordeal last night."

"Not the typical Monday evening shift, that's for sure. When Chief Becker showed up at the scene, I thought he'd call in Garvey to do the investigation, but he turned it over to me. So I got a taste of the kind of work you do every day."

I tugged the cellophane wrapper away from the sandwich with my teeth.

Smoke swung his legs down to the floor. "And how'd you do?"

I shrugged. "I have a lot to learn to be a decent detective," I admitted.

"You have a good, level head, Corky. Good instincts. You like people. You're thorough. You have the investigative skills—you just need to hone them a bit. You get it, better than most." He reached over and gave my arm a small squeeze.

"You trying to steal my sandwich?" I teased.

"I might be tempted if I could identify what that meat might be." He feigned disgust, a chuckle escaping from his throat.

"It doesn't matter. That's what mustard's for. I try not to think about the sometimes disgusting things I consume in the name of nourishment. The alternative was lunch with Mother." I rolled my eyes.

"How is Kristen?" His voice took on a special, smooth-as-silk quality when he spoke of her.

"Keeping herself too busy, as usual. I think she needs a man. Got any ideas?" I swallowed bread, mustard and mystery meat, thankful my stomach was lined with steel.

Smoke's eyes held mine. "Carl would be a tough act to follow. I've never had a friend like him . . . except maybe you," he added.

I studied him a moment. "You're not kidding? You're serious." When he blinked a "yes," I said, "Thanks. That means a lot, and . . . ditto."

Smoke squeezed my hand again. "Well, I'm going to wrap things up here and swing by Clarice's, see if she needs anything. She was a big help when I moved back here. I'll never forget that. Man, she sure went out of her way to find me just the right spot."

"Yes, she did, and I know she can use your support right now. I felt so bad for her last night. She was really shaken up."

"Who wouldn't be, huh?"

Smoke Dawes was my mentor and the best friend I had in the department. He had returned to Oak Lea twelve years before, after living in the northern Minnesota boonies forever. Smoke had served first as a deputy, then several terms as sheriff in Lake County. His professional life had been more successful than his personal life. Smoke was in love with a woman who wouldn't make long-term promises. He wanted marriage; she preferred a more open-ended affair. Smoke couldn't continue seeing her without a serious commitment, so after years of trying to change her mind, he gave up and moved back to his roots.

Mrs. Moy had found him a prime piece of real estate—forty acres of wooded land complete with a small lake and private duck slough. Smoke built a log home near the lake. He enjoyed fishing, hunting, canoeing, strumming his guitar, and tying flies to lure fish. His life seemed a little lonely to me, but he didn't complain. One of his brothers lived in Minneapolis, and they saw each other fairly often.

The first draft of my report was lying on my desk with a post-it note from the sheriff simply stating "GOOD."

I inserted my zip drive into a computer, located the report, and printed two more copies to submit to administration.

It was a sad summary of a prominent man's end.

Chapter 6

Alvie

Alvie picked up a copy of the *Oak Lea Daily News* at the Holiday station and drove home, beside herself with excitement to read it.

It was the front page story.

But it couldn't be true! It wasn't true! How in the love of mercy did they decide Judge Fenneman had died from "accidental drowning"? It clearly looked like a suicide. It was perfect, flawless. There should be no question at all. Accidental? Were they just saying that to protect the judge's reputation?

Her son's death story had been splashed all over, not only in the local newspaper, but in the *Minneapolis Star Tribune*, too. Neither one had had any trouble saying Nolan had killed himself. It was not fair, not fair at all.

Alvie had planned well, and she wanted the judge's family to suffer as she had. Maybe they believed he had done himself in after all. Yes, that made sense. How could they call it an accident? Well, she would make sure next time there was no doubt at all. She was smart. She would find out what she could about her son's probation officer, the lawyer that was supposed to defend him, the damn lawyer for the county who wanted him put away, and anyone else who was responsible.

Oh, yes, and Jason Browne, the turncoat, the traitor. Maybe he was the worst of them all. If you couldn't trust your best friend, who could you trust?

Yes, Alvie, good old Alvie had finally found purpose in her life; besides raising Rebecca, of course. But this was for Rebecca. For Rebecca, and for Nolan, and for her. She knew if Nolan was watching from wherever, he would be smiling, maybe laughing.

What about that classmate of Nolan's, the sergeant? Nolan had never bought a school yearbook, but there were probably some at the library. Alvie would look her up. She wasn't a cop when Nolan died, so Alvie couldn't blame her for what had happened to him. Rebecca had warmed to her right away, and Alvie had to respect that. The sergeant had been kind to her granddaughter, and to the memory of her son.

Maybe Alvie could work with her a little, provide some clues to let her think the judge really had killed himself. But how? Her mind was tired of thinking about the judge. She needed her brain to plan the next suicide.

Alvie sat on her La-Z-Boy with a notepad and pencil. She quickly scrawled out five names.

Jason Browne, double-crosser
Marshall Kelton, useless public defender
Sara Speiss, spineless probation officer
Arthur Franz, merciless county attorney
Detective Dawes, heartless cop

Each one had put a nail in Nolan's coffin. Why had it taken ten long years of misery and suffering to avenge her son's death?

The question was, where to next? Should she scope out each of them then play it by ear as the opportunity arose? No, that was too unorganized. She might never have the perfect set-up like she had at the hospital again.

Alvie tore a sheet of paper into five pieces and put a name to each piece. She shuffled the papers for a minute, then laid them on the coffee table. She would move, left to right, to eliminate each one, in order of the draw.

It was as good a system as any.

Chapter 7

My Grandfather Brandt, "Gramps," was watching television when I walked into his living room. He had gotten addicted to *Guiding Light* sometime during his retirement and usually stayed tuned to see what Dr. Phil had to say.

"Hey, Gramps. Who is doing what on that soap, now?" I yelled over the loud volume of the set.

"Hello, sweetheart." He knew I really wasn't interested in the lives of his soap families. I heard enough of those stories in real life.

I bent down to kiss his cheek then looked around for the remote. "Are you set for some serious fishing?"

"Didn't you see the pole and tackle by the door when you came in?" He patted my hand.

"Yes I did, so let's go!"

Gramps pushed himself out of his chair with effort and shuffled to the television to shut it off. He was too stubborn to use his cane, and Mom even had me worrying he was a bad fall waiting to happen. I hooked my hand on his arm, and we eventually got to my car.

"Have you heard where the fish are biting?" I wondered.

"South side of Bison, by the public access. They're catching sunnies from shore." He didn't get out much, but he always had the answer to that question.

"Should we pick up sandwiches from the deli, Gramps, for an early supper?"

He waved his hand as a "no." "Your mother's bringing me pot roast for dinner, so I'll pass. There will be plenty for you, Corky, you know that."

"Sounds great. We'll see what time we get back. I have my ballet class tonight." I climbed behind the wheel, but looked at my grandfather before turning the ignition. "Gramps, did Mother tell you about Judge Fenneman?"

Gramps clicked his tongue. "Yes, and I heard it on the radio this morning, too. He was a good man. A real shame. And drowned, for Pete's sake. At this age, you pray you go in your sleep."

Gramps was elderly, past expected longevity, but I hoped he would be around for a long time to come. He kept me sane when his daughter, my bordering-on-eccentric mother, drove me crazy.

I attended ballet class Tuesday evenings when I was not working; otherwise it was Saturday mornings—not ideal when I was on duty late Friday night. A new six-week session was starting that night. I pulled on my sleeveless leotard and a pair of exercise shorts, grabbed my bag, and headed out the door.

My work cell phone rang halfway to town. "Sergeant Aleckson."

"Don't you check your messages?" It was my friend Sara, a probation officer for Winnebago County. We had met shortly after I hired on as a deputy. She'd joined me in a jail conference room for an interview with one of her clients following his arrest. Her jade green eyes flashed with fury at the young man for committing another crime while he was on probation. I admired her spirit and spunk from that first day. She was small, but as tough as she needed to be with her probationers.

"You know I do," I said and grabbed my personal cell phone from the car seat. Three missed calls, one from Sara. "Oh, gosh, sorry, I was with Gramps until about fifteen minutes ago. You know how he hates when I bring my cell phone fishing, so I left it in my car. The fish were really hitting on Bison, so he didn't want to leave, which almost made me late to my class, which I'm driving to as we speak," I explained.

"Whew, take a breath! That's right, my friend the ballerina." I could hear the smile around her words.

"I haven't heard from Baryshnikov yet."

"Who?"

I laughed. "Never mind. What's up?"

"I bought some chicken breasts to throw on the grill. You eaten yet?" she asked.

"No, I even passed up Mother's pot roast."

"Are you crazy?"

"You have to ask?"

I could see her smile again. "Touché."

"Actually, I just didn't have time before class." I pulled into the last available parking spot in the back of the dance studio in downtown Oak Lea.

"So, you want to stop over after class? You'll be hungry. I even bought a bottle of Australian wine Arthur recommended." Arthur was the county attorney and knew his wines.

"Sure. I'm here, so see you in a little over an hour." Sara said a quick "bye," and I turned off my cell phone.

My mother had started me on ballet lessons as a child, but I had hated them. Climbing trees and playing sports was much more fun. She finally let me quit in junior high, after I had begged for two long years. Mother had been more surprised than pleased when I started going again three years before.

I had pulled a muscle in my thigh after chasing a suspect across a pasture in the dark. I caught my foot on an exposed tree root. My right leg stopped, but the rest of my body kept moving. I tumbled, jumped up, and took off again. Fortunately, the suspect had run out of breath by then, so I didn't have to go far on my injured leg. By the time I had him cuffed and stuffed in my squad car, I was hurting and needed a good program for stretching, toning, and rebuilding. A former classmate of mine taught ballet. She suggested I give it a try, and I got hooked. Who'd have thought?

My skin was glistening with sweat after the workout. I pulled a towel from my bag to dry off. Students for the next class were beginning to file in and put on their shoes. I dropped to the ground to change back into my sandals when I felt a presence hovering.

"Sergeant, is that you?"

I looked up at hospital administrator Nicolas Bradshaw. That morning I doubted I'd ever see him again, and the dance studio was the last place I would have picked for a chance meeting. I stood up and took the hand he was offering.

"Good to see you in a more relaxed setting," he said and continued to hold my hand.

"Are you taking ballet lessons?" I asked, trying not to sound as surprised as I felt.

Bradshaw's baritone laugh filled the room and drew everyone's attention. First my face flushed, then the rest of my body joined in.

"Sorry," he said. "I was just trying to imagine myself in a leotard. Your body is much better suited for one." He slowly perused the body in question, fueling the spreading burn.

A young girl of eight or nine appeared at Bradshaw's side. He put a protective arm around her shoulder. "Sergeant Aleckson, I'd like you to meet my daughter, Faith. Darling, this is Sergeant Aleckson from the Winnebago Sheriff's Department."

Her lips curved into a small smile. "Nice to meet you, ma'am."

I took her tiny hand. "Very pleased to meet you. What a lovely name, Faith."

"It was my grandma's. She died," Faith said matter-of-factly.

"Then I'm glad you got her name."

"Me, too."

Faith was fine-boned with delicate features. She had her father's dark eyes and hair, but her complexion was fair. I would never have picked her as Bradshaw's daughter.

"Dad, class is about to start." Faith gave his arm a little tug.

"All right, I'm gone. Sergeant . . ." He turned to me. "Will you consider joining me for a coffee, or another refreshment, while my daughter takes her class?"

"Oh, thank you, but I'm going to a friend's for dinner. In fact, I better run, but thanks."

A slight frown narrowed the space between his eyes, revealing his disappointment. I sensed loneliness.

"Another time?" he asked.

"Ah, sure." I ran out the door.

Well, Mother, I almost had a sort-of date. Nicholas Bradshaw, a gorgeous widower with a little girl.

"Come in," Sara yelled from inside.

"Hey, Sara. Thanks for the invite—I'm starving." The smell of chicken on the grill wafted from the deck into the kitchen. Sara handed me a glass of white wine. "Thanks, but I best down some water first." I helped myself, then leaned against the counter with the wine.

Sara added dressing to the green salad she was tossing. "Tell me about Judge Fenneman. I heard you took the call, did the investigation."

"Not much to tell. Not much of an investigation." I filled her in on all the details, the death scene, Mrs. Moy, the hospital, the administrator and staff, the alarm not working, the lack of a real cause or satisfying answers. I decided to reserve a personal conversation about Bradshaw for another night, after I had sorted out my feelings.

"I got to interview one of yours," I told her.

Sara looked up from her salad preparation. "Who's that?"

"Bart Rogers. He's on the same wing as the judge was."

She shook her head in mock disbelief. "Ah, yes, the famous Bart Andrew Rogers. We have an appointment set up for his last offense, and now he almost kills himself doing the same thing!

Some people are more challenging than others, and Bart definitely takes more of my energy than most."

"Be glad you aren't married to him."

We laughed, then I thought about my talk with little Rebecca Eisner. Sara was four years older than me and not originally from Oak Lea. It occurred to me that she might not have heard about Nolan.

"Sara, do you remember a Nolan Eisner—were you here then?"

Sara dropped her spoon and stared at me. "Oh, Lord. He was my first case in Winnebago County. Why, of all the people in the world—or in his case, no longer in the world—did you think of him? I didn't even know you then." She was visibly distressed, her face paled, brows knitted together in an uncharacteristic frown.

"You're upset. Sorry, I had no idea he was yours." I filled a glass with wine and handed it to her.

Sara accepted the drink. "Since I tell you everything else, I'm surprised I never told you about that case." She stared at the wall for a moment. "But I guess it was a few years before you started as deputy—before I ever met you."

Sara sank onto a bar stool by the counter. "You knew Nolan Eisner?"

"He was in my class at school. When he wasn't in detention, that is," I said.

Sara leaned her body forward across the counter and rubbed her arms. "I almost quit my job after he killed himself. I was this close . . ." she drew her index finger and thumb within a quarter inch of each other ". . . chucking my career and moving back home."

Sara was originally from Brainerd, about two hours north. She picked up her wine and took a long sip.

"I'm glad you didn't. Did you ever meet his mother?" I wondered.

"Unfortunately, I saw her every day during the trial, sitting like a statue in the courtroom, mostly just staring. Nolan was in jail, so I did the pretrial investigation and other meetings there. She wasn't at those meetings, thank God!"

Sara took a gulp of wine before going on. "The only time I spoke to her was after Nolan died. She came to my office, walked in without an appointment, about quitting time, and just stood by the door and stared. It frankly scared the bejeebers out of me. I finally managed to tell her I was very sorry about her son.

"She didn't change her expression, kept staring at me for the longest time, then finally said, 'You shouldn't have sent him to prison.' I got kind of choked up and looked down at my desk for a minute, trying to think of what to say. When I looked up a few seconds later, she was gone."

She downed the remainder of her wine.

"Oh my gosh, Sara. That's all she said, just, 'You shouldn't have sent him to prison'?" Sara nodded.

"How strange is that?" I poured a little more wine in my glass. "I can tell you, she hasn't changed."

"What do you mean?"

I told her all I knew about Nolan and meeting Rebecca and Ms. Eisner.

I shuddered, a surprise given the heat and humidity. "I have an eerie feeling every time I think of her. I can imagine her staring at me, even now."

"Stop it." Sara gave me a small shove. "You're giving me the creeps."

Chapter 8

Alvie

Alvie sat in her Chevy on the street southwest of Sara Speiss' house. She parked so she had a clear view through two trees and over a hedge of bushes. She could see the probation officer and the little sergeant in Speiss' kitchen. The P.O. was cooking something on the grill and had stepped outside once to check it. Alvie thought she was well hidden on the tree lined street, but sank down in the seat anyway.

Alvie had gone through her father's clothes, ones she hadn't gotten around to throwing away in the thirty years since his death. She found one gray work jumpsuit he had worn once or twice, so it looked pretty good yet. It didn't take her father long in his job as an auto mechanic for his uniforms to get covered with grease. They just didn't get clean going through the wash. So Alvie had herself a jumpsuit with a "George" name patch above her left breast. She added a black ball cap, sunglasses, and a fake mustache Rebecca had used the past Halloween to complete her disguise.

Alvie felt very clever indeed.

The sergeant being with Speiss was a surprise. Maybe she lived there, too. That could make things a little more complicated, but Alvie told herself she could handle it. Actually, it could make things more interesting.

Alvie had gotten some information on the little sergeant at the library. She remembered seeing yearbooks in the reference section where she'd found the *Physician's Desk Reference*, so it wasn't as nerve-racking when she made a second trip to the library.

The *Oak Lea Almanac* was purple leather stamped with white lettering. Purple and white, the school colors, from what

Alvie remembered. The Student Index listed the entire school in alphabetical order. *Eisner, Nolan, Page 111.* She flipped to the page and found Nolan's name in the "Not Pictured" list. Alvie had forgotten he didn't have a senior picture taken.

Aleckson, Corinne "Corky," Pages 19, 43, 46, 51, 67, 71, 75, and 105. Alvie located each page and the sergeant's smiling face in page after page of smiling faces. Happy little groupies. Student Council, Yearbook Committee, Homecoming Royalty, Band, Volleyball, Girls' Basketball, Girls' Track Team, Senior Picture: the only one she was alone on. Popular and busy. Like her mother and her father had been. Alvie recalled from her short time at Oak Lea High. The kind of people you either liked or hated.

Maybe Alvie was a little jealous that everyone else seemed to have a normal life, except her and Henry. So what? That was in the past. What was important was what she could do about it, how she could make a good future for Rebecca. Get rid of all the people who had killed Nolan.

Speiss was listed as S. Speiss in the phone book. Corinne or C. Aleckson was not listed. Maybe she lived with her mother. Kristen Aleckson was in the book. Corinne was probably hiding from the bad guys. Ha! Alvie would have to do a little more investigating to find out where the little sergeant lived.

It bothered Alvie deeply that the newspaper had written Judge Fenneman died accidentally when it clearly looked like a suicide. She would get a note off to Sergeant Corinne Aleckson at the Winnebago County Sheriff's Department. The sergeant would be sure to get it there.

But Alvie didn't want to think any more. It was more fun to watch, and to know it wouldn't be long.

Did you hear that, son?

Chapter 9

"**S**moke, look at this." I had stared at the words for a full minute before tracking him down at his desk. It was Thursday, my "Monday" of a five-day stretch.

"What is it, Corky?"

I handed him the unlined piece of paper with the words computer-printed in capital letters: "WHAT MAKES A SUICIDE AN ACCIDENT?"

"What the hell? Where did this come from?" Smoke squinted and held the letter up to the light.

"The mail—it was in my box, mailed to me. Here's the envelope."

"Postmarked Oak Lea, mailed locally. Your name and address is printed in block letters—no writing I recognize."

"What does it mean? What are they talking about?" I was puzzled.

Smoke leaned back and read the words again. "How many unusual deaths have you had lately that were ruled accidental?"

I bent over his desk, taking in the words once more. "Oh. So someone thinks Judge Fenneman killed himself?"

"That would be my guess." We stared at each other, each of us hoping to pull an explanation from the other.

"What do you think?" I asked, breaking the long silence. "Does someone know something about the judge, maybe knew he was depressed—something no one else seemed to know—and couldn't bring himself, or herself, to tell Mrs. Moy, or the doctors, and let's not forget, the police?"

Smoke blew out a long, steady breath and shifted in his chair, bringing out the squeaks. "Corky, you're most likely the next in line for investigator, if Hughes ever officially throws in the towel, that is. This is a high-profile death, so be careful."

"What are you saying?" I asked.

"Be discreet. According to the doctors, the death was accidental. According to Clarice, it had to be accidental. I think we need to talk to the sheriff. Damn."

"This is a helluva deal on the day we're going to bury Judge Fenneman." Sheriff Twardy's ruddy tone darkened and his features tightened into a scowl.

"Who were the judge's closest friends?" Smoke asked.

"Besides his late wife, his former law partner, John Wallace. He joined us for golf when he could."

I knew Mr. Wallace. He and his wife had recently moved to an assisted living apartment. According to my most reliable source—my mother—his wife had some physical difficulties and her husband could no longer care for her at home.

"Do you think he would write this note?" I asked.

Sheriff Twardy snapped the note in front of me. "For godsakes, Corky, why would John do something like this? He'd give me a call, or stop in to see me. What would be his motivation for telling *you* his friend committed suicide and didn't die accidentally?"

"I don't know, sir."

"A helluva deal on the day we bury the judge."

The pews of Bethlehem Lutheran, the largest church in Oak Lea, were packed. People had to sit closer together than on any given Sunday morning, with the exception of Easter morning. The funeral was set for five o'clock in the afternoon to accommodate most people's work schedules. A dinner at the VFW hall was to follow the interment at the cemetery.

Smoke took my arm when he spotted my mother and dragged me to her. "Hello, Kristen," he said quietly.

"Elton, Corinne." Her lips curled slightly, the smile she reserved for somber moments when she was nonetheless glad to see you.

Smoke leaned over slowly and put his cheek on hers. They both closed their eyes for a moment, and I watched their brief intimacy with interest.

"Let's find a seat in back. Corky's on duty," Smoke said.

I checked to make certain my pager was on silent/vibrate. Communications knew my radio was off and would page me for any emergency. Half of the county was present: hospital board members, county and town officials, court personnel. Bradshaw was sitting near the front with his secretary.

The small family filed in: Mrs. Moy, Allan and his wife, Heather, her husband and two children, Mr. and Mrs. John Wallace. Even the infamous Mr. Moy was there, minus the new wife. There were a few others with the family group, perhaps siblings, in-laws or cousins of the judge. I scanned the church and sensed Smoke doing the same. My mother, seated between two sets of roving eyes, didn't even notice. Her own were filled with tears.

I watched Mr. Wallace for a moment. He looked more stricken than Mrs. Moy did, if that was possible. The sheriff was probably right. What motivation would Wallace have to send the note? A deep-seated desire to set the record straight? The sheriff might not approve, but I was investigating the matter, and I owed it to the judge to find out.

The late afternoon sun pushed a rainbow of colors through the stained glass windows, adorning the guests and the countless bouquets of flowers. The service was a tribute to a man who had dedicated his life to public service. The music, the eulogy, the reassurances of the minister, and the Bible readings were designed to give comfort and hope, but the unanswered questions put an added damper on the day.

The family followed the minister and pallbearers with the coffin out of the church to the waiting hearse. The congregation began to file out slowly behind. A mysterious chill ran through me, and my eyes locked with Nolan's mother's. She was standing about ten feet away, holding Rebecca's hand. For a second I considered saying "hi" to the little girl, telling her I was glad she was out of the hospital, but I noticed her grandma looking from Smoke to my mother, then back to me. *What a strange woman,* I thought for the countless time as I left the church.

Chapter 10

Alvie

Alvie had to be there. She hated crowds and most people, but she had no choice—she had to be at the funeral. It gave her great comfort to see the judge's family and friends in pain. Of course, there were all the people who had to be there for political and professional reasons. The sheriff; she hadn't thought much about him before. He was the top law enforcement dog in the county, and had been back when Nolan got sent away. Maybe she should add him to the list. She'd think about that.

Alvie was able to spot just about everyone on her list—the county attorney, the probation officer, Nolan's attorney, the detective. That was another surprise, Detective Dawes seemed pretty cozy with the little sergeant and her mother. She didn't even want to know what shenanigans they might be up to.

Alvie remembered Kristen Brandt and Carl Aleckson from school. Her father had moved her and Henry to Oak Lea during Alvie's sophomore year of high school. Kristen and Carl were popular seniors and probably did not even know Alvie existed. Of course, she had only attended school for four months before she began to show with Nolan and had to quit before people asked a lot of questions.

She felt a slight twinge of guilt the sergeant would be losing two of her friends, but it couldn't be helped. They had helped destroy Nolan and had to pay for their crimes; it was that simple.

The sergeant looked like she was going to talk to her and Rebecca. It was better she didn't. Alvie had never taken Rebecca to a funeral before, and if the little sergeant started asking questions, Rebecca might start asking Alvie questions, and the whole thing would get more complicated. It was a funny thing. Alvie did kind of like the little sergeant, but of course they could

71

never be friends. She might have been kind to Rebecca and the memory of her son, but she was, after all, one of them.

Alvie overheard a dozen conversations. What a wonderful man the judge was, what a tragic way to die, how his only daughter will be lost without him, on and on. "There was no suicide note, so the authorities dismissed that right away." The words got louder and louder in Alvie's brain: "no suicide note, no suicide note." She had messed up. All her careful planning, and she had not thought of that one detail. One small detail had become one large mistake. What had Nolan's note said? "Sorry, Mama, I love you."

She started to sweat—time to leave. Right away. And Rebecca needed to get home to rest anyway. She was going to camp the next week and needed to be completely well. It was difficult for Alvie to let Rebecca have friends, but Rebecca was very social—a trait she had gotten from her mother—so Alvie let her spend time with Tina. Tina went to a church camp every year, and Alvie had finally said Rebecca could go with her. As it turned out, the timing could not have been more perfect. Alvie needed to do some more planning, and it would be easier to work with Rebecca away.

How would she write the suicide notes? She had her computer. That would make them look neat, professional-like. And she had letters, signed letters and things from at least some of the people who needed to die. She'd have to look at the file. She had never wanted to see it again, but she'd kept it anyway. Alvie finally knew why—she would need it for the signatures.

After she got home, Alvie waited until Rebecca fell asleep, then pulled the box from under her bed and blew the dust away. There was no reason to label it. She knew what was inside. The arrest report signed by Elton Dawes, Deputy Sheriff, and witnessed by Arthur Franz, County Attorney. The pre-sentence investigation completed and signed by Sara Speiss. The letter of agreement to represent Nolan signed by Marshall Kelton, Public Defender. The execution of sentence signed by Judge Nels

Fenneman. Well, it was too late for that signature. She wondered what the little sergeant was doing about the note she had sent her, hinting that Judge Fenneman's death was no accident, that maybe he had done himself in, after all.

The more she thought about it, the more Alvie realized she might just have to let that one go. Maybe the judge's family did think he'd killed himself, but didn't want the press to have a field day with it. She had to concentrate on the rest of the jobs at hand, make sure they were all done right, commit the perfect murders, bing, bing, bing. So much to do, so little time. It was the fifteenth of July, and she wanted all of her work done by September first, Nolan's twenty-ninth birthday.

So little time.

Chapter 11

I was on my way back from the evidence room when my pager went off: the sheriff. I felt like a child summoned to the principal's office, only worse. When the sheriff paged me, I was usually in trouble, and I knew what I had done.

"Yes, sir?" I asked outside his open door.

"For godsakes, Aleckson, get in here and close the door." I did as commanded.

"You questioned John Wallace? You actually questioned him?" The sheriff's hands were in balls of fists on his desktop. His face was a literal beacon, and I would have felt very guilty if he'd stroked out or dropped dead from a heart attack.

"Sir, please. I did not question him, I merely asked him a few questions," I offered quietly.

"In my book, and in his, too, for that matter, that constitutes questioning." He pounded his fist on the desk for emphasis, and the tips of his ears were glowing red. It was not the time to argue what constituted questioning, legally speaking. The longer he glared at me, the tighter my stomach got.

"I'm sorry, sir. He seemed happy to talk to me, to be part of the investigation."

"Well, John Wallace apologizing for being late for our golf game because he was being questioned by one of my sergeants is a helluva way for me to find out about it, in my opinion."

"I'm sorry, sir." What else could I say?

"Okay. Enough said. Point made." He relaxed a moment, leaning back to an upright position in his chair, folding his hands and resting them on his stomach. "So, tell me everything. John didn't say much."

"To me, either. I showed him the letter, and his response was about the same as ours. 'Who in the world sent this, and why?' He said Nels Fenneman had been his best friend for over fifty years and he could not imagine a reason for him to kill himself. He was a survivor and a devout Christian. If the judge had been depressed—and Mr. Wallace said he wasn't—he would have gotten professional help."

The sheriff nodded. "I think it is probably some nut who was mad at Fenneman for a decision somewhere along the way and saw the opportunity for one last jab. Accidents usually raise more questions than they answer."

I pondered his words.

Sheriff Twardy noticed the bag I was holding. "What's in the evidence bag?"

I laid it on his desk. "It's the judge—there's something about his death I can't let go of. As you just said, 'accidents raise more questions than they answer.' I get this bag out of evidence almost every day I'm here and look at it—like that does any good. I keep thinking something will come to me. Kinda strange, huh?"

"What have you got in there?" the sheriff wondered.

"Not much. The fingerprint slides from the push bar on the emergency exit. A hair from the judge's glasses that obviously wasn't his. The IV bottle and tubing. The sheet from the bed is in a paper bag in the drying locker. I have copies of the photos I took in my desk. Between this bag and the pictures, and now this goofy note."

I pulled a copy of it out of my breast pocket. "I keep thinking something will jump out at me—some missing piece that will solve this puzzle," I said.

"Don't beat yourself up over this. The fingerprints came back to the judge, four nurses, one maintenance man, and one unknown. Maybe a patient, maybe a visitor; they aren't on file. The hair didn't match anyone on duty that night, and it will be weeks before the DNA test results come back from the BCA. Who knows how many different people's hairs might have washed into that pond, for godsakes?"

He paused before going on. "I can't believe he went in such a bizarre way, either. There are things in this life we never get answers for." Sheriff Twardy's voice quieted. He was uncharacteristically subdued.

"And what about the door alarm?" I wondered out loud. "They tested it twenty-five times the morning after he died, and it worked every time. Why would it not work the one time it was really needed, the one time a patient got out and ended up dying because of it?" My voice was a little too loud, and the sheriff flinched. It was difficult for him, a man used to tragedies, but hit especially hard by that one.

"More questions raised than answered," the sheriff repeated.

"**S**ergeant Aleckson?" I opened my eyes to see Nicolas Bradshaw standing in the doorway. "How can I help you?"

I jumped to my feet. "Hi. I, ah, the receptionist said the room wasn't occupied. I hope my being here is okay. I didn't touch anything." Except the chair I sat in.

Bradshaw stepped into the room. "The receptionist called to tell me you were here asking about room one-twenty in B-Wing, and I wondered why. Are you looking for anything special?" he asked.

"No. I mean, I am, but I don't know what it is. It seems silly, but I came here hoping something would jump out at me. I have walked the path from this bed to the back exit door a dozen times. Why, and how, did Judge Fenneman get out of bed, go directly to that door, and push it open without activating the alarm?"

He shook his head. "I wish to God I knew."

"Would the judge have known the door code?" I asked.

Bradshaw shook his head. "Only hospital personnel have access."

"I got this in the mail the day of the funeral." I handed a copy of the note to Bradshaw.

He studied the note and my face. "An odd letter. What does it mean?"

"I don't know, except someone apparently doesn't like the ruling of 'accidental death' for the judge."

Bradshaw handed the note back to me. "It doesn't say anything about Judge Fenneman."

"No, but he is the only one who even vaguely fits, given the cases I've had in the past, say, six months. And it was sent directly to me," I explained.

Bradshaw moved closer and put his hands on each of my shoulders. "I have a bad feeling about this."

"Tell me about it," I said in agreement, then offered the note back to him. "Why don't you keep this copy and show it to the doctors, nurses? Maybe someone has an idea. It's not always easy for those closest to a case to think outside the box. Be casual about it, though. It may mean something, it may mean nothing."

"Of course." His hands moved to the backs of my arms, and I heard the note crinkle. "See you tomorrow?"

"Tomorrow?" I racked my brain. Tomorrow was my first day off. What was I supposed to do that I had forgotten about?

"Ballet class."

I smiled and nodded an "oh, yeah."

"This time will you join me for a drink, or a bite to eat, or even a walk by the lake? Unless you're seeing someone. You aren't, are you?" His voice was earnest, his eyes searching.

"Well, no, but . . ."

"I really want to see you again."

Oh! "Why not? Okay, I'll bring a change of clothes."

Bradshaw smiled. "I liked what you were wearing last week." My face grew warm, remembering the embarrassment I had felt during the encounter with him.

"I'll bring a change," I repeated.

My radio clicked. "Winnebago County, Six-oh-eight." I stepped away from Bradshaw and turned the volume up.

"Six-oh-eight, County, go ahead."

"We have report of a personal injury accident on Highway Fifty-five and County Road One-thirty-seven. My partner is dispatching the ambulance."

"Ten-four. Put me en route from Oak Lea Memorial, with an ETA of three to four minutes." I glanced at Bradshaw in way of a goodbye and sprinted to my squad car. Like always, I said a prayer for the injured as I drove ahead of the wail of my sirens to the scene.

Chapter 12

"**Y**ou look very . . . nice. Lovely." Bradshaw was admiring the delicately flowered sundress—a gift from my mother—I had changed into after class. "Where would you like to go?"

"What are my choices?"

"Have you eaten?" I shook my head. "Then your choices are French, German, Italian, Chinese, or American. Or, we can pick up deli and eat in the park."

"What about Faith?" Forty-five minutes wasn't very long for dinner.

"Jody Ashe, a mom with twin daughters in the class, is taking her to their house to play. Faith has gotten to know them pretty well this summer. They only live a few blocks from us. We discovered that through ballet class." He slipped his hand on my elbow and guided me outside. "So, what are you hungry for?"

"I haven't been to the new French restaurant yet. And it's close."

"Good choice. After you."

C'est la Vie was located on the east bank of Bison Lake, two blocks from the dance studio. The building had been remodeled when an interior decorator retired and some yuppies from Minnetonka thought it would be an ideal location for a restaurant. They were right, I had to admit, sitting at the outdoor patio table across from Bradshaw, sipping wine and eating striped sea bass. I hadn't decided whether I would tell Gramps how much fish cost when it was prepared and served at C'est la Vie.

After dinner we took a walk along the lake. Two paved pathways ran from Central Avenue to Town Park, one for use by pedestrians and one for bikers. To accommodate swimmers, fishers, and boaters for their sports, three municipal docks were rolled out into the water each spring and taken in before winter. Various residents adopted garden plots, scattered here and there along the path, and filled them with flowers of every color imaginable.

The humidity had lifted, and we had a window of about thirty minutes before dusk brought out the droves of hungry mosquitoes from their daytime hiding places. Bradshaw took my hand and wrapped his larger one around it. We walked in silence for a bit. I liked the firmness of his hold and relaxed in the security of his grip.

How ironic.

I had fought my mother's protection most of my life, yet it seemed natural, comfortable, with Bradshaw. I forgot about the demands of my job and family for those minutes with him and simply enjoyed the sparkling orange pathway the sun cut across the lake, the trees nodding at each other in the breeze, and the way the flowers held their faces high, proud of their beauty.

A lazy, Minnesota summer evening.

We sat down on a bench near the walking path. Boats of hopeful fishers were anchored throughout the lake. We watched a couple propelling their paddleboat about twenty feet from shore, and the occasional jogger ran past. The troubled world I worked in was brushed aside, all but forgotten, and I felt calm, at peace.

"Do you live here in Oak Lea? You aren't in the phone book," Bradshaw said, competing with a croaking frog and happy, childish squeals from the nearby park.

"I do. I built a house west of here, off County Road Thirty-five. I took an unlisted phone number when an unhappy camper started harassing me," I told him.

"And that turned out okay?"

"Oh, yes, six months in jail gave him time to think on the error of his ways. He was going through a bad time—he lost his job and his wife and started drinking. I arrested him for DWI, and he snapped. He wrote me a letter of apology from jail and seems to have his life back in order." I hadn't thought about that for a while.

"You live alone?" I nodded. "Ever been married?"

I laughed and shook my head. "I have never even had a serious relationship."

"I find that very hard to believe. You are what, twenty-five, twenty-six?"

"Twenty-nine, next month."

"And you have never had a serious relationship?" He leaned closer to me, his eyes fixed on mine.

I shook my head. "No."

"Why not?"

"I'm not sure." The pattern in my dress became instantly fascinating. "The boys in high school were all just good friends. At college I spent the week studying, and on weekends I went home to see my mother, who was in crisis having both of her children gone." I looked up again. "The last few years, I don't know, I suppose I haven't wanted to date anyone I work with and I haven't met anyone else."

Bradshaw reached over and squeezed my hand.

"How about you?" I asked. "Tell me about yourself. When did you move here—how did you choose Oak Lea?"

"Three years ago, the hospital in southeast Minnesota I was running was bought out by the Mayo Clinic. Oak Lea was looking for someone to replace Sheldon Loch, who was retiring. Faith and I took a few days, scouted the area, visited the schools. I thought it was a good fit for us, and it certainly has turned out to be a great move. I was worried about pulling Faith out of kindergarten midyear, but actually it was a good time. She made friends her first week."

"What happened to her mother?"

"Liver cancer. She died when Faith was three. Just over four years ago."

"I'm sorry, it must have been very difficult for both of you." I squeezed his hands.

"My biggest regret is that I had been so busy trying to carve out our future, I didn't live in the present when Jenny was sick. Jenny needed me, Faith needed me, the hospital needed me, and I kind of shut down for a while. I had no idea Jenny would go so fast. It was only four months after she was diagnosed." His eyes glistened with unshed tears as he searched the lake.

I didn't know what to say. I heard sad stories every day, but my heart went out to this man who had been left to raise his daughter alone, like my mother had been left to raise John Carl and me. I moved closer to Bradshaw, and he slid one arm around my shoulder and rested his other hand on my lap, playing with my fingers, one by one. I told him the story of my father and mother.

"Is that the real reason you haven't dated—you're afraid you'll fall in love, then he'll die and leave you alone? Like your father's death left your mother alone?" His look was tender, his voice soothing, and it took me a minute to realize the meaning of his words.

"No, I, not at all, I . . ." That wasn't true, was it?

"It's okay, Corky, it's okay. I have a confession of my own." It was a moment before he spoke. "You are the first woman I've asked out since Jenny died, the first woman I have even wanted to ask out. I couldn't believe it. I met you under the worst of circumstances, but you were like a light in a dark forest."

My heart beat fiercely in my chest when he hooked his fingers under my chin and leaned his face toward mine.

"Hi, Corky!" A voice called from the walking path. I glanced up to see a friend from high school jog by.

I waved back and popped to my feet. "It's getting to be dusk, and mosquito time," I offered as an explanation.

Bradshaw stood and looked at his watch. "You're right, and I told the Ashes I'd pick Faith up by nine." He reached out for me, grasping my hand. "Come with me."

"Oh, ah, I'd love to, but I'm pretty wiped out. The accident call you heard me get at the hospital was the first of many calls last night. I promised my body an early night."

Bradshaw kept an arm around my waist on the way to our cars. He looked around the parking lot. "Which one is yours?"

"The oldest one in the lot, the GTO."

Bradshaw forgot me for the moment and strolled around my car, taking in every detail, whistling low.

"My uncle had a GTO, different year. She is a beauty. If we had more time, I'd beg a ride."

His approval pleased me. A lot. "I do love my old car. It was my dad's."

"She is a beauty," he said again.

He took a second walk around it then turned his attention to me, closing the space between us, pulling me into his arms. I saw the pulse in his neck beating fast and felt my own heartbeat pick up speed in response.

"Corky, will you see me again?"

"Yes, I'd like—"

"This?" he asked and his lips closed over mine as his hands crept around my waist and up my back. The kiss started gently, then grew deeper and deeper until I was literally breathless, finally lifting my head for oxygen. Nick rested his forehead on mine and exhaled little bursts of air while his thumbs massaged my upper arms.

"Corky, I don't want to say goodnight, not yet. Come home with me," he invited.

I took a step back, resting my hands on Nick's waist, studying his face. His color had darkened and his eyelids were lazy, making him even more appealing. A short battle waged inside me. I wanted to go home with him, wanted this night to go on forever, but . . .

"As much as I'd like to, I don't think that would be a good idea tonight." Things were moving a little too fast, and I was afraid we were both getting carried away by the moment.

"I'll reluctantly accept that. How about tomorrow night?"

I couldn't help laughing. "Okay."

Nick picked up my hand, drew it to his lips, then caressed it with his cheek. "Corky, this is new ground for me, and for Faith too. I've haven't dated since her mother died, I'm not certain how she'll react. You know, it's just been the two of us for a long time now. Since I'm gone all day and have meetings some evenings, I try to spend as much time as possible with her. Do you mind if we include her, at least for part of the evening?"

"Of course I don't mind. It's a great idea."

Nick smiled and kissed my fingertips. "I can cook, in fact I'm pretty good at it, all modesty aside. Does seven o'clock work for you?"

"Sure." He gave me his address, and we exchanged telephone numbers.

"Thanks for dinner, Nick. Goodnight." Before my hand reached my door handle, I was back in Bradshaw's—in Nick's — arms again. His fingers tangled in my hair and his lips gently nibbled my jaw, my cheek, my lower lip. His lips touched mine for only a second before he pulled away.

"Until tomorrow."

I grabbed the door handle to support my weak legs, slid into my car, and watched Nick walk away, taking in as many details of him as I could. His straight, elongated spine, broad shoulders tapering to a narrower waist and hips, legs that carried him with smooth, long strides, arms swinging gently. He turned and raised his hand as goodnight. His smile worked its way inside of me, warming me from head to toe. I turned the ignition in my GTO, found my cell phone, and hit number three on speed dial as I eased from my parking spot.

"Sara, can I stop over for a minute?"

"Corky, you sound different. Is everything all right?"

Chapter 13

Alvie

That little sergeant again. Alvie sank down in her car when Sergeant Aleckson pulled into Speiss' driveway. Alvie knew it was at least the third time in a week the sergeant had been there. Every time Alvie was there, the sergeant showed up. Maybe it was a message that Speiss shouldn't be next. She had been so sure choosing the names by lots was best, but maybe there was a better way. What would that be? Alphabetically? By first or last name?

Problem questions led to such headaches. She would just keep watch and not think. Her best ideas came to her when she wasn't working so hard at it, right? The sergeant was leaving. That was quick. She was only there about fifteen minutes. She'd follow her, see where she went to all dressed up to the nines.

When the sergeant drove off, Alvie started her engine, but kept her headlights off. She stayed about two blocks behind her until the sergeant turned unto County Road 35 and headed west. Where was she going? Alvie had taken the same road the past two days following that county attorney character, Franz, to his lunchtime getaway. She waited a minute, turned her headlights on, and followed. She couldn't risk being stopped for driving with her lights off.

Alvie watched the sergeant's car turn south on Brandt Street. All the little rural roads had names since enhanced 911 had started about ten years before. Brandt. That's where K. Aleckson lived. Maiden name Kristen Brandt. A street named after the family.

Alvie waited a minute before braving the left turn. It was safe to turn her lights off on this rural road. In the distance, she saw the sergeant turn again. Alvie coasted her car to a stop. She could watch from where she was. The garage door went up and the sergeant drove in. It must be her home. Lights came on inside a minute later. It was her home. Did she live alone? That didn't matter, at least not yet. She'd be back another time.

Chapter 14

I wanted one more day off. My normal rotation was seven on, three off, five on, two off, six on, three off, then my favorite, six on, four off. I loved my job, but I loved my days off almost as much.

On my way in to work I replayed my time with Nick on Tuesday night and with Nick and Faith the night before. His kisses were the first thing I thought of that morning. When I told Sara about my attraction for Nick, and my confusion because of it, she interrogated me relentlessly: "Describe him in detail," "What do you like most about him so far?" "How old is he?" "Is he a good kisser?" and on and on.

What I knew was, Nicolas Bradshaw was a devoted father, a successful administrator, a wonderful date, and a great cook. His daughter Faith was a sweetheart, kind and well-mannered, like an adult in a little body. My opinion of Bradshaw had changed considerably since the night we'd met in the hospital. Was that only ten days before?

My work shift started at two-thirty. It was ten after two when I walked into the muster room for my briefing from the day sergeant.

"Nobody's seen him. He had an important arraignment at one-thirty. He didn't come back from lunch, or even call to say he'd be late. It's not like him. He is the consummate professional and insists on being prompt." It was an assistant county attorney, Julie Grimes, talking to Sergeant Chip Roth. She was about my age, very smart, and a hard worker. I had testified for many of her cases the past two years.

They both glanced my way when I walked through the door. I laid my briefcase on the table and listened.

"Do you know where he went for lunch?" Roth asked.

"No. I think he usually brings his lunch, but he always goes out somewhere to eat it. He says it's his time to 'meditate and commune with nature.' He can be an odd duck sometimes." Julie smiled and looked at me.

"Who are you talking about?" I asked.

Julie's face turned serious. "Arthur . . . Franz."

Consummate professional was an apt way to describe the county attorney. He ran his office with an efficiency everyone admired and many envied. Before I appeared in court, Franz always ensured I was thoroughly briefed and well prepared. He had little time for the courtroom dramatics of some of the defense attorneys and didn't allow any from his assistant county attorneys.

On a personal level, Franz was a quiet man, soft-spoken, and small in stature. His manner might not call attention to himself, but his appearance certainly did. He shaved his head, sported a large mustache that seemed to cover half his face, and dressed with a dramatic flair. One day he'd wear a gray pinstripe suit with a pink and purple tie, and the next it would be a fine leather sports coat with a silk shirt and ascot. Arthur Franz had an extensive wardrobe.

"Did he go to lunch alone?" Roth asked.

"As far as I know. I never hear him make plans with anyone, or see him leave with anyone, but that doesn't mean he doesn't, I guess," Julie said.

"Does he have a cell phone?" I asked.

"Yes, we tried calling many times, but it goes to voicemail after four rings. The judge had to order a continuance on the arraignment. The other attorneys and I aren't sure what to do. They sent me down here to ask you guys." Julie's eyes shot back and forth between Roth and me.

"No one in your office knows where he went?" Roth asked.

"No. But Ray Collinwood walked out of the courthouse behind him. He said Arthur got in his car and drove away." Collinwood was another assistant county attorney.

"I'll talk to Ray," I told Roth. "I know you're worried, Julie, but I'm sure Arthur has a good reason for being late."

I sensed she wanted to believe me, but didn't. Something was wrong, and we all knew it.

Sergeant Roth gave me a rundown of the day shift. Mostly routine, except for a domestic assault which wasn't routine on a weekday morning.

"And here are two warrants they want you to serve, if possible. Some people are never home."

I stuck them in my briefcase and gathered my things. Roth was in a hurry to get home. He was newly married to a teacher who had the summer off and spent as much time as possible with her.

I found Ray Collinwood in his office. Ray reminded me of Santa Claus without the beard—round, red-faced, white-haired, and usually jolly. He was on the phone, but ended the call shortly after waving me in.

"I'm here about Arthur Franz," I said.

"Any word?" he asked, not even a little jolly.

"Not yet. I understand you saw him leave for lunch." I sat down and pulled out my memo pad.

Collinwood smoothed his tie over his ample belly. "That's right. He took his car."

"Did you see which way he went?"

"I wasn't paying much attention. Let me think." He closed his eyes. "I was parked on First Avenue, on the street. He drove past me and had his right turn signal on. I didn't actually see him turn, you know, because the hill is there."

"You mean the hill between First Avenue and County Road Thirty-five?" I asked.

Ray extended his arms on his desk and folded his hands. "That's right."

"So, your impression is, Arthur was going to take a right on Thirty-five, but you didn't see him do it?"

"That's right."

"I wonder where he'd be going? Not much out there except farms, lakes, and the two or three small housing developments. He doesn't live there," I said.

Ray shook his head in agreement. "No, he still has his house in Plymouth."

"Julie said he used his lunch hour to 'meditate and commune with nature.'"

"That's what he would say after a difficult morning. 'I'll feel better after I meditate and commune with nature for a while.' It got to be kind of a joke around the office. We wondered if 'nature' is the name of someone he's seeing—he's pretty secretive about his personal life." His grin brought a twinkle to his eyes.

I smiled, then shook my head to dismiss the joke as I handed him my card. "Give me a call if you think of anything else, something he may have said along the way about where he went or what he did."

"Sure, Corky. I can't imagine him just running away without an explanation. He is so ultimately responsible, always." His phone rang, so he gave me a brief wave as he lifted the receiver.

I was able to serve the warrant on Jessica Jean Christy for issuance of worthless checks. When she opened the door of her apartment, I saw a small pile of designer clothes with the price tags still on lying on her couch, evidence she had not overcome her addiction. I took her into custody and drove her to the county jail to be booked. It wasn't my first encounter with Jessica. She had a problem with compulsive shopping and was caught in a vicious circle of writing bad checks, getting arrested, paying fines, and serving time. Like anyone with an addiction, she needed treatment to get at the core of her problem.

I was about to stop a vehicle for speeding and recklessly passing a semi-truck when I got paged. "Winnebago County, Six-oh-eight."

"Six-oh-eight, County, go ahead."

"Sergeant, phone communications, ASAP." I glanced at my watch: Five-twenty.

"Ten-four." I found my phone and punched in the two digit code. "Corky here." I continued to follow Mr. Reckless.

"Sergeant." It was Jerry. "Just got a call from a citizen, Jake Morrow. He's on the east side of Bebee Lake. He found a man dead in his car there. License comes back to Arthur Franz."

I braked and whipped my squad around to head south and east. "He's sure he's dead?"

"What he said was, 'I just found a guy that killed himself.' He's pretty upset; my partner has him on the line."

"Ten-four. Tell him I'm on my way and will be there in a few minutes. Have you called the sheriff?"

"My next call," Jerry said.

"Copy that. I'm about five miles out. Oh, Jerry, radio the One twenty-six squad to keep watch for a red Corvette, Minnesota plate, Henry-Robert-six-Edward-eight-one, heading west on Fifty-five from Oak Lea. He's speeding and did a reckless pass."

"Ten-four."

There was no reason to go code three—red lights and sirens—but I drove very, very fast. My heart pounded from the adrenaline release. I knew how unnerving it was to be alone with a deceased person. There was not a thing you could do, but you felt a responsibility to stay with the body until it was safely taken away. One of those unwritten rules no one is taught, but people somehow do instinctively, I had learned in my years with the department.

I turned south on Beacon, a gravel road a mile east of the one where I lived. Bebee Lake was small and pristine with good fishing. Most of the lakeshore was surrounded by privately owned farmland. When Malcolm Johnson had retired from farming some years back, he deeded a road and lake frontage for public access. The road to the lake was little more than a tractor trail through a field of corn. I steered my squad car down the path.

A stocky man about forty was pacing back and forth by his late model Ford pickup truck. A connected trailer held his fishing boat. He saw me coming and walked up to the front of my car, forcing me to stop so I didn't hit him. His face was tight and pasty white, a stark contrast to the tanned hand he used to wipe the sweat from his brow.

"Thank God! How can you do something like this to yourself in such a beautiful spot?" He asked a rhetorical question I couldn't answer.

I extended my hand. "You're Jake Morrow?" He nodded and shook my hand. "I'm Sergeant Aleckson, Winnebago County." He followed me to the beige Taurus parked facing the lake.

Clearly, the death was not an accident. One end of a clothes dryer hose was attached to the vehicle's exhaust pipe, and the other end was secured in the front passenger side window. The window was open just enough to accommodate the hose. A pillow was stuffed in the rest of the opening, banning unwanted, life-giving oxygen. I was careful not to disturb the immediate area around the vehicle.

The car was not running. Apparently the engine had run out of gas. I glanced in the front windshield, then in the driver's window. My stomach rose in my throat, and I swallowed a few times to erase the bitter taste, but it didn't go away. I stared at the body of Arthur Franz, his head back, mouth open, arms dropped on the car seat.

Arthur's face was bright red, the telltale sign of carbon monoxide poisoning. His death wasn't natural, but at least it was painless. I stared for long moments, trying to believe what I was looking at. Arthur was successful, a prominent county attorney, and a man I personally respected, both in and out of the courtroom. What on earth had gone so wrong?

I spoke into my radio. "Six-oh-eight, Winnebago County."

"Go ahead."

"Send Detective Dawes and Dr. Melberg to my location." Dr. Gordon Melberg was the county coroner.

"Ten-four, at seventeen-forty-six."

I looked at my ashen companion, close by my side, then reached over and patted his forearm. "I know this is very upsetting, but I need to ask you a few questions. How are you doing? Okay?"

Morrow nodded, looking anything but. I walked him over to my squad car, and we leaned against the front hood. I withdrew the notebook and pen from my breast pocket. Morrow was visibly tense, his hands clenched into tight fists.

"It looks like you were planning to do some fishing. Do you come here often?" I asked, hoping he'd relax a little.

"Usually once a week, or so. The lake is full of northerns. A lot of people don't like 'em, cause the Y-bones are hard to remove, but I pickle 'em. We love pickled pike, better than herring."

I nodded and smiled, then switched to the information I needed for my report: name, date of birth, address, phone numbers. "What time did you get here today?"

Morrow looked at his watch for an answer. "I'm trying to think. Okay, I left home at five o'clock. I must have gotten here about five-fifteen."

"You pulled in here and then what?"

"Okay, I saw that car sitting there when I pulled in. I saw someone inside, and didn't think much of it. I mean, not too many people use this lake, a shame, but I guess that's why the pike get so big." He stretched his hands apart as an indication of how big they grew in the lake.

He pointed to the back of the Taurus. "Anyway, I drove my truck behind the car there and started to back my trailer to the lake to unload my boat. When I got next to the car, I looked over and saw the guy sitting there, red as a beet, not moving. That's when I noticed the dryer hose in the passenger window. It was kind of hidden by the underbrush there." He pointed again and sucked in a deep breath.

"I jumped out of my truck, ran over and got a closer look. I could see he was dead and called nine-one-one right away. For once, I was glad my wife makes me carry a cell phone when I go fishing." He thought for a moment. "You got here a little while later."

"Did you touch anything, move anything?"

"No, I almost opened the car door, but the nine-one-one officer said not to touch anything when I said it looked like he had been dead for a while—with his tongue hanging out like that and everything." Morrow frowned at the awful memory.

"Three-forty, Six-oh-eight." It was Smoke.

"Go ahead, Three-forty."

"I'll be there in five."

"Copy that." My cell phone rang. "Sergeant Aleckson."

"Sergeant, it's communications. Sheriff Twardy should be pulling in any minute, and the coroner is on his way back from a meeting in Minneapolis. His ETA is eighteen hundred."

"Thanks, Robin." As I hung up I heard the sound of tires crushing gravel on the narrow road. Sheriff Twardy. He hopped out of his car with the ease of a much younger man and jogged over to the beige Taurus.

"I'd hoped it wasn't Franz," the sheriff said, peering in the window. "You the one who found him?" he directed at Morrow. Morrow nodded.

"Helluva thing." The sheriff kicked at a small rock in the gravel, then looked at me. "Talk to Dawes yet? He's the one on call." He must not have heard him on the radio.

"Yes, sir. He'll be here any time now. I've already interviewed Mr. Morrow, but we'll see if the detective needs any more info."

The sheriff nodded and walked around the Taurus, peering in the windows.

Morrow had had more than enough of Arthur Franz's death scene and wandered down to the lake. He stood on the shoreline, staring at the gentle ripples on the otherwise smooth-as-glass surface of the water. I wondered if the magic of that fishing spot was gone for him forever, replaced by his shocking, tragic discovery.

"Take any pictures?" Sheriff Twardy asked.

"Not yet, sir. I thought I'd wait on Smoke."

The sheriff nodded his okay.

We heard a vehicle, and within seconds Smoke's Crown Victoria drove into the access. His car was barely in park before he had joined us by the Taurus.

"Damn," was all he said when he saw Franz. He screwed up his face in disgust, then nodded toward Morrow. "You interview him yet?"

"I did." I followed Smoke to the shoreline.

"Good. I'll introduce myself and give him my card in case he thinks of anything else," Smoke said.

He shook hands with Morrow and soon had him on his way home with instructions not to talk to the press, or the general public, until the sheriff issued a press release. He told the fisherman to be sure to call, however, any time if he needed help or wanted to talk to one of us.

"Where's your camera?" Smoke asked me.

"In my car. I'll get it." We worked together for some minutes. Smoke took the pictures, and I noted what each one was.

"Does this make any sense to either of you?" the sheriff asked.

Both Smoke and I shook our heads.

Smoke rubbed the back of his neck. "Something definitely went wrong, that's for sure. We'll talk to his friends, family, co-workers. I see a suicide note next to him, but we'll preserve the scene until Melberg gets here. My biggest question right now is, why go to all this trouble, the dryer hose, pillow? Wouldn't it be easier to drive in his garage, close the door, and leave the car running?" Smoke asked.

"Maybe he didn't want his family, or housemate, to find him," I offered.

"As far as I know, he lived alone. You know different?" the sheriff asked.

I shrugged, shaking my head. "No, just speculating. I don't think anyone in Winnebago County knows much about his personal life, from what I can gather. I talked to Julie Grimes, who made the initial missing report, and Ray Collinwood, who saw Franz leave for lunch. Both of them told me no one knew where he went for lunch, except Arthur's lunch hour was his time to 'meditate and commune with nature.' The joke around the office was that 'nature' was a person."

"Male or female?" Smoke said.

"I think that's one of the burning questions. Was Franz straight or gay?" I asked.

"Did he live alone, or with someone?" Smoke added. "I'll phone his home later to see if anyone is there. If not, I'll go to Personnel, get a court order if need be to look at his file. We'll need contact information. How can we know so little about a man who's been with the county for what, ten, eleven years?"

"I can't tell you the number of times we had coffee together, either in his office or mine. He didn't say much about his personal life, except what restaurants he liked or where he traveled to. That's about it. He mainly talked about the cases his office was working on," the sheriff said.

Robin's voice came over the radio, "Winnebago County, Six-oh-eight and Three-forty."

"Six-oh-eight, County."

"Six-oh-eight, Dr. Melberg is in town and phoned for directions. He's on the way."

"Ten-four."

"Did you notice the footprint back here?" Smoke was bent over near the exhaust pipe. The gravel drive and park area was surrounded on three sides by bushes, ferns, and other foliage growing in black dirt. It was an area that had filled in naturally by either the wind, or by birds spreading the seeds, between the gravel and the planted corn and soybeans.

Smoke went on, "Looks like it could be either a man's or a woman's shoe, long and narrow. I'd say about size ten. Franz would be smaller than that. It had to have been left today, 'cause it rained last night. Must have been someone fishing here this morning, before Franz got here."

We were still looking at the print when Dr. Melberg pulled in, followed by two Winnebago County squad cars.

"Sergeant, start a sign-in sheet," Sheriff Twardy ordered.

Natural curiosity and a sense of duty brought deputies to crime and accident scenes to offer any needed support to the lead officer on the case. It was department policy to make everyone sign in when they showed up at an investigation scene, and consequently, write a report, if need be.

Dr. Melberg stepped out of his Lexus with a small case. Whenever I saw him, I wondered how he had chosen medicine. He reminded me more of a professional athlete or coach. His pants were a little too snug on his muscular thighs and his shirts a little too small for his biceps. Melberg kept his graying brown hair cropped close to his head and had deep squint lines around his eyes, like he had been protecting them from the sun for years. But, despite gray hair and some wrinkles, he was a young looking forty-something with a gorgeous wife and a teenage daughter.

Dr. Melberg looked more tired that night than usual, almost weary.

"Hello, Doc," Twardy said for all of us.

Melberg tipped his head back a hair and narrowed his eyes. "Franz?"

The sheriff nodded.

Deputies Brian Carlson and Todd Mason signed in via the clipboard, and all the sheriff's department personnel gathered to watch at a reasonable distance from the Taurus, allowing the coroner to do his job.

"Pictures taken of the scene?" Melberg turned to ask the sheriff.

"Yes."

"Any contamination?"

"Sergeant?" The sheriff passed the question on to me.

"Not that we know of. The civilian who found him didn't touch anything. He just walked around the vehicle and looked in the windows. And we only did a sweep outside the vehicle."

"Good, good," Melberg said.

Dr. Melberg set the case down, pulled on two sets of latex gloves, and opened the driver's door. The speed of decomposition accelerated on hot, humid days, especially in a car baking in the sun. Melberg pulled a thermometer from his case and set it on the dashboard of the Taurus. The mercury began a steady, rapid climb, then settled on 140 degrees Fahrenheit.

Sweat dropped from the doctor's head onto his notepad as he jotted some information down. The smell of death from inside the car reached us in seconds, about the same time flies gathered on Arthur's body to begin their work. They were an efficient crew, knowing where to go and what to do.

"When was Franz last seen alive, anybody know?" Melberg asked.

"Right around noon, when he left for lunch," I told him.

Melberg confirmed that with a nod. "He could easily be dead five, six hours. Looks like suicide—here's a note, here." He pointed to a paper on the passenger seat. "Can someone call

Anderson's Funeral Home? We'll transport him to Hennepin County for autopsy after we notify the family," Melberg instructed.

"I'll call Anderson's," Mason volunteered.

The sheriff cleared his throat. "We're not sure who he has for family. But, of course, we'll find out." He pointed at a deputy. "Carlson, call communications and have them track down one of the county attorneys and tell them to call Detective Dawes on his cell phone. And we'll need a tow to take the vehicle to the crime lab for processing," Sheriff Twardy instructed, then clapped Carlson on the back.

"Yes, sir."

"Ready to take pictures of the inside of the vehicle?" Melberg asked Smoke.

"Yeah, go ahead, Sergeant," Smoke told me.

I held my breath while the camera and my brain captured one picture after the next of the body and surrounding area. Franz was beyond being irritated by the flies buzzing around us and landing on him. I tried, unsuccessfully, to ignore them, growing increasingly tense with each passing second. When I finished the photography, I looked for Smoke and saw him standing by his squad car, talking on his cell phone.

The transport van from Anderson's Funeral Home arrived. Dr. Melberg supervised and assisted the two middle-aged Anderson brothers with the removal of the remains from his vehicle. Flies were everywhere, but any clinging to the body of Arthur Franz would soon be suffocated when sealed in the vinyl bag. Dr. Melberg needlessly advised the brothers to put the body in their cooler to await transport to Hennepin County.

"Call my cell after you make notification, or if anything comes up," Melberg called back to us and followed the Anderson vehicle away from the scene.

"You got a county attorney to meet you at their office?" Twardy asked Smoke.

He nodded. "I just got off the phone with Collinwood. He's coming in. I told him we'll call when we're finished here and ready for him."

Smoke reached in the Taurus and removed the suicide note with a pair of tweezers.

"What does it say? Read it out loud," the sheriff instructed.

"'This is best for all concerned. Arthur Franz.' It's typed, except the signature. One sentence. Kind of odd." Smoke held it up so we could see the words.

"Very odd. And that's it? 'This is best for all concerned. Arthur Franz'?" The sheriff frowned.

"That's it," Smoke confirmed.

The sheriff shook his head. "What the hell kind of explanation is that?"

Smoke added, "And why the devil would he bring a lunch with him if he was planning to off himself?" With gloved hands he picked up an open can of soda from the center holder and a small red lunch cooler from the passenger seat. "Got a bag for these?" he asked me.

Carlson pulled a plastic evidence bag from his back pocket. "Here."

"Thanks." Smoke dropped the cooler in then fixed his eyes on the soda can. "Hey, look at this." He slid his readers on his nose and moved the can closer to his face. "Some kind of powder residue on the top of the can. We'll have it tested. I'll need another bag."

Mason ran to his squad and returned with another evidence bag.

"Winnebago County, Seven-fourteen." Jerry's voice.

"Seven-fourteen, County, go ahead," Mason answered.

"Domestic assault in progress at Four-four-zero-one Dayton Avenue Southwest. We have a child on the line reporting her father is hitting her mother."

"Ten-four. Show Seven-fourteen and Seven-twenty-three en route." Mason and Carlson were gone in seconds, leaving the sheriff, Smoke, and I standing in a cloud of dust.

I held the plastic evidence bag, and Smoke dropped the can inside. Arthur had downed most of the soda as the can felt nearly empty.

"Got a Sharpie with you?" Smoke asked, searching for a permanent marking pen as he patted his pants pocket. "Never mind, I got one." He handed it to me. "Fill in the info on these evidence bags, will ya? I'll see if there's anything else we need here."

Sheriff Twardy followed behind Smoke. "I have the county commissioners' meeting at seven and need to get cleaned up. Page me when you make notification. The press is going to be all over this in no time, so I'll need to prepare a statement."

"Will do, Sheriff," Smoke said.

I finished my task then walked to the lakeshore. It was my home turf. I lived less than a mile away, as the crow flies. As badly as I felt about what Franz had done to himself, I could imagine why he had chosen this place, a snapshot of nature's peaceful beauty captured in the small haven. A pair of mallard ducks skidded across the lake and landed with a splash, oblivious to human matters of life and death.

For no apparent reason, the hairs on my arms and the back of my neck stood on end. I felt like someone was watching me. Strange. I looked around, scanning the opposite shore and nearby cornfields, but Smoke was the only living thing I spotted besides the ducks.

"Smoke, I have been having the weirdest feelings lately."

He quit writing in his notebook and slid his glasses to the top of his head. "What do you mean?"

"Don't think I'm crazy, but it's actually two separate feelings. One is that there's something wrong, like an evil presence. I can't really explain it better than that. And the other is that I'm being watched. It's happened a few times now and started the night Judge Fenneman died."

"Doo doo, doo doo, doo doo, doo, doo." Smoke sang the eerie little tune, then smiled. When I didn't smile back, he said, "Where did my friend lose her sense of humor?"

"It's just kind of freaking me out. Is it from stress, do you think? Not that I really feel any more stressed than usual."

He slipped his pad and pen into his pocket. "I think you are paying attention to your gut feelings, that's all. Maybe there *is* an evil presence and maybe you *are* being watched."

"That makes me feel much better."

Smoke closed the space between us and put his arm around my shoulder. "So tell me exactly when you've experienced these feelings."

"The first time was in Judge Fenneman's hospital room, after his death. It was a strong sense there was something I had missed, overlooked. Something that would explain why the judge left his hospital bed, made his way out the back entrance, and ended up in the pond. And it felt creepy, bad, evil. It's happened a few other times, like when I got that strange note. And a while ago, when you asked about the footprint by the tailpipe."

I took a breath. "And the weirdest thing of all? Do you remember Nolan Eisner?"

"Boy, the name is familiar, but I can't think why."

I gave him the rundown.

"Oh, sure, I should have remembered—one of the cases I handled my first year back. That was a bad deal all the way around. What brings him to mind? You weren't with the department back then."

"I interviewed his daughter. She was a patient on B-Wing the night the judge died. Her grandmother, Nolan's mother, came in about the time I finished and just stared at me. I hate to admit it, but she kind of scared me."

"How so?"

"I don't know. She just looked at me so intensely, like she could read my mind or something. Anyway, when you asked me about the footprint?"

Smoke nodded.

"Well, for a second, I was back in that hospital room with Mrs.—or Ms.—Eisner looking right through me. Isn't that strange?"

Smoke shrugged.

"Then, a few minutes ago, when I was standing by the shore, I could have sworn we were being watched. That's happened a couple of times, too."

Smoke sucked in a deep breath. "You know, there are coyotes around here. Maybe they are watching the goings on here. Not your usual day of maybe one fisherman, two if they're lucky."

"Are you serious, Smoke?" I looked for his teasing grin.

"Absolutely. When I lived in the north woods, it wasn't uncommon for me to feel I was being watched when hiking through the forest. An old timer up there said it was the wolves. We couldn't see them, but they could see us." He scratched the back of his neck.

It seemed a little far out to me. "I don't know. You think there are coyotes by Sara Speiss' house? I feel I'm being watched every time I'm there lately."

"I don't know where she lives," he said, so I told him. "Well, it's a pretty populated area, but lots of trees. I suppose it is possible, but not likely, coyotes are watching you there. Probably a nosy neighbor, or an admirer." He winked and smiled. "All kidding aside, I'm the last one to tell you to dismiss your gut feelings. By all means, cover your backside."

The tow truck arrived. Smoke handed Lou the Property Release Form, and Lou loaded the vehicle where Arthur Franz had breathed his last. The dryer hose and pillow were left as they had been found. The crime lab would go through the vehicle. All evidence would be examined, labeled, and placed in the property room. What they couldn't test on site would be sent to the Minnesota Bureau of Criminal Apprehension for analysis. The vehicle and personal property would eventually be released to the family. Lou pulled away with his load.

"I'll give Collinwood a call to meet us at the office." Smoke's phone rang before he could dial. "Detective Dawes . . . Uh huh . . . Right . . . What did you tell her?" He pulled the notebook and pen from his pocket and slid his glasses down from the top of his head. "Her name again? . . . Okay. She's on her way there? . . . Copy. Sergeant Aleckson and I will meet with her there. Thanks."

"What?" I asked.

"No need to call Collinwood in. Franz has a significant other on her way to the sheriff's department. She's coming from Plymouth, so it will be about a half hour."

We walked to our vehicles. "She? Franz has a significant other who no one knows about? How did they get in touch with her?"

"She called communications, finally, after not hearing from Arthur since he left for work this morning. She knows something is wrong, but communications wouldn't tell her what, of course. They told her an official would contact her as soon as possible. She said she was on her way to Oak Lea and hung up."

"Who is she?" I wondered.

"We don't know her, at least I don't. Marion McIllvery. She called Franz her husband."

"Why would Arthur be secretive about having a wife?"

"Who knows? Let's get out of here. We'll meet with Miss Marion then write reports until tomorrow morning."

Smoke called Collinwood to say thanks anyway, and I took a last look around the area. Was I developing a weird sensitivity to death scenes?

Chapter 15

Alvie

There was sure a lot of monkeying around to get rid of one body and one car. Alvie thought the little sergeant and that ace detective would be there forever. Even the sheriff had left long before. Her cigarettes were burning a hole in her pocket, but she didn't dare light up as long as they were there, to risk being discovered. She had the perfect hiding spot, across the lake behind a clump of sapling birch trees, with weeds nearly as tall sprouting from the bases.

It was one hot day, low nineties, high humidity. Alvie unzipped the workman's jumpsuit to the top of her breasts to release some of her skin from the synthetic, clinging fabric. A little better. She sipped on her last soft drink, impatient for them to leave already.

What luck to happen onto that set up. Alvie had stashed her Chevy in the cornfield, waited in her hiding spot for Franz to show up, and no one was the wiser. Her ball cap helped keep the sun from her face as she kept her lookout. Franz was five minutes later than the day before; five measly more minutes to be alive, that's all it meant. She watched him pull in and park then quickly made her way to the other side of the small lake, about the length of a football field.

Her supplies were stashed by a small bush, out of sight. Franz walked along the shoreline in the opposite direction. Just like the day before and the day before that. Alvie ducked down and crawled to the passenger side of his car, opened the door, dumped the contents of the crushed tablets into his cola can, and used a straw to stir them in. She licked a granule that was clinging to the straw. No detectable taste other than cola.

Alvie crouched in a ball in an attempt to be invisible behind the small bushes. A few minutes later, she heard a car door open, and Franz climbed back in the driver's seat. He was parked in the shade, but left the door open for apparent ventilation. Alvie snuck a look in time to see his head tip back to get a last sip of beverage from the can. He settled against the headrest and closed his eyes.

She waited as long as she could stand it, then grabbed the dryer hose and pillow and went to work. Franz didn't move when she opened the passenger door. She rolled down the window, inserted the hose, and rolled the window back up. She leaned over the seat and turned the ignition key. The car started right up.

Alvie noticed a little instrument, about the size of a calculator, lying on the seat by the county attorney's hand. It looked like a Palm Pilot, one of those appointment calendars like the administrator of the nursing home used. Franz wouldn't need that anymore, and it was something for Alvie to save as a souvenir, so she slipped it in the zippered pocket of the coveralls.

She pulled the door handle out, then eased the door shut as quietly as possible. She leaned her weight against it for a tight close and repeated the process on the driver's side. Franz was snoring by the time she stuffed the pillow in the open space of the window.

The windows started fogging up, and the car doors didn't open so after twenty minutes or so, Alvie figured he was dead. Slick as snot. Slicker. She hiked back to her vantage point to sit tight. She had no idea how many people fished in that lake, but someone was bound to come by sooner or later. She'd wait until dark, then come back the next day if need be. She had to cover a day shift for someone the next day, so she could come after that.

Franz's car stopped running at about three o'clock, and Alvie's heart practically stopped beating. She figured it had run out of gas when she spotted no movement whatsoever around the vehicle.

Except for the "cah, cahs" of the crows every once in a while, it was quiet until a truck loaded with a boat trailer rumbled in next to Franz's car. Five minutes later the little sergeant showed up, followed by the others, and they all worked like busy little bees, walking around, taking pictures, writing, loading up the body, and finally hooking up the car to a tow truck.

The little sergeant acted strange. She stood by the water for a long time and stared. Why? At what? Of course, she did live on the other side, not far from where Alvie was. Maybe she swam in that lake. Who knew? Alvie was just glad when they finally packed up, got in those police cars, and drove away.

She wouldn't have to come back after all, and she couldn't wait to hear the news about the lawyer's suicide.

Chapter 16

$\mathbf{I}$ was in the squad room working on my report when communications phoned. I found Smoke at his desk.

"Marion McIllvery is at the south entrance," I said.

Smoke looked up from his writing. "Will you meet her and bring her here? It will be more private at my desk."

"Sure."

I opened the secured door to a tall, slender woman who looked like someone I should know, but couldn't place. Her eyes were red and she was biting the inside of her cheek.

"Ms. McIllvery?"

She nodded.

"I'm Sergeant Aleckson. Please follow me. Detective Dawes is waiting for us."

She hurried in and looked around. "Where's Artie?"

"The detective will explain everything."

We snaked our way through the unoccupied sheriff's department to Smoke's cubicle. He rose, came around his desk, and offered his hand. "Ms. McIllvery, I'm Detective Dawes. Please sit down."

Marion McIllvery took his hand and held it. She didn't sit down. "What's happened to Artie? Where is he?" she pleaded, her knuckles white as she squeezed Smoke's hand.

Smoke moved his free hand to her arm. "It's my sad duty to tell you he died this afternoon. His body is at Anderson's Funeral Home."

"Oh, God. Oh, God . . ."

Her legs gave out, but between Smoke holding onto her arm and me stepping in behind her, we prevented her fall and eased her into a chair. McIllvery tried to speak, but no words came out for a long moment.

"What happened?" She choked on a sob.

"It appears he took his own life." Smoke spoke in a soothing tone, perhaps to ease the pain of his words.

"Killed himself? You're wrong, mistaken, there is no way!" She shook her head back and forth, tears spilling from her eyes and down her cheeks, denying the ugly words and their meaning. I reached for a box of tissues on the corner of Smoke's desk and set it in front of McIllvery. She snatched up two.

"He was found in his car with a dryer hose from the exhaust to the passenger window. And there was a note," Smoke explained.

Marion McIllvery scrutinized Smoke. "Why didn't you call me? There was no one in his office this late, so I finally called the sheriff's department. I hadn't heard from him all day."

Smoke reached over and put his hand over hers. "We didn't know how to reach you, or even who you were. We were on our way to Arthur's office when we learned you had called."

"He carries an 'in case of emergency' card in his wallet with my name and number as the contact person," she said.

Smoke took a minute then glanced at his memo pad. "His wallet wasn't on his person."

"He puts it in the glove box when he drives. It bothers him to sit on it, he has trouble with his sciatic nerve," Marion explained.

"We haven't done a thorough search of the vehicle yet," Smoke said.

The impact hit her again and Marion let out a whimper. "Oh, God. What did the note say?" She bowed her head.

Smoke picked up the evidence bag containing the note from the top of the pile on his desk. "Here, you can read it."

Marion lifted her head slowly and blinked, pushing the unshed tears from her eyes. She slowly accepted the plastic bag from Smoke with trembling hands. "Oh, God, he typed it on the computer?"

She stood up and walked back and forth for a few minutes, her eyes glued to the paper. "This doesn't sound like Artie, and the message doesn't make sense. 'Best for all concerned.' Concerned in what? For what? He's happy. He loves his career, and our personal life is almost perfect."

"Communications said you were his wife?" Smoke said.

"Common law—it's a long story," she started. Marion paused, appearing uncertain of what to say. "You see, Artie and I are cousins." The words came out slowly, deliberately.

"Cousins?" Smoke said, his voice steady.

"First cousins."

My eyebrows went up involuntarily, and I was glad Marion couldn't see the expression on my face. Smoke was a seasoned professional and didn't even blink.

"Like I said, it's a long story," she confirmed.

"It could be a piece of the puzzle. The people here at Winnebago County know virtually nothing of Arthur's private life," Smoke said.

Marion sank back down on the chair. "Now you can guess why. I met Arthur when I was hired by Ramsey County as an assistant county attorney. He had been there, I think, five years."

Smoke sat on the edge of his desk looking relaxed, like he had all the time in the world. He opened a bottle of water and set it in front of Marion. "Let me get this straight. You're first cousins, but didn't meet until you were adults?"

McIllvery captured Smoke's eyes, then mine. "Our mothers were sisters, but they were estranged, hadn't spoken for years. In fact, neither of us even knew we had a maternal aunt. Arthur grew up in Duluth. I was from Iowa. I came to Minnesota to attend college at Saint Thomas and loved the area. I went to law school at William Mitchell and started with Ramsey County eleven years ago. I'm still there, at Ramsey." She pulled another tissue from the box and dabbed at her eyes and nose. Every movement McIllvery made was graceful, flowing.

"When we met, there was an immediate attraction between us. Not just physical, but intellectual, spiritual, even. You hear about soul mates? We are, truly we are. We dated for two months, then Artie took me home to meet his mother. Oh my God, you should have seen the look on his mother's face when he introduced me." Marion took a moment to smile through her tears at the memory.

"She recognized my name right away, of course, and I look a lot like my mother. Auntie didn't say a word, just left the room for the longest time, and we just stood there, wondering what was going on. Artie was embarrassed. He couldn't understand his mother's behavior.

"When Aunt Mary came back in the room, she was carrying a photograph. She held it out and said, 'Do you know who these children are?' It was a picture of Artie, his brother, a baby boy, and me. Artie was four, his brother six, I was eighteen months, the baby was three months old. We were lined up next to each other on a couch. I recognized myself, Artie recognized his brother and himself, but neither of us could understand why we were there together.

"Artie's mom told us the story, pretty gingerly, of why she and my mother hadn't spoken for over twenty years. My family was visiting the Franz family for a weekend. We lived about six hundred miles apart, so visits were rare. And our mothers were never close, even as children. My parents were visiting school friends in town. Artie's dad had taken the boys and me to the neighbor's—they had a kids' swimming pool. Artie's mom stayed home with the baby, who was taking a nap. The baby was my infant brother—I didn't even know about him, can you imagine?"

Smoke discreetly shifted, and I sat down next to Marion.

She watched us a moment, then continued, "Anyway, when my mother got back, she went to check on the baby. He had died of SIDS, or something, in his sleep. My mother blamed Artie's mom, saying she had killed her baby, and it went from bad to worse. Artie and his brother spent the night at the neighbor's, and we left Duluth that night, never to return.

"Artie's mom tried to make amends, but my mother never forgave her. My mother eventually drove my father away. He was a saint to put up with her under the best of conditions, anyway. She kept the secret of my brother, her sister and family, from me until the day she died." Marion locked her eyes on mine.

I mouthed the words, "I'm sorry."

She went on. "You can imagine how shocked Artie and I were by the story. When he saw the picture he had a vague memory of the day, but I had none, of course. I was just a baby. That night the three of us—Artie's father had died a few years before—had a very quiet, very polite dinner. During the night his mother must have started wondering about the depth of our relationship. The next morning she had a long conversation with Artie and made him promise to break off with me immediately. She even made him swear on the family Bible."

Marion stood and paced the small area in Smoke's cubicle, her movements fluid, even in the confined space. "It was a long ride back to St. Paul that day, you can imagine. We agreed to stop seeing each other. Honestly, we were, both of us, a little grossed out about our personal relationship. We both had paternal cousins we had grown up close to that seemed almost like siblings.

"When Artie dropped me at my apartment, we held each other for a long time, like the final goodbye. The next morning, he was back. We were hopelessly in love, but Artie couldn't hurt his mother, and neither could I, especially after the way my mother had treated her. So that's how we began our secret that snowballed into a secretive life."

A life none of us in Winnebago County knew about, a secret Arthur had kept until his dying day.

"Our dearest friends, Ann and Bill Jacobs, are the only two people—besides you, now—who know the whole truth. Artie left Ramsey County for Winnebago. We moved to Plymouth, about halfway between the two counties. I took a post office box for mail. Artie's mom and brother have our individual cell and work phone numbers if they need to call.

"Fortunately, Artie's mom never leaves Duluth, and his brother lives in Illinois. So it's been easy that way. I'm always invited to her home for holidays, as the long lost niece, and when I've gone, Artie and I have somehow managed to hide our true feelings from her." Marion sighed deeply and stared at nothing for a while.

I would never be able to keep my mother in the dark like they had, even if I lived on the moon.

"That's quite a story. It must have been difficult living like that," Smoke said, maintaining his pacifying tone.

Marion's head inclined to the side and she inhaled a sigh. "It is. We wanted to tell Mary the truth, but couldn't. It's a small world, and you know how it goes. Mary, Artie's mother, works in a gift shop in Canal Park, you know, downtown Duluth, and talks to people from all over. She's told Artie over the years of all the people she's met from Winnebago County. It would take just one innocent comment from someone about Arthur and me to absolutely destroy her. We couldn't take that risk.

"So, as far as most of the world knows, Arthur is a hard-working county attorney, married to his profession, a bit unsociable. He adopted an artistic, dramatic way of dressing. He got the idea because of the nickname I gave him, 'Artie.' It sounds pretty silly now. He knew people were curious about him, wondering if he was gay, wondering why he didn't talk about his life outside of work. But it's almost impossible to have normal conversations with people without mentioning your personal life, so Arthur brought his lunch and even ate alone."

"Sounds kinda lonely," Smoke said.

Marion's lip quivered. "It was, sometimes, but we always talk during lunch. In the summer he usually goes to the same lake, takes a walk, eats lunch, has a little nap, then phones me." She licked a tear that found its way down her cheek. "Oh, God, when he didn't call me, I called him and got his voicemail. I thought maybe he had forgotten his phone at the office and he'd call later. Why didn't he call to say goodbye? He could not have done this to himself." Marion bunched a tissue and squeezed tightly.

Neither Smoke nor I spoke in response. We had been at the scene, looked at the evidence. No sign of a struggle. What else could have happened?

"I have to see him," Marion decided.

"I'll call Anderson's," Smoke said.

It was heart wrenching watching Marion say goodbye to Arthur. When I took her hand to lead her out, she gripped mine so tightly I hoped I would someday regain the use of my trigger finger.

The Andersons prepared to transport the body of Arthur Franz to Hennepin County for autopsy. It would be several days before we would get the results. Maybe a brain tumor had affected his reasoning, or perhaps it was a fatal illness Arthur couldn't deal with, not even to tell his family.

More secrets, added to the list of secrets Arthur Franz had already been keeping.

Ann and Bill Jacobs drove to Oak Lea to pick up Marion, at Smoke's suggestion. It wasn't safe for Marion to drive in her state of shock, plus Smoke didn't want her alone with her grief. I wondered what Marion would tell Arthur's mother. She could protect her aunt from the whole truth of Arthur's life, but the truth of his death would be impossible to avoid.

We were on the way back to the sheriff's department when Smoke said, "I think I've heard it all, and every day I hear something new."

"You mean about Arthur Franz being with Marion?" I asked.

"Yeah, he always struck me as such a straight shooter, so black and white when it comes to the law. 'Course, I guess he didn't actually marry her." Smoke keyed open the south door to the sheriff's department and motioned me in ahead of him.

"Is it even legal for first cousins to marry?" I knew the criminal and traffic codes of the Minnesota Statutes, but there were volumes and volumes of others.

"Yeah, with conditions, but I'm guessing it's pretty rare, excluding, of course, rural areas where first cousins would be considered distant relatives." He gave me that lopsided grin.

"Smoke."

"Well . . ." He settled behind his desk, and I leaned against his cubicle partition.

"Ever have a crush on one of your cousins?" I asked.

"That would make me gay." I shot him a puzzled look. "All my cousins are male," he explained.

"Wow, no sisters or girl cousins."

Smoke pulled open a drawer and looked inside. "Yeah, boys run in the family."

"You know, I don't have any cousins at all," I reminded him.

"That's right. Kristen and Carl were both only children. Truth be told, when I was young I used to envy how spoiled they must be. No little brother to get into your stuff."

I shrugged, knowing they probably were spoiled. I reached over and patted Smoke on the shoulder. "If only someone could spoil Kristen now."

"I'd like that." That grin again.

"You may have to try a little harder."

"I'm thinking about it." The same old story.

"Think less, act more."

Smoke shuffled the papers around on his desk. "Little lady, it's your mother we're talking about. What would she say if she knew you said such a thing?"

I put my hand over his. "Don't tell her. I repeat, think less, act more."

"You are tenacious."

Chapter 17

Alvie

Alvie took her lunch break at eleven-thirty a.m. She slipped out of the nursing home, not far from the hospital, and drove downtown. She parked in a public lot kitty-corner from the old square red brick building that housed the public defender's office and waited. Alvie felt naked without her man disguise, but there hadn't been time to go home, make the change, and return. She decided to stay put, making do with her sunglasses and large straw hat for a disguise.

A little after noon, Marshall Kelton left the office on foot and crossed the street. Alvie had a clear view of him going into The Sandwich Shoppe. He was out in a matter of minutes, carrying a bag. He returned to the office and remained there until she had to get back to work. Alvie figured she wouldn't be so lucky again, to have the sitting ducks Fenneman and Franz had been. Was it only the day before that Franz had checked out of the world?

The newspaper would be out around four p.m., and she couldn't wait. The local radio station reported the "apparent suicide" of the Winnebago County Attorney every half hour, and the nursing home staff had talked about it off and on all day. Most everyone knew who Arthur Franz was.

Alvie got off work at four and thought about picking up a newspaper, but decided she might miss Marshall Kelton. Maybe she already had. She slipped on her glasses and hat and drove back to the parking lot she had left several hours earlier. A little after four-thirty, she spotted Kelton walking toward his office with a briefcase. Most likely returning from court. Probably some other kid who hoped his defender would do a decent job and instead found himself on his way to prison for making a little mistake, trusting the wrong person who got him in trouble.

Another fifteen minutes passed, and Alvie thought she would pass out from the heat. There seemed to be no end to the hot weather in sight. It had rained the morning before, but not enough to break the humidity.

Three people left the office before Kelton. At five o'clock on the dot, he walked out the door, talking on his cell phone with a silly smile on his face. She had to admit he was handsome, tall, dark eyes and hair, with only a hint of silver by his temples. About her age, but she had gone gray years before, so most people probably thought she was older, if they even cared.

Kelton walked to the parking lot where Alvie was and got into a black Ranger pickup. Not the vehicle she would have picked for him. He seemed like he'd have some fancy, sleek sports kind of car. Alvie watched him turn right then pulled out from her spot to follow at a safe distance. He led her to the American Legion Club near the industrial section west of town. Sure, Friday night. The old "Thank God it's Friday" mentality of needing a few drinks after work to celebrate getting through another long work week.

When Kelton walked into the club, Alvie drove to the nearby Holiday Station and bought a slice of pizza and two bottles of mineral water. She figured he'd be at happy hour awhile.

Alvie rolled down her window and downed the first bottle of water with the pizza. She'd save the other bottle for later. She didn't want to have to leave to pee in the middle of it all and lose her tail on Kelton.

That was fast. Kelton was back in his truck by five-thirty-five. He took the same route Alvie did to her own house. Past the golf course, on the south edge of town, Kelton took a right, then an immediate left into the first driveway. Alvie continued driving, did a U-turn at the next intersection, and parked. Kelton had pulled into the garage, so it had to be his place. A townhouse: another surprise. She'd figured he had a big house and token wife.

Not much traffic on the street at all. Good. She waited awhile then drove home. Surveillance was a tiring job.

Chapter 18

Marion McIllvery arranged a Sunday afternoon memorial service in Oak Lea for Arthur Franz three days after his death. Then his body would be taken to Duluth for a funeral at his home church and burial in the family plot. Maybe Marion *could* keep the details of her intimacy with Arthur from his mother, her aunt. They were attorneys; perhaps provisions had been made in the event Arthur died before his mother. That scenario seemed likely since he had chosen the time of his death.

Sara reached me on my cell. "Are you planning to go to Arthur's service?"

"Yes, but I'm working, so barring an emergency—"

"Will you be lining up with the sheriff's department?" she asked.

"No, I may have to leave, so I'll sit in the back."

"I'll get there early and save you a place."

"Sounds good. Thanks, Sara."

Two funeral services in less than two weeks. Both Judge Fenneman and Arthur Franz had died unexpectedly, leaving unanswered questions and unresolved issues. I sat in the second pew from the back next to Sara and scanned the sea of county employees, from the black clothing the county attorneys had chosen collectively to wear, to the block of brown, crisply pressed uniforms of the sheriff's department deputies. I felt proud to be among them, united in their support of Arthur, his work and his life, despite the circumstances of his death.

Arthur's death. The thought sent chills through me, and I had the same weird feelings, both that something was wrong, and that I was being watched. I fought against turning around to see who was behind me. When the service ended, I whispered goodbye to Sara and scooted past her before the procession of mourners began down the center aisle.

I glanced sideways down the pew behind me and was a little shocked, but somehow not surprised, to see Ms. Eisner looking at me. She gave me a half-smile. How odd. Did she make a practice of attending funeral services? Probably right up her creepy alley. At least Rebecca wasn't with her. The more time spent away from her grandmother, the better.

I was barely outside the church when my pager buzzed. Communications. I depressed the call button on my portable radio.

"Six-oh-eight, Winnebago County."

"Six-oh-eight, are you clear to take a call?" It was Robin.

"Ten-four." I opened the door to my squad car.

"We have report of a home burglary. The party just got home from a weekend at his cabin and found his back door jimmied open. Ready to copy the address?"

"Ten-four."

"One-fourteen, that's one-one-four, Stony Creek Way, Rockwell. You'll be meeting with Max Cromley."

"Copy that and show me en route."

"At eighteen-thirty-five."

Rockwell sat ten miles southeast of Oak Lea on the Crow River, the eastern border of Winnebago County. Cromley lived in an upscale neighborhood overlooking an upscale golf course. It was the first home burglary I could recall in the area, and I hoped it wouldn't be the start of more. I asked him all the usual questions. The only person he suspected was a young man who cleaned his pool once a week. Cromley had refused to give him a requested raise, and he'd quit. I took pictures of the damaged door lock and dusted for latent prints.

Investigation was becoming a favorite part of my job.

Nick called me on my cell phone a little after ten. "How is work going tonight? Busy?"

I had finished writing a fix-it ticket for a broken taillight a minute earlier. "Pretty steady all night. And, you know, Arthur's service was this afternoon."

"How was that?"

"Okay, I guess. Arthur was a very private man, personally, but he had lots of professional colleagues and contacts. There were hundreds of people. Very sad."

"A real shame."

"How was your weekend with the family?" I asked.

"Oh, I'm glad we went. Faith and her grandmother are crazy about each other. They get too lonesome if we don't make the trip at least monthly." Nick's voice quieted to a near whisper. "Corky, I miss you. Why don't you stop over after work?"

"I'd love to, but it could be late, and you need your beauty sleep."

"Are you trying to tell me something?" he invited.

"You know, if you start getting all tired and haggard looking, the little old ladies on the board who have a crush on you might blame me," I kidded.

I was falling in love with his baritone laugh.

"Who says the little old ladies on the board have a crush on me?"

"It's common knowledge."

He laughed again. "How about lunch tomorrow, before you go to work?"

Monday. "Sure, sounds good. Where and when?"

"Come to my office at twelve-thirty; I'll order from the deli. Sure you won't stop by, at least for a goodnight kiss? I've never kissed a woman in uniform before, and I want to see what it's like."

"I'll wear my uniform to lunch tomorrow, so don't order Sloppy Joes or juicy fruit," I instructed.

"Yes, ma'am. Goodnight, dear Corky."

"Night, Nick. Sleep well."

Dear Corky. What was I going to do about that man?

I was pulling into the sheriff's department lot shortly before eleven when my personal cell rang again.

"Corky, it's me." Sara on the other end of the line. "In the middle of something?"

I keyed my way into the office. "Just about to file my reports. What's up?"

Sara spoke in hushed tones, unusual for her. "I just got home from Brian's, and I think someone was in my house. I would have called Brian, but there were still a few people at his house when I left." Deputy Brian Carlson was one of Sara's good friends.

"A break-in?"

"Not exactly. My back door wasn't locked."

"Sara!"

"I know, I know, don't lecture me. I went to Brian's after the service and didn't plan to stay so late. He had some other friends over, and time got away from me."

There were times I could wring her neck. "Is anything missing?"

"Not that I can see."

"How do you know someone was there?" I asked.

"Some things are moved."

"Did you talk to anyone else, another friend who might have stopped by? Maybe your family was down to pay you a surprise visit?" I suggested.

"They would have left a note, but they never do that anyway. It's a two-hour drive, and they always call before leaving. None of my friends would come in my house when I'm gone and move things." I could hear her opening and closing cupboard doors and drawers.

"Good point. You sure no one's in the house now?"

"Gosh, I didn't look everywhere, like the basement."

Oh, Lord! I spoke calmly. "Okay. Go out to your car and lock yourself in. I'll be right over." I ran back outside and jumped in my squad car.

"Corky, I don't think anyone's here."

"Probably not, but just do what I ask. Are you on your cordless?"

"Yes."

"Take it with you and call if you see anything suspicious." I heard her screen door squeak open and close.

"Okay, okay."

Sara didn't live far, maybe two miles away. I phoned communications. "Will you send an Oak Lea officer to Four-zero-two Willow Drive, Sara Speiss' house? She came home and suspects someone was there when she was gone. I'm heading there now, and as a precaution I'm requesting back-up in case someone is still in the house."

"Any indication there might be?" Jerry asked.

"No, but Sara didn't go through the house. I'll wait for Oak Lea."

"It shouldn't be long. The midnight officer went ten-eight a minute ago and has nothing else pending."

"Thanks." I was at Sara's by the time the call ended. The development she lived in was about ten years old and had been carved out of a wooded area of maple, elm, and oak trees. It was unusual to have so many old, mature trees in a relatively young development. The residents were a mix of first time homeowners and people who had retired and downsized from larger family homes. The developer had constructed mostly ramblers, with a few split-entries intermingled. Sara had moved out of an apartment and into her two-bedroom rambler a few years before.

I spotted Sara sitting in her vehicle in the driveway. She had a detached garage without an automatic opener and rarely parked in it, except in the winter. I pulled my squad to a stop at the curb, out of sight from the house, and walked to her car. Oak Lea Officer Casey Dey joined me in less than two minutes.

We planned our entry as though a person was in Sara's home. Officer Dey went in the back, via the sliding glass door, and Sara unlocked the front door for me. We did a sweep through the main level then met at the top of the basement steps to go down together. Officer Dey stood on my left. We drew our guns and sat on the first step, then scooted to the second and third. Sara threw on the light, and we scanned the basement for intruders. The basement was unfinished: one big open space with a little furniture and some storage containers.

I waved Officer Dey down the remaining stairs and we walked through the lower level. Sara joined us when it was evident no one else was there. "Anything out of place or missing down here?" Officer Dey asked.

Sara looked around a few minutes. "It doesn't look like it."

"Okay, let's go upstairs and I'll take a report," Dey said.

"Is that necessary?" She shot me a "thanks a lot" look, but I merely shrugged in return.

"It's just a formality. Only take a few minutes," Officer Dey assured her.

Sara repeated for Officer Dey what she had told me on the phone. She didn't think anything was missing. "But my things have been moved, and my cupboard doors have been opened."

"What do you mean?" Officer Dey asked.

"See how you have to shut the left door first, then the right door fits tight?" She demonstrated, and we both nodded. "Two of them are closed with the right door first. And the crock on the counter?" We looked where she pointed. "I keep it here." She slid it over a few inches.

"And that rug is pushed. I straighten it if it gets bunched up, so I don't trip. I know it doesn't seem like much, but I know where I keep things, and since I'm the only one here, they can't move themselves. And I never close the doors that way." She pointed at the cupboards again.

Officer Dey recorded her words in his memo pad. "Anyone you know might have been here?" he asked.

"No."

"Okay. Could be neighborhood kids. As long as nothing is missing, I'll file my report as a 'Trespass, suspect gone on arrival.' If you discover anything else, let me know. And keep your doors locked," Officer Dey said as he handed Sara his card. They stared at each other for a moment before he left.

"He's pretty cute," Sara said. "I've never seen him before. Know anything about him?"

"A little. He grew up here, a couple of years older than me. Let's see. I remember he was on the football team. And I heard he enlisted in the service for a few years after high school. He worked as a cop for Saint Paul for a while and got hired here last month. I don't know him well, but he's a decent guy. No scandals in high school, and he passed background investigations for two departments."

"It sounds like you know quite a bit about him, but you left out the most important part—is he single?"

"I know he's not married, but I don't know if he has a girlfriend or not. You have his card—call him sometime."

She tacked his card to the bulletin board by her kitchen phone. "Maybe I will, or else we're bound to run into each other in court one of these days."

"True. Hey, back to the reason I'm here. It's probably nothing to worry about, but I'll feel better spending the night here." I depressed my radio button. "Six-oh-eight, Winnebago County."

"Go ahead, Six-oh-eight."

"I'll be ten-seven." Off duty.

"You're ten-seven at twenty-three-twenty-eight."

"Cork, you really don't have to stay," Sara argued.

I countered, "I know, but you are my best friend, and we haven't had a sleepover for a long time."

"Sorry, I got an early day tomorrow. I need to crash. Help yourself to food, drink, a shower, bed. And thanks, Corky. I'm glad you're here." She gave me a hug.

"Now, get some sleep. I'll pull my squad into your driveway. Oh, can I borrow a pair of pajamas?" I didn't feel like driving home for a change.

"You left some here last time. I washed them and put them in the spare room dresser." Sara was much more organized than I.

I lay in bed wondering who had gone into Sara's house, apparently to snoop around. There was no doubt in my mind someone had been there. Sara was particular without being a fanatic about it. I knew what it was like to live alone—your things stayed where you left them. Sometimes I wished a magic elf would come to my house when I was gone and clean up my messes, but an uninvited person in your home was another concern.

Could it be neighborhood kids, not realizing they were doing anything wrong? Or one of Sara's probation clients? She must have one hundred, maybe two hundred cases a year. More than one of them was bound to be angry with her, but they seemed more likely to storm into her office than sneak into her home. I was more worried about someone obsessed with her, stalking her, wanting to touch her things. We'd talk to the neighbors and see if any of them had observed a stranger hanging around lately.

I needed to change the subject to relax. I turned my thoughts to Nick and fell asleep with a smile on my face.

Chapter 19

Alvie

Things had started out so good. She knew the little sergeant was working and wouldn't be in the way for once. Alvie slipped out of the church and into her man disguise and got to Speiss' house ahead of her. She didn't even have to hide. The back door was open, easier than she'd thought it would be. Until the probation officer didn't come home, that is. Where could she have gone? Alvie waited two whole hours and couldn't wait any longer.

What was the reason for these interruptions and delays? Speiss was slated to be number two, then got bumped to number three, then bumped again. What was Alvie supposed to do? What if Speiss didn't make it home at all tonight? Rebecca was due home around seven o'clock, and Alvie had to have another one done by then. It was the twenty-fifth of July, and time was running out.

Good thing she was prepared. A smart planner was always ready. If plan A didn't work, you went to plan B. As long as Speiss wasn't the last one, it was okay. Jason Browne had to be last. Save the best, or in Jason's case, the worst for last. Dirty double-crosser deserved double the punishment.

Wasn't that the way you wanted it, son?

Chapter 20

My pager went off at four minutes after seven Monday morning. My hand fumbled on the bedside stand to retrieve it as my mind struggled to remember where I was. I focused my eyes, saw it was Smoke paging, and dialed his cell phone number.

"Corky, you up?"

"No," I groaned softly.

"The day sergeant called in sick, and we've got a situation. Can you come in early?"

The urgency in his voice propelled me to a sitting position.

"How early?"

"Now?"

"I'm at Sara's. I'll have to go home, get a clean—"

He interrupted. "How long will that take?"

"What's going on?"

"I'm on my way over to Marshall Kelton's. He's dead—apparent suicide."

"You have got to be kidding me! What is going on? Arthur, now Marshall?" The shock pushed me into full consciousness.

"I'll know more when I get there. Officer Dey from Oak Lea is securing the scene."

The Oak Lea Police Department investigator, Detective Garvey, was on vacation for two weeks, and the sheriff's department was assisting with some of the cases in the city.

"I'll be there shortly."

I had seen clean underwear in the drawer next to my pajamas, and my uniform was clean enough to pass inspection. I brushed my teeth and hair, splashed water on my face, dressed, and donned my duty belt and gear. I heard Sara's alarm ring, then stop. I called out a quick, "Thanks, talk to you later," and was out the door in under seven minutes.

I depressed the talk button on my radio. "Winnebago County, Six-oh-eight."

"Six-oh-eight?" It was Carmen, one of the day shift communication officers.

"I'm in service and en route to Detective Dawes' location."

"Copy that. You're ten-eight at seven-twenty."

Marshall Kelton was a public defender and had moved in with his brother to a townhouse on the south side of Oak Lea when his wife kicked him out a few years before. He enjoyed partying more than being a family man. His wife had finally said, and rightly so, that enough was enough.

We were at the same retirement party one night and Marshall had surprised me by asking me on a date, but didn't push the issue when I politely turned him down. Marshall was at least fifteen years older than me, divorced with teenage kids. The only thing I could see we might have in common was the time we spent together in the courtroom. As the public defender, he represented most of the people I arrested, so I was called to testify in his cases on a fairly regular basis.

I had caught a glimpse of Marshall Kelton at Arthur's memorial service, so I knew he was alive the previous afternoon. So Marshall had left the service, went home and killed himself? That was very, very peculiar. Was suicide something he had been thinking about for a while, and that night he'd snapped and done it? Maybe his life of partying and carrying on had taken a depressing turn, or gotten him into some trouble he couldn't face.

As I pulled into the driveway, I saw a man I guessed was Marshall's brother sitting in a lawn chair with his head in his hands. A silver Suzuki sport utility vehicle screeched to a stop on the street, and Stefany, Marshall's ex-wife, ran over to the man. He stood up, and they embraced and sobbed. Neither one seemed to notice me as I made my way to the house.

Officer Dey was standing guard inside the front door. Oak Lea officers worked twelve-hour shifts, from either seven a.m. to seven p.m. or vice versa. Since he was the one securing the scene, he would be working until we cleared. Dey nodded at me and handed me a clipboard. I signed in. "Detective Dawes is waiting for you in the living room."

I pulled on a pair of latex gloves.

"Winnebago County, Three-forty?" Communications was calling.

"Three-forty," Smoke answered.

"The coroner is on his way from another call, ETA, zero-seven-thirty."

A closet on the right partnered with the opposite wall to provide an entryway for the townhouse. I walked the short distance past it to the open area and saw Smoke taking pictures of the body of Marshall Kelton. Kelton was in a sitting position on a couch, his head resting on his chest, drained of all color. His right hand was on his leg, a razor blade lying beside it. His left arm was dangling with dark, dried blood on his wrist and hand. The front of the couch and carpet were stained with the same.

He had been dead for a while. Rigor mortis had come and gone.

Smoke looked at me and shook his head. "Two lawyer suicides in less than a week? The prosecutor, and now the defender? You know how you can think of the dumbest things sometimes? I have spent the last few minutes feeling a little guilty for all the dead lawyer jokes I've told in my career."

I nodded and walked closer to Smoke, careful not to step on a book and a beer can lying on the floor by the end table. I noticed another can on the table next to a typed piece of paper. The television was turned on to a sports channel.

"Think he was drunk?" I asked.

"Not on two beers, and I don't see any other empties lying around. They'll do a blood alcohol with the other tests."

I walked around, taking in the scene. "He came home from the memorial service, drank beer, and sometime in the middle of watching a sports event on TV, cut his wrist and bled to death? Where was his brother when this happened?" I asked.

Smoke glanced my way. "Spent the night at his girlfriend's, came home to get ready for work, and found Marshall. He's been outside since I got here. Big blow to him. Officer Dey had communications call a chaplain to talk to him," he said.

"His ex-wife is out there, too. She got here right after me and seems as upset as Marshall's brother."

"Did you talk to her?" I shook my head. Smoke set the camera next to his briefcase on the floor. "Okay. We'll interview them when we finish up. Doc Melberg will be here any time now."

"I am here," Melberg said as he entered the room. "You two again," he offered in greeting.

"I can't say we're too happy to see you, either, Doc," Smoke said.

"I get that a lot." He moved to Marshall's body and performed a brief exam and rigidity tests. "So, last week the prosecutor and this week the public defender?" He leaned over to read the note on the end table, then moved his head back and forth several times, lost in thought.

"They question the meaning of their lives, and we question the meaning of their deaths. We'll send him to Hennepin for autopsy, check for contributing factors, but it appears he cut his own wrist," Dr. Melberg concluded.

"Doc, this is the first time I've seen a man kill himself by slashing his wrist," Smoke said.

"Very rare. I had one case a few years ago. The guy was in jail and took his safety razor apart during morning hygiene. When the officer came back to collect the used razors, they found him in his cell."

"Not in our jail?" I asked, thinking I'd remember that.

"No, Meeker's," Melberg said, referring to our neighbor on the west. Melberg was the coroner for two other counties that neighbored Winnebago.

"Contact me if you need anything," Dr. Melberg said.

Smoke nodded as he picked up his camera, and Melberg left without a goodbye.

"You got any evidence bags on you?" Smoke asked.

"One."

"Will you read me the note?" He pointed to the table.

"'This is the end of a big problem. Marshall Kelton.' He makes it sound like Marshall Kelton is a big problem and his death ends it. One liner, typed, except the signature, like Arthur's was."

"And makes about as much sense. Two lawyers, both used to doing a lot of talking, explaining, arguing, and they both leave one-line suicide notes that say nothing."

I slipped the note into an evidence bag. "Oooh!"

"What is it?" Smoke looked around.

"That awful feeling I've had with every death lately."

"The evil presence?"

I nodded.

Smoke shrugged. "I don't feel it. Are you due for a vacation?" He looked at me with concern.

I shook my head.

"Days off?"

"I have one more day then off for three."

"Good."

"Smoke, look at this."

I pointed to the beer can on the end table. There was a white residue around the opening.

Smoke found his glasses in his breast pocket and slipped them on. "Damn. Either this is one big coincidence, or there is something way beyond that going on here."

"You don't mean like a suicide pact between Arthur and Marshall?"

"I can't speculate on anything, especially something that sounds so crazy when you say it out loud."

"Dawes, Aleckson." We both turned at the sound of Sheriff Twardy's voice. "Oh, for godsakes," he said to Marshall's body. "What in the Sam Hill is going on here?" he asked as if we could give him an answer. "Bud is outside talking to the brother and ex-wife. You talk to them yet?"

"No, but we will shortly. We're about done here," Smoke relayed.

"Anybody call Kelton's office, tell them what happened?"

Smoke looked at his watch. "No. Someone should be there about now if you want to send an officer to tell them."

Sheriff Twardy pulled out his cell phone and walked away as he dialed a number.

Chief Bud Becker filled the room with his presence and his girth. "I saw Marshall Kelton yesterday at the service. Just goes to show you never know. His wife wants to see him before they pick him up."

The sheriff returned a minute later. "The chief deputy will walk over and give them the bad news, and tell them to keep it quiet for a while. They'll have to figure out court—Monday is a busy day there. I don't have to tell you that. You can talk to the folks at his office later. See if anyone knows what brought this on."

Smoke pulled an evidence bag from his jacket pocket and picked up the beer can. "Sheriff, see this?"

The sheriff leaned forward and frowned at the can. "What is that? Same stuff as on Arthur's soda can?"

Smoke raised his eyebrows. "Lab tests will give us the answer to that. We don't know what the residue on Arthur's can was; no results back yet."

"What are you folks talking about?" Chief Becker asked, and Smoke told him we had found a similar looking residue on the can in Arthur's vehicle on the day he died.

"You think there's a connection between the two suicides?" Becker asked.

"I wouldn't even want to say possibly at this point," Smoke said.

"For godsakes," was all the sheriff added.

Stefany Kelton came in clutching her ex-brother-in-law's arm. I knew of them through casual conversations with Marshall, but had never met either one. Stefany was pretty, round, and maternal looking. Brock Kelton looked like he was related to Marshall, but was much younger and more physically fit. Marshall had kidded about the boring life his brother led, eating nutritious food, playing racquetball and tennis, and going to bed early almost every night.

Stefany wailed at the sight of Marshall, and Brock gasped when she did. "Why would he do this when things were getting so much better?" Stefany asked.

The sheriff directed us into the kitchen, away from the body and scene of the death.

"You said things were better. How so?" Smoke asked Stefany.

"We've been seeing a marriage counselor. Marshall was really pushing to get back together, and I wanted that, too, I just wasn't quite ready," Stefany choked out, her voice broken by sobs.

Brock agreed. "He did a one-eighty a few weeks ago and realized how much he had lost, you know, Stefany and the kids. I think he had a midlife crisis, myself, when he started all that running around." Brock rubbed the back of his neck. "This doesn't make any sense at all."

That was becoming an all too familiar theme.

"And the beer cans? He never—and I mean never—has more than one beer, or any other alcoholic drink. Even during his party hardy days, he usually stuck to colas." I had assumed, like most people did, his colas were mixed drinks.

"Was Marshall on any prescription medications?" I asked.

"No," Stefany and Brock answered together.

"How about over-the-counter drugs for headaches, stomach aches . . ."

Stefany looked at Brock. "Not that I know of," he said. "We can check the medicine cabinet, see if there's anything new in there. But he didn't complain of anything."

"To me, either," Stefany said.

"Chief Becker," Officer Dey called from the entry.

"Yeah?" the chief asked.

"The chaplain, Pastor Boyd, is here."

"Ask him to wait outside in the front yard. We'll be through here in a few minutes."

Smoke got back to the interview. "Was there a particular problem either of you were aware of that Marshall was dealing with? Any trouble he had gotten into recently?"

"No, I already told you things were going the best they had in years," Stefany said.

"Take a look at this note." Smoke reached toward me, and I handed over the evidence bag with the note.

Stefany made no move to take the note. Brock's hand was shaking as he slowly removed it from Smoke's grasp. Stefany let go of another loud cry, an unnerving sound to our ears.

"I don't believe Marshall wrote this, and I don't believe he killed himself. He told me everything, and if he had a problem, big or little, I would know about it. He may have made some dumb choices the past few years, but he wasn't depressed. And if he had a problem—even a horrible one—he would face it, not commit suicide over it," Brock said emphatically.

"Chief," Officer Dey called out again.

"Yeah?" Chief Becker answered.

"Anderson's is here."

"Are you close to wrapping this up?" the chief asked Smoke.

Smoke nodded. "One more question."

"Dey, you can send the Andersons in," Becker said as he walked toward the living room.

"Was Marshall close to Arthur Franz?" Smoke asked.

"The prosecutor who just died?" Stefany spoke. "Close, as in friends?" She shook her head. "They've been on opposite sides of the courtroom for years. They got along fine, but I don't think they ever saw each other outside of work."

Brock agreed. "No, Marshall was, you know, shocked Franz had killed himself, and felt terrible about it, but not in the same way he would for, you know, a close friend. He went to his memorial service yesterday—at least was planning to. I left around one and didn't talk to him after that." The impact of his own words hit him hard. He pulled his tee shirt up, covering his eyes, and sobbed.

"Let's go find the chaplain," Sheriff Twardy said, once again leading us, this time to the back patio. Smoke appeared with Pastor Boyd a minute later.

"What do we do next?" Brock wondered, looking at Chief Becker and Sheriff Twardy.

"We'll need an autopsy, then you can talk to Anderson's, or whoever you choose, to make the arrangements," the sheriff said, his voice low and steady.

Chief Becker took over. "For now, spend some time with Pastor Boyd here. And call if you have any questions, or think of something else."

Chief Becker, Sheriff Twardy, and I followed Smoke to the side of the townhouse, where he stopped and turned to face us. "When I went to get the chaplain, guess who was talking to him and the Anderson brothers? Paul Moore. He's pushing the line between reporter and fire chaser. And there must be another dozen people watching from the yard across the street."

"Nothing like a few squad cars and a hearse to get an audience. Paul's a decent guy. I'll find out what he's up to," Chief Becker said.

When we reached the front yard, I glanced at the neighbors across the street, then focused on Moore. Chief Becker marched over to him.

"Geez, Paul, what are you doing here?"

Our group stood like an army around the chief, the offense to anything Moore might say in defense.

Paul held up his arms in surrender. "Hey, officers, no scare tactics, please. I'm not the only one." He nodded his head and waved his hands toward the neighbors. "I live two blocks down. On my way to work, natural curiosity had me wondering what was going on. So, Chief Becker, are you ready to make a statement?" Paul asked, his pen poised above his pad.

"Not yet, Paul. You know the ropes. There are people who need to be notified ahead of the press."

"Okay, somebody died here. So are you talking about next of kin? I know Marshall Kelton, the public defender, lives here with his brother. Is it one of them, or a visitor?"

"Geez, Paul, shut up and quit fishin'. You'll know soon enough," Becker said.

"In time for the evening edition?" Moore persisted.

Chief Becker gave him a stern look in place of an answer and walked to the front door. The rest of us watched the Andersons roll their gurney, with Marshall Kelton's enclosed body, to their transport van.

"How late you want to work, Sergeant?" the sheriff asked, pulling me aside.

"Not a double, sir, if I don't have to."

Sheriff Twardy nodded. "I'll have the chief deputy work on the schedule."

"Thank you."

"I'm going to talk to Bud. I'll see you back at the department later on." The sheriff shook his keys, fingering the one to his Crown Victoria.

Smoke and I walked to our vehicles. "You have the feeling we're being watched?" he chided.

"We are being watched," I countered.

"And knowing you're being watched is different from feeling you're being watched?"

"I guess. I don't think I can analyze that right now, so give it a rest." I sounded crabby, but didn't apologize.

"Look at that old blue Impala." Smoke pointed to a car sitting a little over a block away on the opposite side of the street. "You don't see many of those around, anymore. I had one like it about fifteen years ago, different color. Mine was brown."

"You didn't get enough driving brown squad cars?" I asked.

He smirked. "I got a good deal on it."

"That looks like the same car that was parked next to mine at the hospital the day I talked to Rebecca Eisner." I had noticed it because it was the second oldest car in the lot after mine. "It's a strange place for someone to be sitting in their car reading the newspaper."

"Probably picking someone up. A lot of people in these townhouses are elderly and don't drive. Or it could be another curious onlooker. Not many dramatic incidents in this town," Smoke reminded me.

"Until a few weeks ago. Oak Lea will be in competition with Wellspring if we don't watch out." Wellspring was a community on the western edge of the county and a magnet for lawless people.

"I can't say I look forward to that area of assignment."

The county was divided into six areas of service, and the detectives were rotated every three months.

"But the untimely deaths here are not in the same category as the downright criminal behavior there."

Christine Husom

"True." I pointed to the Impala. "That car is backing into a driveway and turning around. Probably was just someone checking what was going on."

"Not much to watch, now Anderson's is gone," Smoke said. "Hey, I got this call before breakfast. You hungry?"

I nodded. "More importantly, I haven't had my morning coffee."

"Let's grab a bite before we go to the public defender's office. We might be there awhile."

We got into our separate vehicles, and I followed Smoke to Brookings, a local mom and pop restaurant. I thought back to the first death call I had had as a rookie. It was pretty gruesome, and I couldn't eat for two days. Death calls continued to be difficult for me—especially when I knew the person—but they were a regular part of my job, and I had learned I needed to eat well to stay healthy.

Chapter 21

Alvie

The detective and the little sergeant seemed to come out of nowhere, then stood and stared right at her for way too long. Alvie was parked a whole block and a half away. How had they even spotted her? Alvie was dripping wet with sweat thinking they would walk over to her car and talk to her. What if her mustache came unglued from all the perspiration running down her face and fell off? The little sergeant would probably have recognized her, even with the ball cap and sunglasses on. How would she have explained what she was doing sitting in her car, in that neighborhood, at that time of the day, dressed like a man?

As soon as they looked away for a second, she turned her car around and drove away. She went down streets she didn't know existed in Oak Lea. Not that she could tell much about what they looked like. That was a blur. Her main focus had been watching the rearview mirror to make sure they hadn't followed her. And getting home before Rebecca woke up. During the summer, Rebecca usually slept in until nine o'clock, which had worked out especially fine that morning when Alvie had a little errand to run.

But then that damn detective had picked her out, and even had the little sergeant look at her. No one, not the nosy neighbors, not the police chief, not the sheriff, not one of them had looked her way until then. Why was that? Speiss should be the next death, but maybe the detective had to be. Or maybe it should be the little sergeant, so Alvie could get to Speiss easier. Speiss never seemed to be alone.

Alvie's head was practically splitting open. Okay, time to regroup. She'd get home, redraw the three names, and see what that told her. Didn't they say things happened in threes? Okay, she'd gotten the first three done; she just had to figure out what to do about the last three. But the little sergeant made four. If she did Speiss and the little sergeant together, a murder-suicide, that would count as one, wouldn't it? That deserved very serious consideration.

Chapter 22

There were a few tables of mostly older people eating breakfast when we got to the cafe. The working crowd had eaten earlier and gone to their jobs. It was the place to go for home style cooking in an old-fashioned cafe. Smoke and I greeted the patrons as we made our way to a back corner booth. The waitress served us the breakfast special of eggs, bacon, and toast.

Smoke sipped his coffee, then leaned forward and spoke in a tone one step up from a whisper. "I can't help thinking there is some kind of nonprofessional connection between Arthur and Marshall. The question is how deep do we dig to find out?"

"What kind of a connection? Stefany and Brock Kelton both said Marshall didn't hang out with Arthur."

"True. So if it was personal, it was secretive."

"Smoke, that sounds like a movie from the TrueLife network," I said.

He added more coffee to his cup. "I know. I'm just bouncing ideas around. Another possibility is they got mixed up in some kind of illegal activity."

"Like what?" I put my hand over my cup and shook my head to decline more coffee before he poured it.

"Don't know, cutting a deal with a client in exchange for money, drugs. Like I said, I don't know, I'm just throwing scenarios out there," Smoke explained.

"Way out there."

"Look at how Arthur managed to keep virtually his entire personal life a secret. What's one more secret?"

Smoke's words were worming their way through me, raising questions and doubts about two men I thought I had known. "And Marshall?"

"His personal life doesn't seem to be much of a secret, but what do we really know? A major crisis could explain what happened to Marshall and to Arthur. Marion McIllvery might provide an insight for us."

"But, Smoke, why investigate this? I mean, aren't their families going through enough right now?"

Smoke nodded. "But, if there was something corrupt involving the two of them, we owe it to the county and the citizens to get to the bottom of it and stop it before someone else gets hurt."

The previous day I had loved investigation. But at that moment, it was the least favorite part of my job.

The public defender's office was trying to function in the midst of their collective state of disbelief and shock. Despite his personal failings, Marshall Kelton had been well liked and fun to work with. No one in the office could believe, or understand, why he had killed himself. Yes, he had a stressful, way too heavy workload, but that had been true for years.

No one had ever seen Marshall and Arthur together outside of work, but of course, it seemed strange Marshall had chosen to die on the day of Arthur's service. In addition to the personal loss, they were scrambling to get help from public defenders from reciprocating counties, or from private attorneys, to help manage the caseload until another attorney was hired.

Smoke and I were on our way into the sheriff's department when I remembered I had a lunch date at noon.

"Oh, my gosh, I forgot all about Nick!"

"Nick? Who's that?"

I gave him an abbreviated rundown.

Smoke looked both pleased and concerned. "I talked to your mother last night. I'm surprised she didn't mention him. That would be big news for her. If she knew about it, that is."

Smoke knew me too well.

"I haven't exactly told her yet."

His words sunk in.

"You were talking to my mother?"

He nodded. "I'm making a little progress. She invited me over for dinner tonight."

"Smoke, I am so happy." I reached over and bumped his arm with my elbow.

"Any words of wisdom or advice?"

"Just one—she's always right. After I finally figured that out, our arguments almost completely disappeared."

The sheriff was in a closed door meeting with the chief deputy and lieutenant. His secretary said she would page us when they had finished. I went to the squad room to file my reports from the previous evening and start my report on that morning's call. It was after ten, so I dialed Nick's number before I started writing.

"Corky, hello! Just rolling out of bed?"

"I wish. Actually, I got called in for the day shift, and the bad news is, I don't think I can break away for lunch. The good news is, I should be off duty by three or so."

Nick didn't miss a beat. "Then how about dinner? We're grilling tonight. Will you join us?"

Monday night. No plans. "I'd love to, if I can bring something."

"All right, well, how about a salad?"

"Sure. What time?"

"Six?"

"See you then." A salad. I'd either have to call my mother or check online for a good recipe.

Smoke stuck his head in the squad room. "Sheriff wants to see us."

The sheriff was pacing behind his desk, pounding his right fist into his left hand. "Close the door," he called. Smoke did.

"Just got done talking to Kenner and Randolph, prepared a public statement. Gilbert is sweating tacks over this whole ordeal." Kenner was the chief deputy, Randolph was the lieutenant, and Michael Gilbert was the county administrator who oversaw both business and personnel issues for Winnebago County.

The sheriff continued, "It doesn't reflect well on Winnebago. Two prominent legal figures kill themselves—might be interpreted the stress of their jobs got to them. Like we work 'em to death around here, for godsakes."

Politics.

"Well, that might be better than the truth," Smoke said, his blue eyes intense, darkening to navy.

"Which is?" The sheriff raised his eyebrows.

"I have no idea, Denny. Still, if it turns out they were involved with each other personally, it might be a lot for people to digest, but a whole lot easier on the county."

"What in the hell are you talking about, Dawes?" Sheriff Twardy's frown deepened.

Smoke explained the possibility of the attorneys being involved in some sort of illegal or unethical activity.

The sheriff's face turned a deep shade of red. "You don't believe that?"

"Sheriff, it's my job to keep an open mind. I've got both cases. If there's a connection, I'll find it. If not, life just got a whole lot easier," Smoke said.

The sheriff rested both hands on his desk and leaned his body toward us, staring first at me, then at Smoke. "This theory of yours stays with the three of us. Be more than discreet. The reputations of two fine men are on the line here."

As we walked down the corridor, Smoke directed me toward his cubicle. On the way, we passed three other detectives at their desks, reading or on the phone. Smoke indicated the visitor chair, and I sat down. He swung his long leg onto the side of his desk and half-leaned, half-sat close to me.

He spoke quietly. "You have Marion McIllvery's phone numbers?"

I nodded.

"Good. I'm putting you in charge of talking to her. Ask her what she knows, if anything, about a connection between Arthur and Marshall. We'll do a follow-up with Stefany and Brock Kelton in a week or so. Meantime, I'll get a search warrant for the county attorney and public defender files." He stopped at the thought of it. "Damn. How are we supposed to do that without arousing suspicion in their offices?"

I shrugged and whispered back, "I guess you'll have to be honest. It's an investigation of something you can't discuss, but will explain it when it's over."

Smoke raised his eyebrows and nodded.

It was three-thirty-five when I went off duty. I was usually barely beginning my shift at that time of day. I remembered Marion McIllvery was in Duluth for Arthur's burial. Smoke said it was fine to wait until I got back from my days off to contact her. I debated whether to phone my mother or to stop by her shop for a salad recipe. I settled on the visit.

Mother put down the dress she was holding and gave me a hug. "Hi, dear. You got my message?" she asked.

"No."

"I didn't talk to you yesterday, and I tried to catch you before you went to work." My mother didn't have a cell phone and never called mine.

"What's up?"

"Well, I called the first time before I heard about that public defender, then I called again after I heard." I waited patiently for her go on. "You never stop in when you're working," she finally realized.

It saved time for me to summarize my life and activities since the last time we had spoken, which was Saturday morning. I gave her the details of the memorial service, why I had spent the night at Sara's, and how I had gotten called in for the day shift.

"I know who the Keltons are, but I really don't know them. Do they think there's a connection between the two suicides? KRKW, you know, the Winnebago County radio station, is saying there isn't any known connection, but that the sheriff's department is looking into it. What's that supposed to mean? I don't know how you can do what you do," Mom said.

"Just routine investigation." The official reason for the investigation was under wraps. "Mother, you didn't tell me what your phone message was."

"Well." She picked up the dress and slipped it on a hanger, not looking at me. "Elton is coming over for dinner tonight."

"Good for you, Mother, good for both of you."

Mother hung the dress on a display rack. "It's not really a date. We have been friends for many years, you know."

"It's a start." I watched her work for a moment. "Actually, I have a dinner date myself."

She finally braved a look at me. "Corinne May Aleckson, you have a date! With whom?"

"Nicholas Bradshaw—"

"The hospital administrator?!"

"—and his eight-year-old daughter."

"Well, you are old enough to have an eight-year-old yourself."

My ever practical mother. I could envision the wheels in her head turning, processing the information and the potential impact it could have on all our lives.

I didn't want to go there, so I stuck to my original subject. "We're grilling, and I'm bringing a salad. Any suggestions? Something really good, but easy to make?"

"I made a pasta salad as a side dish for tonight. Why don't you take half of it? I made way too much."

Even better than me trying to cook. "Are you sure?"

She smiled. "Of course, dear. What time will you be by to pick it up?"

"Ten to six?"

I drove to Sara's neighborhood to ask whoever was home if they had noticed any suspicious activity the previous day. The couple to the immediate east of Sara were both teachers and had the summer off. The ones on the west side worked in the metro area and were gone most of the time, according to Sara.

I got no response from the first five houses I tried. When I rang the doorbell on the sixth house, directly across from Sara's, a woman's voice called out, "I'm coming."

An older, portly woman opened the door. Her hand flew to her heart, and her brows knitted into a frown. "What is it?" she pleaded.

"Nothing to be upset about, ma'am. I'm a friend of Sara Speiss', across the street?" I showed her my identification and handed her my card. "I'm Sergeant Aleckson from the sheriff's department. And you're Mrs. Sanford, is it?"

"Yes, Mabel Sanford." She squinted for better focus. "Oh, yes, now I recognize you. I've seen you go into her house, but I've never seen you close up before."

"And I'm not usually in uniform when I stop by," I added. "Actually, I wanted to ask you some questions, if you have a few minutes."

"Come in, come in. Let's sit in the kitchen. I have warm chocolate chip cookies cooling on the counter. I'll put some on a plate. What would you like to drink: coffee, milk, water?" She held her hand on her right hip, waddling her way to the next room.

Mrs. Sanford's house smelled friendly, like sunshine and bread baking in the oven and lemon cleaner. There was nothing quite like homemade chocolate chip cookies, and my stomach growled in anticipation. "Thank you. I'd love some milk."

My grandmothers always loved to treat me, so how could I have disappointed this nice old lady? She set cookies, plates, napkins, and beverages down before lowering herself onto a chair opposite me. Mrs. Sanford waved her hand back and forth over the table. "Don't be shy. Help yourself."

The first cookie, then a second one, melted in my mouth and I would have eaten a third, but the thought of saving some room for dinner stopped me.

"Thank you. I haven't had homemade cookies for a while. They are really delicious." Mrs. Sanford beamed. "The reason I'm here is, yesterday, when Sara was gone, someone got into her home. I was wondering if you saw anyone going in or coming out of her house in the afternoon, or evening?"

Mrs. Sanford's expression changed instantly, her smile replaced with a frown. "Oh, my! We haven't had any trouble in this neighborhood before. Let me think . . . yesterday . . . I went to church in the morning, then out to lunch with my lady friends. . . . My husband died last year." She paused for a while, organizing the previous day into a narrative.

"Then I came home and took a little rest and read some. It was too hot to be outside until evening. After I had a bite to eat for supper, I sat in the back in my screened porch and read awhile more. I saw my next door neighbors come home from their open house about six. They're realtors and had an open house yesterday. I watered my flowers in the front around seven, then went inside and watched a little television until bed."

"So you didn't see anyone at Sara's house?"

Mrs. Sanford shook her head. "Not even Sara. This morning—I get up early—I saw a Winnebago County Sheriff squad car parked in her driveway, and the next time I looked, it was gone."

I nodded. "How about Saturday, or another day last week? Anyone in the neighborhood, hanging around?"

"Well, there are people who walk by that I don't know, or sometimes those Jehovah Witnesses handing out their magazines, or people selling cleaning products." Her face brightened. "Wait a minute, there was a man sitting in a car one day last week. I remember because it reminded me of one of those private investigators on television, you know how they sit in their cars and watch people. Maybe take pictures of them doing something they shouldn't be doing."

"Can you tell me what the car looked like?"

Mrs. Sanford squeezed her eyes together, then shook her head. "I guess I can't. It was one of those older ones. I'm not good with cars."

"What color?"

"I'm not sure about that either. Gray, or green, or blue. Oh, I'm not much help, am I?"

"You're doing just fine. Can you tell me where the car was parked?"

"Why don't I show you?"

It took a while, but we got out of the house, walked to the street, and a little way down the block, where Mrs. Sanford stopped.

"Right about here," she told me.

I stood on the spot and looked toward Sara's house. There was a large tree in her neighbor's yard that obstructed part of the view, but her driveway and back deck were clearly visible. Why would a private investigator be spying on Sara? Or anyone else, for that matter? I got goose bumps wondering if Sara was, in fact, being stalked.

Chapter 23

Alvie

It was late afternoon, and Alvie was finally enjoying a more normal heart rate and lower body temperature than she had all day. It had been the most stressful twenty-four hours since her mission began. It had started out pleasant enough, watching the prosecutor's wife and friends mourn the loss of his merciless life. After the judge, the prosecuting attorney had the most power to destroy people, young men like her Nolan who didn't deserve to die in prison.

And Alvie was prepared to take on the little sergeant if she showed up at Speiss' house. Even though she didn't want to kill her, it might be a relief to get Aleckson out of the way. She was always showing up.

The gun had worked so well. Almost unreal how it made men grovel. Alvie was surprised when she found the gun on the shelf in her uncle's closet. Nolan was a toddler, three years old. At nineteen, Alvie had divided her energy between taking care of her baby and hoping Uncle would leave her alone. She kept the gun and hid it under her mattress, just in case.

One night, she woke up to the sound of Nolan crying. She went to the room next to hers, and found her uncle doing awful things to him. It was bad enough he had abused Henry and her, but his own son. Her beloved son. Alvie would not stand for that. She ran to her room, grabbed the gun, and gripping it with both hands, pointed it at Uncle and told him to stop. He laughed at her. "You wouldn't shoot your own uncle."

Uncle stepped away from Nolan's bed, and Alvie fired, pop, pop, pop. It was a mess. Alvie covered Uncle's body with a blanket, picked up her screaming son, and carried him to her bed. She held him until he fell asleep. Eventually, she worked up enough courage to go back to Nolan's room to clean up. Uncle was huge, but Alvie was strong, and she dragged his shrouded body down the stairs and out to the yard. It took hours, but she dug a deep enough hole and got Uncle buried by the big oak.

Alvie almost threw the gun away after using it that one time, but she was sure glad she hadn't. It gave her the power to make people do what she wanted. Yes, she was in control.

Judge Fenneman, Arthur Franz, Marshall Kelton. Three down, three to go. Unless she killed the little sergeant, then she might add the sheriff and that snooty secretary at the public defender's office to the list. Boy, to knock that smirk off her face permanently would be worth whatever trouble it took. That would make six to go.

It was nearly five o'clock. Rebecca would be home for supper in about an hour. Plenty of time for a calming cigarette and a little reflection on the third suicide. What if she hadn't overheard them talking about suicide notes? She was meant to hear that so everyone would know they were suicides. The families had to know that. It made the suffering so much worse.

Alvie lit a cigarette and dragged long and hard as she settled into her La-Z-Boy. Just one quick one; there'd be time to clear the air for Rebecca. She'd have a fit to see her grandma smoking. Not because of her own respiratory problems—she'd be worried about Alvie getting cancer. Rebecca was a dear, always thinking of her grandmother. *Nolan, you'd be proud. She's the best of all of us.* A little sickly, but never complained about that, or anything else, for that matter.

Alvie watched the smoke swirl around her head and thought about her latest triumph. Kelton wasn't quite as easy as Judge Fenneman, or Arthur Franz, but he was gone. The look on his face when she walked into his living room pointing the gun at him! He had the television on loud enough to cover the little sound she'd made coming in the unlocked back door. Alvie crept to the opening separating the kitchen from the living room and spotted the back of his head leaning against the back of his couch. He was a true sitting duck, too interested in the game on TV and drinking a beer to hear her.

Alvie quietly went to the kitchen refrigerator, pulled out a beer, slipped outside to cover the sound of popping the top, poured the crushed tablets in the brew, and waited one long minute for them to dissolve. Once inside the house again, she pulled the gun from her pocket, walked in and blocked the lawyer's view of the game. His jaw dropped so low, Alvie could see most of his bottom teeth were full of fillings. It was a silly thing to nearly make her lose her concentration.

"What are you doing?" he whispered.

Alvie saw he was struggling to identify her, but the man disguise prevented that.

"Drink this. Don't ask questions."

And he did, just like that. He tried to talk a few times before he fell asleep, but Alvie just shook her head and waved her gun back and forth.

She opened the new pack of razor blades, fumbling, a little awkward with the rubber gloves on her hands. Kelton was snoring and barely moved in his sleep when the blood started dripping from the cut on his wrist. His breaths grew slower, and slower, and stopped. Just like that.

Alvie commended herself on the most relaxing suicide yet. She put the blade in Kelton's right hand so his prints would be evident, then watched it drop from fingers that could no longer grasp. Alvie retrieved the note she had left on the kitchen counter. She was about to lay it on the end table, next to the public defender, when she saw a pocketsize appointment calendar there. She picked it up as a keepsake, then placed the note down in its place.

Alvie took one last satisfying look at another job well done and walked calmly back to her car. She didn't spot a single soul as she drove her Chevy south of town to the haven of her little house.

The third suicide had been the best part of the past two days. There was no need to give more thought to the wasted time at Speiss', or being spotted by the ace detective and little sergeant. She needed her energy to pull off the last three suicides, and to take good care of Rebecca. She was back from camp, so Alvie would have to be careful. Rebecca was smart and would notice if her grandmother was gone too much. As long as she kept the man disguise and gun locked in her trunk, Rebecca would never know. She could pull the car in the garage, undress quick as a flash, and stow her gear. Just like that. Yes, she would keep that as part of her routine so there would be no mistakes.

The one thing that was beginning to concern her was, she only had four tablets left of the ten she'd stolen from Henry's prescription. Was it possible to pull off one of the deaths without the drug? Maybe if she did a shooting. That might be a good one for Jason Browne. He didn't deserve to fall asleep like the last two. He should be awake and know exactly how he was going to die. Nolan did. And Jason was the one who had ratted Nolan out, the traitor who'd handed him over to the wolves who picked him apart until there was nothing left to keep him alive.

Time to open a can of soup and toast some bread for sandwiches. Rebecca was due any time.

Chapter 24

Finished with Mrs. Sanford, I made my way back to my squad car. After sitting in the sun, with its black interior, the temperature inside my car was well over one hundred degrees. When I slipped behind the wheel, the smell of death and decay joined me, surrounding me in the heat, threatening to knock me unconscious. I gasped for air, pushed my door open, and jumped onto the pavement. The stench from Marshall Kelton's death was still with me—on me—ten hours later, and I knew the foul odor would forever be ingrained in my memory.

It was the same for Judge Fenneman, and Arthur Franz, and all the other death scenes I had been at. Each one had its own set of smells attached to it. With the judge, it was hospital antiseptics, rain in the air and on the earth, swamp on bedclothes and skin.

Arthur's death was the taste of gravel dust, sunbaked soil, the witness' sweat, and the beginning of decay in the hothouse of Arthur's vehicle.

Marshall's was stale beer, dried blood, and decomposing flesh, not unlike the musty smell of mold.

I climbed back in my car and turned the air conditioning fan on full force. I lifted my arm to my nose and inhaled deeply, but I couldn't tell if the odors from Marshall's house were clinging to my clothes or were springing unbidden from my memory.

I pulled in my driveway, ran into my house, stripped in the laundry room, and stepped into the shower. The hot water blasted over me while I soaped and rinsed twice. I needed reassurance that any telltale stench from my workday was scrubbed from my body, exiled to the recesses of my mind.

Mother had a generous portion of pasta and vegetable salad dished into the multi-colored bowl she often used for summer meals.

"Your face is a little flushed, Mom. You okay?"

"Fine, dear. Just rushing around trying to finish up. Elton will be here soon."

I looked around. "Mother, what is there left to do? Your house is perfect, dinner smells wonderful, and your table is even set, for heaven's sake. Relax, Elton is just an old friend, remember?" The opportunity to tease her was so rare, I couldn't resist.

"Yes, I remember. Now take your salad and go, or you'll be late." She pushed the bowl against me and gave me a kiss on the cheek.

"I really appreciate this. I love you, Mom. Have fun."

"You, too."

Faith opened the door to their two-story brick home. She was supported on either side by lookalike, freckled carrot tops. Each was holding a Barbie doll. I didn't know the dolls were still popular and guessed my mother had mine stowed somewhere.

"Come in, Sergeant Corky."

"Thank you, Faith. Who are your friends?"

"This is Janie and this is Sarah."

"Very nice to meet you, girls. Would you happen to be twins?" All three girls giggled.

"You know, my best friend's name is Sara."

They giggled again.

"Corky, welcome." Nick appeared, and the girls ran off to play. He took the salad from my hands, and I followed him to the kitchen. "This looks good—almost as colorful as the bowl." He set the bowl on his sand-colored granite countertop.

"We can thank my mother for that. She likes to color coordinate." I laughed.

"You're not in uniform?" It was spoken more as a statement than a question.

"What?"

He put a hand on either shoulder and gently pulled my hair. "Never mind, you look better like this." He ran his hands down the back of my turquoise sleeveless shirt and rested them on my capris-clad hips. "There will be other opportunities to kiss my favorite officer when she's in uniform."

"Oh, yes, that weird fantasy of yours," I said as Nick stepped closer, trapping me between his body and the cabinets.

"You think it's a weird fantasy?"

"I do."

"Probably more common than you think. Okay, then we'll just practice for now."

His lips closed over mine, and I heard the shy giggling of little girls nearby. Nick lifted his head and faced the girls. "Faith, Sarah, Janie, it's not polite to laugh when you're spying." He smiled and gave my back a quick rub before stepping away.

"Sorry, Dad," Faith said, not looking the least bit so.

Nick smiled. "Hey, dinner is about done. You girls can set the table. We'll eat on the deck. Corky, what can I get you to drink? Wine, soda?"

"Water is fine." Nick served my drink and laid out the table service for the girls to use. "Something smells good," I said.

"Ribs on the grill, and corn on the cob steaming on the stove."

"Mmm, what can I do?"

Nick pointed to a drawer. "You'll find the serving utensils in there. And you can pour milk for the girls—glasses are in that cupboard." He disappeared to the backyard with a platter and tongs.

Nick and my mother had created a great dinner, and I ate until I couldn't hold another bite. The girls kept us entertained, telling stories and the same knock-knock jokes I had told as a kid.

They thought they were the funniest things in the world and I laughed with them, my sides actually aching because of it. Nick rolled his eyes more than once, but didn't seem to mind being outnumbered four to one.

"May we be excused?" Faith asked after dessert of chocolate covered ice cream treats.

"You may. And take your dishes in with you."

I watched the little girls shift their loads to open the door.

"Faith is so polite. She seems like a thirty-year-old inside a little girl's body."

He chuckled. "More like a forty-year-old. I am grateful she has been so easy to raise. So far. We're a few years from the teens yet."

I couldn't imagine Faith being a problem teen, but I'd seen enough to know anything was possible.

"More coffee?" he asked.

"No, thanks. Let me help you clean up. I should get going soon." I stood, and Nick did the same.

"You work tomorrow?"

I nodded. "Back to the evening shift. You probably heard the news about the lead defense attorney, Marshall Kelton?"

"No. What happened?"

"Apparent suicide. Another one." I told him the story, with more information than I had given my mother. "I'm guessing the press will be all over it by morning, and rumors and speculations will start flying about the coincidence of an attorney killing himself on the day of his rival attorney's memorial service."

"Is there a connection?" he asked.

"I have no idea. Actually, this is an open investigation, so if I do find out there is a connection, I won't be able to say anything until it's over."

Nick set his load of dishes on the kitchen counter and faced me. "That's like letting me read the first nine chapters of a book, and right when it gets to the best part, you make me wait weeks to read chapter ten."

I shrugged. "Pretty much—sorry."

Nick put his arm around my waist. "You can make it up to me. Let's sit on the couch and cuddle for a while."

I pointed to the other room. "Nick, there are three eight-year-olds in the house."

"You're right, and they laughed at me the last time I kissed you. Doesn't do much for a guy's ego."

I poked his chest. "You do seem pretty fragile." I laughed.

He captured my hand and flattened it over his heart.

"Forget my ego. Feel what being near you does to my heart?"

It thumped hard and fast against my hand. I rested my ear where my hand had been and listened to his heart tap its rhythm, contentedly lost in his embrace until waves of youthful cackling from another room broke the moment.

"It's your kitchen. Want me to wash or dry?" I asked.

"How about I load the dishwasher, and you find the most comfortable spot on the couch."

"I do need to go."

I stopped at my mother's house to drop off her bowl so it wouldn't get broken riding around for days as the unprotected passenger on my front seat. Smoke's vehicle was in her driveway. A good sign—he hadn't left the minute they finished dinner. It wasn't quite dark, but the light was on in the kitchen, and I glanced in the window on my way to the back door. My mother and Smoke were in the throes of passionate kissing. And their hands were very busy. My brain didn't immediately register what I was seeing, and when it did, I nearly dropped the ceramic dish.

Oh my gosh. *Oh my gosh!* The words kept repeating over and over in my brain as I climbed in my car and drove home. Sparks were flying in that kitchen, and I wasn't sure how I felt about it. I thought of Smoke as more of a companion for Mother, someone to go places with, eat dinner with, watch television with.

"**H**ello, Corky." My brother was home and answered on the second ring.

"Hey, John Carl. You busy?"

"Naw, catching up on a little work I couldn't get done at the office. What's up?" John Carl rivaled my mother as a workaholic. I heard his fingers striking keys on his laptop.

"Do you think Mother will ever get married?" I settled on the couch.

"Yeah, the day after they put the Minnesota mosquito on the endangered species list."

"Very funny, but I'm serious," I said.

"Then, no, I don't think it will ever happen."

I told him what I had witnessed.

"Wow, maybe our mother is finally ready to accept that our father will never return from Vietnam."

"You think that's it?"

"When I was going through some rough times a few years ago, I talked to a shrink . . . yeah, yeah, yeah . . . don't give me your usual guff."

"I wasn't going to. What did your shrink say?" I drew my feet under me and waited for his answer.

"Among other things, maybe one reason Mom was so smothering is she believed Dad would come home someday and we would all be the happy family they had always planned to be," John Carl said. "She felt as if she had to keep our family perfect for that day."

I picked some fuzz off the afghan I kept on the couch. "Why would she think that? He died—they sent back his body."

"Gramps said he was unrecognizable. His dog tags were the way they identified him."

I had never considered my mother not accepting Carl's death. "What do you think?"

"About Carl?" he wondered.

"No, Mother," I corrected.

"If Smoke can help her move on, it will be the best thing that can happen."

I had to agree.

"When are you going up north to visit Grandpa and Grandma?" John Carl asked.

My father's parents, Grandpa and Grandma Aleckson, spent the month of July at a resort in Nisswa.

"Wednesday and Thursday. I'm looking forward to seeing them, but almost wish now I hadn't committed. There's been a lot going on here."

John Carl and I e-mailed regularly, but I hadn't had a chance to tell him about the two attorney suicides. I gave him the lowdown on the tragic events.

"So, if they set Marshall Kelton's funeral for Thursday, I may just be there Wednesday," I explained.

"The grandparents would be disappointed, but I'm sure they'd understand. Tell them I think about them all the time, and I'll see them next month," John Carl said.

"That's a big ten-four, good buddy."

And goodnight, I said to myself as I climbed the stairs to my bedroom.

Chapter 25

I heard the phone ringing and saw it was light outside. "Hello?"

"Is that all you ever do is sleep?" Smoke.

"What day is it, and what time is it?"

"Tuesday, eight-twenty. I got permission to search both the county attorney's and public defender's offices, and I thought you should be in on it. Sheriff says he'll get your evening shift covered. Meet me here as soon a-sap. We'll start at the county attorney's office. There are reporters camped outside both the courthouse and the public defender's office."

"Great."

"You could say the powers-that-be are none too thrilled."

Ray Collinwood led the way into what had been Arthur Franz's private office. Ray was the senior assistant county attorney and had the only other private office. The remaining six assistants, including Julie Grimes, had cubicles divided by rows of file cabinets.

"Here's the password for Arthur's computer. I've had it on file in case of emergency, but never had to use it." He frowned and handed the yellow memo paper to Smoke. "I'll get out of your way, but give us a holler if you need anything."

Collinwood closed the door behind him. Smoke scanned the room, then turned the computer around and moved the chair to the opposite side of the desk.

"You can start with his desk, and I'll see what I can pull up on the computer." Smoke pulled on his reading glasses and signed on.

"What exactly am I looking for?" I asked, peering into a neatly arranged shallow drawer.

"See if there is a calendar, names in a notebook or on a scrap of paper—anything that seems suspicious. We'll compare what we find here to what we find at Kelton's office, see if we can make any kind of connection."

We worked in silence for over an hour. Smoke was intent on his work, and I didn't want to break his concentration. I read through each page on Arthur's daily planner, but it was mostly notes to himself about court cases. If he kept a personal calendar, it wasn't in, or on, his desk. Since there wasn't one with his personal effects in evidence, I made a note to ask Marion about it.

I pulled the plastic divider trays out of the drawers to see if there was anything hiding beneath them. Nothing. Arthur Franz had had a reputation for being a stickler on the job, and I noticed that also applied to the way he'd kept his supplies and papers.

After taking his desk apart, I moved to the file drawers. *This could take a while.*

"Shit," Smoke said in an exhale.

"What?"

"Well, we can't say he didn't have his affairs in order. At work, at least. Everything seems very organized—I'm almost jealous. I've looked through letters he's written, all work related. E-mails he's sent, e-mails he's received. Aside from the usual junk we all get, the only personal ones I've found are from Marion, his brother, and two friends who seem to be lawyers."

Smoke sucked in a cleansing breath. "Nothing that would indicate any kind of trouble, personal or professional, for Franz. The last fifteen websites he's visited are newspapers—apparently read them online. No mental health sites. And Marshall Kelton isn't in his mailbox or address book, but I haven't looked at his deleted files yet." He tapped his pen on the desktop a few times. "You've been quiet over there."

"Not a thing to report. So his suicide note isn't in his computer?" I asked.

Smoke shook his head. "No reason to save it, I guess."

"What could have happened to make him snap? It wasn't a spur of the moment thing. I mean, he had to buy the dryer hose and the pillow—it was a new pillow."

"Got me. So you haven't got any of your weird feelings going, touching his stuff?"

"Not a one."

"Good." Smoke continued to hit buttons on the keyboard. "It won't take me much longer—not much in the recycle bin."

I pulled a file out of the drawer and paged through it. "You want me to read through each file?" I asked.

Smoke broke his concentration to consider my question. "Naw, take a look at them, see if they're what they say they are. If not, or if they aren't county attorney related, pull them."

After nearly three hours, the only positive conclusion we had was that Arthur Franz was the organized professional everyone had thought he was. If he was hiding something that led to his death, he hadn't left the evidence of it lying around the office.

Smoke clapped his hands together, then stretched. "We need a break before we head over to the public defender's office. Wanna grab lunch at The Sandwich Shoppe? Let's see: Tuesday it's clam chowder or chili."

News vans from four Minneapolis stations, WCCO, KARE-11, News 9, and KSTP, were parked near the courthouse and public defender's office. The reporters jumped to attention as Smoke and I crossed the street after leaving The Sandwich Shoppe and headed toward the office of the public defender.

"Detective Dawes, any idea what led to the suicide of two Winnebago attorneys within days of one another?" asked a young WCCO woman, one who knew Smoke.

Smoke turned his head, so the camera caught his profile. "No, no idea."

"Can you tell us why you were in the Winnebago County Attorney's office all morning, and why you're going into the Tenth

District Public Defender's office now?" a sandy-haired man from News 9 asked.

"No."

I broke into a jog to keep pace with Smoke's long legged strides. A KARE-11 reporter caught up with us and extended his microphone. "What did you find in County Attorney Arthur Franz's office?" he asked.

Smoke looked into the camera and said, "No comment."

He pushed me in the door ahead of himself when a reporter stuck a microphone near my face.

Marshall Kelton's desk was piled high with files. Glancing around the room, I spotted more piles on the chairs and floor. Going through his office would be like looking for needles in haystacks. "Now this is a guy I can relate to," Smoke said.

"Yeah, I hate to admit the same thing. I think Marshall is a more creative organizer than Arthur is, or was, I should say." I looked around, wondering how to start. "I can't believe they're both dead."

Smoke pinched the top of his nose between his eyes, making them water. "It's best to just concentrate on the job at hand. If we can find out why they died, everyone can move on in the grieving process."

I moved several stacks of papers on Kelton's desk to uncover his large desk calendar that also served as a placemat, given the coffee stains on it. "Nolan Eisner."

"What?"

"Nolan Eisner," I repeated. "Marshall wrote his name on July fifteenth."

Smoke walked over, stopped beside me and bent over the calendar. "That was the day of Judge Fenneman's funeral. Funny he didn't write that in—he was at the funeral."

I nodded. "It doesn't look like Marshall uses the calendar for appointments. He mostly has little notes scribbled here and there. You know, I just met Nolan's daughter and mother in the hospital the day after Judge Fenneman died. Rebecca was a patient on the same wing, and when I was talking to her, her grandma came. And now Marshall has Nolan's name on his calendar on the day of the judge's funeral. Isn't that strange, kind of a weird coincidence, like when you hear a word you've never heard before and then you hear it all the time after that?"

Smoke was so close I could smell chocolate brownie on his breath. "Yeah, more of your doo, doo, doo stuff."

I gave Smoke a little nudge with my elbow. "There must have been a reason why Marshall wrote Nolan's name down. I mean, he's been dead for eleven years."

"Something could have triggered a memory of that kid and he jotted it down, more as a doodle than anything else." Smoke lifted the calendar sheet to look at the month of August. "Nothing written there."

"Probably right. I did see Nolan's mother at the service. Maybe Marshall talked to her that day."

Smoke nodded. "Marshall couldn't help but feel bad when the kid hanged himself. We all did. Marshall was a good attorney, did his best to represent his clients, whether he knew they had done the crime or not. He did the job he was hired to do."

I sat down on Marshall's brown desk chair, and the wheels clicked against the front of the desk. "What happened at Nolan's trial?"

"To tell you the truth, from what I remember, it was pretty routine. The other kid, what was his name . . ." Smoke closed his eyes to think.

"Jason Browne."

"Oh, sure, that's right. They were both in your class?"

I nodded.

"Anyway, remember, Browne confessed and named Eisner as his partner in crime. When they were found guilty, Eisner got the worse end of the deal. Browne went to jail, but Eisner got years in prison. Kelton didn't have a chance of getting him acquitted," Smoke said.

Smoke stepped out of the room and returned with Barbara Jacobs, secretary and receptionist for the attorneys. Barbara was somewhere over sixty, and she was the pulse of the office. For at least four years in a row, she had said she would be retiring, but hadn't. Her co-workers were her adopted family, and I suspected leaving them would make her too lonesome. Barbara's normally flawless makeup of powder, blush, mascara, and lipstick was smudged and tear-streaked. Her eyes were puffy and bloodshot.

Smoke wandered over to Kelton's desk, and Barbara followed. "Barb, any idea why Marshall would write 'Nolan Eisner' on his calendar?"

"No. I saw that there and thought it was more than a little curious. Marshall also had the Eisner file pulled, but it's been such a zoo around here lately, I never got the chance to ask him why. Heavens, the Eisner case was years ago." Her spitfire business front was back in place.

"Was he working on a similar case and wanted to review his notes?" Smoke asked.

"None that I can think of. You know, Marshall Kelton was a unique man. His office was always a mess, yet he kept few notes. He was brilliant and remembered the minutest details." Barbara studied the desk calendar for a few seconds. "I can't imagine why he was looking at the Eisner case."

Smoke glanced around the room. "Where is the file now?"

"Put back in the drawer in the file room. Do you want to see it?"

"Yeah, thanks."

Barbara returned with the file, then went back to her own office. Smoke scanned the pages and handed them to me. The criminal complaint was three pages long and contained the details of the armed robbery as reported by Terry Holmers, night clerk at the store, to Deputy Vince Weber, who had taken the call and written the initial armed robbery complaint.

Detective Elton Dawes had arrested Nolan following Jason Browne's confession and filed the report. The case sheet, containing Nolan Eisner's personal information, had been completed by Marshall Kelton. Arthur Franz had signed the Winnebago County versus Nolan Eisner criminal complaint, and Judge Nels Fenneman's signature was on the sentencing decree.

I wondered how many criminal cases Marshall Kelton and Arthur Franz had tried on opposite sides of the aisle before Nels Fenneman, and all the other district judges, over the years. And Smoke and I had the unpleasant job of scouring their offices and personal effects to find out why they had killed themselves in the same week.

I read through Nolan's case sheet. "Smoke, under 'Father's Name,' it says, 'Unknown.' What do you think that means?"

Smoke raised his eyebrows. "That his mother slept around?" He shrugged. "I have no idea. See anything that reminds you of any case pending in Winnebago right now?" I couldn't think of one and shook my head. "Not to me, either," he said. "So, let's finish up here and you can have a talk with Nolan Eisner's mother, see if she knows anything."

"Like what?" I asked.

"Like why Nolan's name is written on Marshall Kelton's calendar eleven years after the fact."

"Maybe she asked Marshall something about the case at Judge Fenneman's funeral, since Nolan's name is written on that date."

Smoke let out an audible burst of air. "There you go—a speculation that needs to be settled."

"Ms. Eisner is just so strange," I said.

Smoke flinched slightly. "She is that. When I went to their house to arrest Nolan, I can tell you I have never gotten a colder stare from anyone in my life. And that's saying a lot, considering all the characters I've dealt with over the years."

That was easy to believe. "Where does she live?"

"If she's still there, south on County Twelve, then west on Barton about a mile. Check the number on the file. Old farmhouse."

I looked at the address listed for Nolan. "Is that the place on the right, long driveway, remote?"

"Yup."

"I get all the fun."

Arthur Franz had kept copious notes and Marshall Kelton very few. If there was any kind of personal or suspicious connection between them, we couldn't find one in our sweep through their offices.

On the way out we stopped at Barbara's desk. "Have the funeral arrangements been made for Marshall yet?" Smoke asked.

"Yes, Stefany Kelton phoned earlier. It's set for eleven a.m. Saturday at St. Mark's Catholic Church. His folks live in California, so they need to make travel arrangements." Barbara's voice cracked. "Stefany says they are just devastated."

My heart went out to the Kelton family: Stefany, Brock, the children, parents. My mother had told me many times that children should never die before their parents.

I drove to the Eisners' convincing myself it would at least be nice to see Rebecca again. The driveway ran about a quarter of a mile and was lined with twenty-foot-tall Norway pines, the house barely visible from the road. I don't know what I expected, but what I found was a small, white two-story home with a detached garage, a small red barn, and two modest outbuildings. Everything was orderly and neat. There was a tire swing hanging from a mammoth oak tree on the side of the house, swaying slightly in the breeze, the only movement I detected on the farmstead.

I walked to the front door and knocked loudly. No answer, so I knocked again, harder and louder. Still no answer. I wandered to the side of the house and admired the old twisted oak for a minute. At least Rebecca had a decent place to live and the simple pleasure of swinging on her tire from this sturdy tree.

Chills prickled up my arms and spine. On that hot, humid July evening. "Someone walked over my grave" popped into my mind. It was an old expression my Grandma Brandt said from time to time when she had one of her "intuitions." I wasn't sure what it meant. Finally, when I asked her, the only explanation she could give was, "I got a chill for no good reason." And now I had a chill for no good reason.

I moved away from the oak tree when a little creature creeping close to the barn caught my eye: a tiny tabby kitten. I wasn't soul-alone at the isolated farmstead.

I reached Smoke on his cell. "Eisner's not home," I said.

"I suppose she could be at work. It's not quite three."

I glanced at my watch. "Any idea where she works?"

"Seems to me she is a janitor at one of the nursing homes. Call Barbara, I think it's listed in Nolan's file," Smoke suggested.

"No, when I read the file I noticed it gave her occupation, but not employer. Thanks, I'll call Sara. She was Nolan's P.O."

"Corky, it's probably not a good idea to show up at Eisner's place of employment. She seems like the kind of person who would be especially put off by that."

"Okay, then how about a phone call?" I strolled around the oak tree, appreciating how old it was, a survivor of countless years of climate extremes in Minnesota.

"That'd work." Smoke talked through a yawn. "You're off for the next three days?"

"Yes."

"If you don't find Eisner today, this can keep until your next evening on. Marshall isn't going anywhere fast." Smoke sounded a bit defeated.

"True." I walked back to my squad car, ready to change the subject. "Smoke, I didn't get a chance to ask you, how did dinner go last night?"

There was an extended moment of silence on the other end. "Ah, your mother is a wonderful cook—dinner was wonderful."

Two "wonderfuls" from a man of few words. "What did you have for dessert?"

"Ah, I guess we didn't have any."

Right.

Pushing the image of Smoke kissing my mother to the back of my mind, I dialed Sara's number. "Hey, you with anyone?"

"No, just keeping company with my usual stack of paperwork. What's up?" Sara asked.

"I'm trying to locate Nolan Eisner's mother. Do you know where she works? I'm just leaving her place."

"Does it look like the movie set for Frankenstein or Dracula?" she asked in a low voice, trying to sound scary.

I laughed. "Actually, it's pretty pleasant, an old farmstead. Of course, having grown up in the country, I love old farmhouses. I felt a little creeped out walking around the place, but I think I'm just tired."

I heard a file drawer open. "I got his file here. Well, eleven years ago, Alvie Eisner worked in the housekeeping department of Parkside Nursing Home."

"Got a phone number?" I jotted the number in my memo pad. "Thanks. I'll check with them."

"Still working on Judge Fenneman's case? I thought that was closed," Sara said.

"As much as it can be. His death was ruled accidental drowning. It's true, we never did get an answer to why the emergency alarm didn't go off. And I got a strange note, but that's another story."

"What?" Her voice took on an edge of worry.

"I'll tell you about it sometime. It's more of a curiosity at this point. Actually, I need to talk to Ms. Eisner about something else, not about the night the judge died. Marshall Kelton had Nolan's name scribbled on his desk calendar on July fifteenth, and we're wondering why."

"Of this year? Yeah, that is odd."

"You don't have any idea why?"

"Not at all." Sara was silent for a second. "You think there's a connection between Nolan's case and Marshall's suicide?"

"There's no reason to, but that's why I have to talk to Ms. Eisner."

Sara let out a little "ooh" then said, "Better you than me."

"I think that's why Smoke sent me to talk to her. He didn't say it, but I think she creeps him out at least as much as she does the rest of us. Change of subject—I'm heading to Nisswa tomorrow. You still going back home Friday after work?"

"Yeah, my monthly journey. Too bad we'll just miss each other, since Nisswa is only about ten miles from Brainerd. We could have gotten together for a meal or some shopping. My folks keep asking when you'll visit again," Sara said.

"One of these months my weekend off will coincide with your Brainerd trek again. Tell your family 'hi' from me. I miss them, too."

I phoned the nursing home, but Alvie Eisner wasn't working. I spoke with the scheduler, who was happy to cooperate with the sheriff's department and gave me Eisner's work schedule. She was working the next day and Thursday from eleven a.m. to seven p.m., then off Friday and Saturday. I would try to catch her at home one more time instead of trying to talk to her on the phone.

I preferred talking to people in person, even when that person was Alvie Eisner.

Chapter 26

Alvie

When Alvie saw the Winnebago County squad car coming down her driveway, her mouth went dry. Rebecca was napping, and her car was safely hidden in the garage. Alvie slipped upstairs and closed Rebecca's door, then went to her own room to watch. The squad car parked, and who but that little sergeant got out and walked right up to the door?

What on earth would she want? To ask Rebecca more questions about that fateful night in the hospital? The sergeant knocked and Alvie held her breath, but there was no sound from Rebecca's room. The sergeant knocked again, but soon gave up that anyone was home.

Instead of leaving, she hung around in the yard, awfully close to where Uncle was, next to the oak tree and under the tire swing where Rebecca could stomp on his grave without even knowing it. He wasn't fit to be her grandfather, or Nolan's father, or Alvie's uncle. It gave Alvie real satisfaction watching Rebecca have fun on his final spot, knowing he could never hurt her, or anyone else, again.

To top things off, the little sergeant pulled out her portable phone and talked for a while. The window was open, but she was far enough away so Alvie only made out a few words: "works, Sara, dinner." Probably was setting up something with that probation officer. She finally got in her squad car, still yakking on her phone, and drove away. Couldn't have been too important.

Alvie wracked her brain, wondering if there was any way they could trace anything to her, but she knew there wasn't. She was too smart and had planned too well. But what could the little sergeant want that would bring her to Alvie's house? Maybe it had nothing to do with her. Maybe it was about the neighbors. Alvie suspected they grew marijuana, but that was their business. The more she thought about it, the more it made sense the visit probably was about the neighbors.

Chapter 27

"**C**orky!" Both Grandma and Grandpa Aleckson came out of their cabin to greet me, their white hair bright in the sunshine. Grandpa's face was deeply creased, weathered from years of crop farming during the long days of summer. Grandma had spent most of her time indoors doing the many household tasks and keeping the farm's business records. She had a faint frown crease and some laugh lines that deepened when she smiled. They had both gotten a little too heavy in their retirement and moved more slowly. But they stayed current and vital and counted each healthy day as a blessing.

Grandma and Grandpa gave surprisingly strong hugs, and I rested in their warmth for a long moment. My grandparents' excitement over my arrival made me feel a little guilty for waiting until the end of their resort month to visit. I knew they missed me when they were away.

"We didn't expect you until later in the day," Grandma said.

"I got an early start," I said as I pulled my overnight bag from the back seat. Grandpa immediately snatched it out of my hand. Each of them put an arm around me as we headed inside.

"So, we'll catch up first then you can tell us what you want to do." Between the two of them, my grandmother did most of the talking. "Have you had breakfast?"

"Yes, thanks, but the coffee smells good."

We talked for over an hour. They didn't know Judge Fenneman well enough to return home for his funeral, but wanted to hear all about it and how his family was doing.

"Oak Lea has been on the statewide news with those lawyer suicides," Grandma said. "We saw Elton Dawes on both WCCO and KARE-11. He sure wasn't saying much."

That was an understatement.

"Yeah, I just missed my fifteen minutes of fame. I was standing next to him when the reporters were questioning him." I paused. "The two suicides were awful, and we hate to have them plastered all over the news."

"Why did Arthur Franz and Marshall Kelton kill themselves?" Grandma wondered.

"We have no idea, but we're working on it."

"Oak Lea has always been such a quiet little town," Grandpa added.

Grandma changed the subject. "How is Arnold doing?" My Grandpa Brandt. "I wish you could have talked him into coming up here for a few days," she said.

"No such luck. He has become even more of a hermit, but I did get him out fishing last week. You know, Mom dotes on him, does his laundry, brings him meals." *Speaking of Mom.* "Which reminds me, guess who had dinner at Mother's the other night?" They both shook their heads. "Elton Dawes."

My grandma inhaled an audible "ah" and smiled broadly. My grandpa nodded and said, "Could do worse."

Nisswa was one hundred miles northwest of Oak Lea and about ten degrees cooler, a welcome break from the past weeks of temperatures in the eighties and nineties with high humidity. Rainfall had been above average for two weeks, then there wasn't a drop for almost a week. I was content to soak up the northern sun, do a little swimming and fishing, and tag along with my grandparents through the crafty shops of Nisswa. I even bought a few things.

Thursday morning, my grandfather joined his Nisswa cronies in their usual game of golf. My grandmother enjoyed the sport on occasion, but she didn't want to leave me for those few hours. Grandma and I took our coffee to lounge chairs by Woman Lake, about twenty feet from the back door of their cabin. There were several resorts and over fifty private cabins on the lake: a quiet place to escape from the corporate world, carpools, and stresses. Parents and young children played on the shore, some teenagers battled over water tennis, and still others sat in boats hoping to catch a meal of walleyes.

On another day I could have completely relaxed, but the deaths of Arthur Franz and Marshall Kelton—and even Judge Fenneman—weighed heavily, an anchor pulling on my mind and heart.

"My Heart," Grandma started.

I thought for a second she was reading my mind, but "My Heart" was her pet name for me when we were alone.

Grandma picked up my hand and searched my face. "You've been a little distracted ever since you got here. You look just like your father did when he had something on his mind. Do you want to talk about it?" Grandma implored, as only she could.

Of everyone in my family, my grandma understood me best. Had she been born fifty years later, I had no doubt she would have been a top cop somewhere.

"Grandma, I know we're missing something in the Franz and Kelton suicides, but can't imagine what it would be. I feel, deep in my gut, their deaths are related, but the reason must be very well hidden, since no one in either of their offices has a clue. We still need to talk to their families some more, see if they come up with anything."

"You think they were involved in something illegal together?" Grandma asked.

I shrugged. "As troubling as it is for the families personally, the county's main concern is making sure there was no criminal activity that would jeopardize court cases, or initiate an investigation by the BCA or FBI."

"What do you think?"

"I'm at the same loss as everyone else seems to be. Why would two successful, respected attorneys kill themselves in the same week?" I swirled the coffee around in my cup, then took a sip.

"And you ruled out foul play?" Grandma asked.

"What do you mean?"

Grandma folded her hands and leaned forward, speaking in a conspiratorial tone. "You know, someone else did it and made it look like suicides."

Sometimes Grandma had a pretty vivid imagination.

I drove back to Oak Lea obsessing about the suicide cases and my grandma's words. Okay, what were the facts? Arthur Franz: a perfectionist, professional. On a Thursday in July, he left for lunch and didn't return. No one knew where he ate lunch, but on that day his body was found by a fisherman, asphyxiated in his car. His uneaten bag lunch was on the passenger seat next to his suicide note. His wallet, containing his identification, was in the glove compartment. Arthur's cell phone, the one he used to call Marion every day at noon—except on that day—was in one cup holder between the seats. A soda can with a small amount of white residue around the rim was in the other.

The questions: Had Arthur been thinking about suicide for a long time and finally got enough nerve that day? Is that why he had his lunch with him? *"If I don't kill myself today, I'll eat my lunch."* Had he been carrying the hose and the pillow and the note in the trunk of his car for a while, or had he purchased them that day? What was the white residue on the can? Did he not call Marion because hearing her voice would make it harder to do what he was determined to do? Was his relationship with Marion a contributing factor? Why didn't anyone in his life recognize some symptom of depression?

And what about Marshall? I had read that if someone was thinking about suicide and knew someone who had killed himself, the chances were greater he would too. I didn't know if that was true, but it sounded logical in an illogical way. Marshall had sown some wild seeds and hurt his family, but he was apparently repentant and working toward being a better person. That should make him happy, not despondent.

On the day of Arthur Franz's memorial service, Marshall went home, turned on the sports channel, drank a beer. Then in the middle of drinking a second one, he stopped, went to the computer, wrote a suicide note, sat back down in front of the television, cut his wrist, and watched the blood drip from his body until he passed out and died? And again, wouldn't there be at least one person who would have seen some sign of depression?

Nothing made sense.

I remembered from my training that no one could positively predict a suicide. Of the many suicide scenes I had processed in my career, there were only four where the victim's family or friends had had no idea they were depressed. Three of those people were professionals—a business owner, a doctor and an accountant. It turned out the doctor had a secret drug problem, the accountant had been pilfering money from a client's account, and the business owner's reason was still a mystery, as far as I knew.

The precipitating factors in suicides were usually an accumulation of stressors, one of them being legal problems. If Arthur's and Marshall's deaths shared a commonality, the reason was buried as deep as Arthur's body. And Marshall couldn't tell us, either.

I got to Oak Lea in under two hours. As I drove by the public defender's office and courthouse, I had an ominous feeling Arthur and Marshall were connected in a way we hadn't yet imagined. I pulled in the sheriff's parking lot but stayed in my car. It was after business hours, so I could go in and do some work without having to explain myself, but I thought better of it. I glanced at my watch and figured Alvie Eisner should be home from work.

The sun was low in the western sky, poking holes of bright lights through the rows of pines. My eyes closed involuntarily against the visual assault as I drove down the gravel driveway. Rebecca was sitting on the grass next to the small barn, petting a kitten she held on her lap. She was a cover picture for *Farmer Magazine* with her blonde braids and denim coveralls, framed by the red barn behind her. Rebecca looked at my GTO with a frown, but her little face broke into a broad grin when she saw it was me.

"Sergeant Corky! You have a really different car." She jumped up and ran to me, wheezing a little.

I touched her shoulder, then petted the cat. "Hello, Rebecca. The car was my dad's, so it's pretty old. What a cute kitty."

"We have barn cats that are mostly wild, but this is the runt of the last litter and likes me more than the other cats." She moved the kitty to her shoulder. "Why are you here?"

"I just need to ask your grandmother a question. Is she home?"

Rebecca nodded. "I'll get her, she's in the house. Will you hold Kitty? I can't bring her in."

She handed the little tabby over before I could answer and disappeared inside. A moment later she returned with her solemn grandmother, who was dressed in black slacks and a black tee shirt. Was the woman in perpetual mourning, or what?

"Sergeant Aleckson." Her frigid stare was enough to cool anybody, anytime, even in the heat of summer.

I counted to three to compose myself. "Good evening, Ms. Eisner. I have a quick question to ask you. Rebecca, will you take the kitty? I need to talk to your grandma alone for a minute."

Rebecca looked from me to her grandmother. Ms. Eisner nodded.

"Okay," Rebecca said, not hiding her disappointment.

"What is this about?" Eisner asked.

"You heard about Winnebago County's public defender, Marshall Kelton?" I started.

"Yes."

"Well, going through his things, we discovered he had written your son's—Nolan's—name on his desk calendar and wondered if you knew why?"

Eisner's eyes blinked, the first hint of expression I had seen on her face to date. "No."

"Did Marshall Kelton contact you, or did you talk to him recently about Nolan or his legal case? I understand he was Nolan's attorney," I said.

Eisner's unblinking icy stare returned. "He was my son's attorney, but he has not contacted me since the trial."

I pulled a small memo pad from my jeans pocket so I could break our staring session. "And you have no idea why he would have written Nolan's name now, after all these years?"

"No."

"Nolan's name was written on the date of Judge Fenneman's funeral. You didn't talk to Mr. Kelton there?" I continued.

"No." If looks could kill.

"Okay, well, thank you for your time, and if you think of anything, please call me. Do you still have my card?"

"Yes."

"Good. Thanks again." I waved at Rebecca, who was still patiently petting the kitty. "Bye, Rebecca, enjoy the rest of the summer," I called out.

Rebecca waved back.

"Goodbye, Ms. Eisner."

She gave me a slight, terse nod in return.

I drove away wondering how that statue of a woman could hold a job and raise a little girl. Maybe it was me that brought out the worst in her. I was her son's classmate, so maybe I triggered a sadness somehow. Or it could be with all the legal trouble Nolan had had, she had a thing against cops. A lot of people do.

I dialed Smoke's cell number. "Detective Dawes."

"Smoke, you owe me."

"Ah, my favorite sergeant. I didn't look at Caller ID. Where are you?" he asked, the soothing, melodious quality back in his voice.

"Leaving Alvie Eisner's driveway."

"You're working? I thought you were at your grandparents' cabin." I heard Smoke's dog, Rex, panting nearby, and the whirr of a fishing rod and reel. I pictured Smoke sitting on his dock casting for walleyes in his small lake.

"I got back a while ago and decided to see if Eisner was home. The good and bad news is, she was home and I actually had to talk to her. Man, that woman is like a stone."

"And?"

Plunk! The jig and bait hit the water.

"She says she doesn't know anything."

"So she didn't contact Marshall, and Marshall didn't contact her?" he asked.

"Guess not."

"Then it was most likely Marshall was thinking about the case, maybe about the suicide. If Barbara or his other co-workers don't know, and Alvie Eisner doesn't know, we probably never will, either."

"Fish biting?" I asked.

"Nah, but it's too nice out to sit indoors."

Gramps would love to fish from Smoke's dock.

When I got home, I retrieved my sheriff's memo book from my bed stand to look up Marion McIllvery's phone number.

"Hello . . ." Arthur Franz's voice spoke to me after the first ring, and I nearly dropped the phone. ". . . We can't take your call right now, but please leave a message and we'll get back to you at our earliest convenience." I didn't leave a message. Marion might not have returned from Duluth, so I planned to try later.

My cell phone rang, and I smiled at the name on display. "Hello, Nick."

"Are you on the road?" His voice sent waves of joy through me, helping to dispel the distress I felt.

I lay down on my back on top of my bed quilt and watched the ceiling fan circulate round and round. "Just got home a few minutes ago."

"How are your grandparents?" he asked.

"They are great. How's Faith?"

"Doing well. Why don't you stop over and see for yourself?"

"I have an errand to run, but we're on for tomorrow night? Movie and a pizza?"

"We are." Nick's voice was playful. "You're going to make me wait until then to see you?"

"Not that I want to, but, yes I am. See you tomorrow."

After hearing Arthur's voice on his recorder, I felt a strong need, a compulsion, to go to the lake, the site of his death. I parked next to where his vehicle had sat. Arthur's embedded tires tracks were broken down, driven over by other vehicles since then.

I turned off the ignition and rolled my window down to listen to the sounds of the evening. The crickets were out in force, their clicking noises amplified by the general quiet of the country. Plop. A keeper-sized northern rose from the water, then quickly disappeared. I wanted to take Gramps fishing there some evening, but he preferred the smaller pan fish, sunnies and crappies, prevalent in other area lakes.

For many years I believed people went to Bebee Lake not only to fish, but also to be wrapped in its small cocoon of serenity. Somewhere overhead a mourning dove sat in a tree, delivering his lonesome call, "Coo, coo, coo, coo." Apt. I listened to the dove repeat his melancholy lament, over and over.

"Who are you sorrowing for?" I called in the direction of the dove.

Every death had a story. There had to be a very good reason for yours, Arthur, but what was it?

I wish you could speak to me.

Chapter 28

Alvie

Alvie was throwing her uniform into the washer in the basement. She didn't know the little sergeant was there until Rebecca called down for her. There was no way she could have pretended not to be home at that point, so she went outside. That old GTO the little sergeant drove was older than Aleckson was. Alvie thought they were popular about the time Nolan was born, maybe a year or two before.

The last thing she expected to come out of the little sergeant's mouth was a question about that useless public defender. Ha, he was even more useless now! Why had Kelton written Nolan's name on his desk calendar? She had seen him at Judge Fenneman's funeral, but she didn't know if Kelton had even seen her. What if he had? Would that be enough to make him write Nolan's name? It didn't make sense, and it was giving her a headache. A bad one.

And the little sergeant showing up at every turn, but not smart enough to figure anything out. Lucky for both of them. Maybe she'd head into town after Rebecca fell asleep and drive by the Speiss house. If the little sergeant was there, Alvie could make it look like a murder-suicide. She had a special note in her trunk for that one, just in case. One of those nights, that Speiss woman would be home.

Or maybe it would be better to wait until Speiss went to the little sergeant's house for a visit. Fewer people around at Aleckson's home in the country. It was kind of hard to figure out what the little sergeant's work schedule was. Like that night, she came in regular clothes and her own car. Most of the time, she was in her fancy uniform—except the first time Alvie had met her, in the hospital. She was in regular clothes then, too. So was she

185

really working, on duty, that night or not? Alvie had followed her once. She could follow her again if she had to.

But the most important business at hand was handling the "suicides" of Sara Speiss, Elton Dawes, and Jason Browne. Alvie didn't know where Dawes lived yet, but she had located Jason Browne. Jason and Ann Browne lived at 1402 Second Street Northwest, Rockwell. It was great satisfaction knowing he was married. She hoped he had kids, too.

Chapter 29

After lazing around up north for a couple of days, I woke up early Friday morning full of energy. I changed into shorts and a tank top and fought heat and humidity on a run down my road. About a mile from my house, I was going past the rows of corn when I noticed some damage to them. Maybe some deer had found a place to make a home, surrounded by plenty of feed.

I jumped across the narrow ditch and walked to the edge of the field to have a look. Up close, it was evident a vehicle had left the roadway and driven into the corn. It appeared an attempt had been made to resurrect the downed rows nearest the road, but inside stalks were broken, some half-standing, others lying on the ground. With all the places teenagers could park to make out, it seemed an unlikely spot for that.

Tire tracks from a vehicle were captured in the dried mud, evidently made shortly after the last rainfall. That was about a week before. Near the tire tracks, I noticed a footprint, then another, and another, in between two rows of corn, leading in the direction of the lake. Curiosity got the best of me, and I decided to follow them. There was a public access on the other side of the lake, so why would someone park in that spot, damaging a farmer's corn crop?

The footprints, long and narrow, had been made by one person. I read *Propet,* a fairly common brand, left by the impressions of the shoe soles. I continued to the edge of the field, which ended about fifty feet from the lake. It was more challenging to pick out the footprints in the weedy area between the field and the lake, so I broke off a stick from a fallen branch and parted the weeds until I found one, then another, compelled beyond reason to see where they led.

A few feet into the weeds, I discovered a little clearing made by someone. The brush had been pulled from the soil in an area of around three feet by four feet. There were two soda cans and a pile of cigarette butts stuck in the ground. I took a closer look: Camels. It was much too far from the lake to do casting for fish. Why would anyone sit there right after it had rained, when the ground was soft and muddy-wet?

I noticed a pathway where the weeds had been stamped down leading toward the water, then veering to the left about six feet from the shore. I continued my expedition on the north side of the lake, around bushes and through the undergrowth, with a growing sense of dread. The last print, and the first one easily visible on the path, was the one Smoke and I had found next to Arthur's car on the day he died.

Dear Lord!

I jogged back to the little clearing, careful not to step on the pathway. I took a quick last look at the cleared area and knew in my heart of hearts someone had been watching us the day we had worked to process Arthur's death scene, and that sick person had killed Arthur.

"You know, someone else did it and made it look like suicides." I spoke my grandmother's words out loud. They had seemed so unlikely the previous day, a fantastic speculation. But there I was standing in the middle of the indication her words could be true.

My heart raced as I sprinted through the cornfield to the road. I sucked hard for air, and the sweat dripping in my eyes was burning and blinding. I couldn't get home fast enough. Why had I left my cell phone there?

I was panting, but there was no time to waste. They were predicting rain that afternoon. "Smoke." Big breath. "Can you come to my house?" Another breath. "Now?"

"What's wrong, Corky? I can hardly understand you. Shit, are you in trouble?" His voice rose and I heard his chair move.

"No, but I found something—evidence—on my run just now, and it's serious."

"What?" he asked. "I have interviews scheduled about the forgery ring I've been trying to crack."

"This is more important. It's about Arthur. I'll tell you when you get here. Hurry."

I had to cool down and get out of my clinging clothes, so I hopped into a tepid shower, soaped and rinsed in about ninety seconds. I pulled on a tee shirt, denim capris, and my running shoes, then brushed my hair into a ponytail. I grabbed two bottles of water and was waiting by my garage when Smoke pulled in a few minutes later. I hopped in the squad car before he could get out.

"What about Arthur?" he asked.

"I'll show you. Head north on Brandt about a mile." We drove to the area in question and piled out of the vehicle. "Follow me." And he did.

Smoke looked at the cornfield, then at me. "What does this have to do with Arthur? It looks like kids parking here to make out, or maybe meeting to pull off a drug deal."

"I wondered about the same thing, but there's more. Don't think I'm nuts, but I think Arthur's killer parked here."

"What?" Smoke was incredulous, his doubt evident in that single word. "You may not be crazy, but you must have heat stroke."

I ignored his comment. "Let's keep going. See the footprints? They aren't very evident once we get out of the corn field, but you can still find them." We trekked to the cleared area. "Stand here and tell me what you see."

Smoke slowly turned a complete circle, his eyes focused. "Among other things, a clear view of the public landing on the other side of the lake." He took a step back and looked down. "And from the number of butts lying there, he must have camped here for quite some time."

"Exactly. Do you know when they must have been made?"

"I'm guessing the day Arthur died." Smoke shrugged.

"It has to be. Remember how it rained so hard the day before, then again the morning of? Well, it hasn't rained since."

Smoke scratched the back of his neck. "You're right. Any prints made the day before would have been washed away that morning."

I pointed to the ground. "See how the footprints are going from, and coming to, this clearing? Come on." I led the way to the bush where the last print had been left in the mud.

"Damn. We talked about this, even photographed it." He stared at the footprint for a long minute.

"I know, so why didn't we see the rest of this before?"

"For one thing, we weren't looking for it. This one print, where there are no weeds, is obvious. The rest of them, until you get to the cleared area, then again in the cornfield, are pretty hidden. There was a signed suicide note, and supposedly no one knew where Arthur had lunch. What was there to think?"

Smoke rattled off reasons, and I didn't have a response.

"This looks pretty suspicious, but there still could be any number of explanations," Smoke said.

"And what does your gut tell you?" I asked, knowing an officer's intuition is often the best tool to start with.

"We should start looking for Arthur's killer."

I agreed. I believed it was not a coincidence I had noticed the damaged cornfield and felt a compulsion to check it out. The night before I had sat by this lake, wishing Arthur could talk to me. It was as if he just had.

"And Marshall's killer?" I asked.

Smoke nodded. "If Arthur was murdered, we probably just found a connection between the two deaths."

"They were killed by the same person who made them look like suicides?" I asked.

"Seems that could be true."

"Exactly what my grandmother said yesterday."

Smoke raised his eyebrows. "No shit? She psychic?"

"Sometimes I think so. But the question is, why would anyone do something like that?"

"To throw us off track so we don't go looking for him. No murder, no need for a suspect," Smoke threw out as an explanation.

We both looked to the western sky when we heard thunder a long way off. "How would he get both Arthur and Marshall to sign the 'suicide' notes?" I asked.

"God only knows—maybe a gun to the head, or another threat of some sort. May not have even known what they were signing." My stomach churned, wondering if that was what had happened. "The sheriff needs to know about this right away." Smoke grabbed his phone and punched in the number with urgency.

Sheriff Twardy told Smoke he would send the mobile crime lab and some deputies to help process the scene. Smoke grabbed a pair of coveralls from his trunk and pulled them over his clothes. We got yellow crime scene tape, stakes, and a hammer from the squad car to enclose the areas in question to help define them in the photographs. The sheriff arrived ahead of the crime lab.

"How on earth did you spot this, Sergeant?" Sheriff Twardy stood with his hands on his hips, scouting the scene.

"I'm not sure, sir. It didn't look right, and I was curious enough to check it out," I told him.

"Thank you for that. Good work."

The Winnebago County Sheriff's Mobile Crime Unit, staffed with two deputies, pulled up just before the still air began to stir. Deputies Vince Weber and Mandy Zubinski got out. Weber was in his mid-thirties, with a square body and no neck. Zubinski was younger than me, with cropped auburn hair and a prominent nose. A Ford Explorer, Todd Mason's personal vehicle, pulled up behind the crime lab. Todd and Brian Carlson jumped out, both wearing street clothes. The sheriff had called them in to help expedite the investigation.

Darkening clouds rolled in, threatening to douse us with rain any minute. The sheriff was the chief law enforcement officer on site, but he turned the scene over to Smoke.

"We have to work fast, ahead of the rain, so let's divide this into three areas," Smoke determined.

The group was gathered on the road. Smoke jogged across the ditch and waved at the area. "Mason and Carlson, you take from the road to, and including, the parking area here."

We all followed Smoke, armed with evidence bags, cameras, measuring tapes, notebooks, and pens. The increasing humidity was stifling. There wasn't a dry forehead or armpit in the group.

"Weber and Zubinski, start here." Smoke pointed to where the prints left the parking area. "And I want a cast taken of that print, unless you can find a better one than that." He indicated the section with the cans and butts. "And you'll process this cleared area."

"It looks like our guy was dumb enough to leave his DNA," Deputy Mandy Zubinski observed, pointing to the cigarette butts and soda cans.

"Unless his DNA's not on file or he's arrogant enough to think we'll never catch him on that," Smoke said. "Okay, Corky, we'll take the last leg. Any purchase receipts, bits of clothing, anything that hasn't blown away by now. By the looks of how soft the soil was on the day of the death, something could easily be stuck in the mud."

We got down on our hands and knees and carefully examined the trail that led from the clearing to the public landing, gently moving the mix of clover, meadow hay, goldenrod, and other wild grasses. Smoke worked one side of the path, I worked the other.

"Anything?" I asked, finding nothing on mine.

"Not that I can see, but with the all the sweat dripping in my eyes, that isn't saying much. I could use one of those headbands you runners wear."

I didn't own one, but after that experience, I thought I might buy one.

"When we get to the end, we'll switch sides to double check each other."

We worked as quickly and carefully as possible, but came up with nothing new.

"I can't believe the rain held out," I said as we walked back to join the other officers. The sheriff was nowhere in sight.

"We can thank the Man Upstairs for that. Are you about wrapping up here?" Smoke asked the four deputies who had gathered by the parking area near the edge of the cornfield. "I think our luck with the storm front is about to run out."

Rain clouds, low in the dark gray sky, were almost overhead. Thunderheads rumbled, warning us to find shelter. A blast of air sent dust, bits of dry hay, and weed seeds swirling around us, first in one direction, then in another a nanosecond later. Carlson's Minnesota Vikings ball cap blew off, and he scampered to retrieve it.

Todd Mason nodded then raised his voice over the sound of the howling wind. "Everything is secure in the mobile unit. We'll send the butts and cans to the BCA for analysis."

"Where'd Twardy go?" Smoke asked.

"Back to the office. He said call, don't radio, if you need anything," Brian Carlson answered, securing his cap back on his head.

Smoke nodded. "I'm going to check to see if one of you can drive the evidence down to St. Paul, save some time. Any takers?"

All four nodded. Carlson said, "Yeah."

"Okay. And I'm sure the sheriff told you to keep this under your hats for a while. It will be up to him to make a statement when we figure out what in the hell we got going on here."

"So, if someone killed Arthur Franz, what about Marshall Kelton?" Zubinski asked.

"We don't know, but we're going to find out right a-sap. That's why I want the results on the residue from the cans found with Franz and Kelton. We can compare them with the autopsy reports to see if the same chemical, or drug, is in both their systems."

Quarter-sized raindrops finally let loose from the clouds, pouring down, immediately drenching our clothes and bouncing off the vehicles. None of us were wearing rain gear, and we were all quickly soaked to the bone.

"Let's all meet in the sheriff's office in thirty minutes for further instructions," Smoke yelled as we ran for shelter.

I hopped in the passenger seat of Smoke's squad car.

"You're a mess," Smoke said looking at me.

Dry soil and brush had clung to my clothes and skin when we crawled around on the ground and the rain turned the dirt to mud. Smoke reached in the backseat and grabbed a towel.

"Here."

I wiped my bare skin, cleaning up somewhat.

"We'll swing by your house so you can change before our meeting."

We made a mad dash for the house. I jumped in the shower for the second time that morning, and Smoke used the half bath off the kitchen to get out of his coveralls and clean up.

I found Smoke leaning against a counter in the kitchen, staring at nothing.

"I talked to the sheriff—he's expecting us. Hope you didn't have any special plans for your day off."

I filled two glasses with water and handed one to Smoke. "No. This discovery pretty much puts everything else on the back burner. All I can think of is Arthur and Marshall. If they were murdered, who did it?"

"And why?" Smoke added. "The only link we've found so far is they were both lawyers." He looked out the window and downed his drink in one long gulp. "Seems like it let up a little, but I should have grabbed my raincoat out of my trunk."

"I have an umbrella my mother gave me. I've never used it," I offered.

"Nah, I'll run." He probably imagined it having a bright floral pattern.

"Meet 'cha there," I said and hopped in my GTO.

Deputies Carlson and Mason were waiting in the corridor outside the sheriff's office, pouring sodas down their throats. The heat and humidity had dehydrated us all. Smoke moved in front of the door to let the sheriff know we were there. Sheriff Twardy was pacing behind his desk and waved us in.

"Where are Zubinski and Weber?" Sheriff Twardy asked.

"Probably securing the crime lab in the garage. Should be here—"

They walked in before Smoke could finish.

"Close the door," Twardy directed at Weber.

The sheriff leaned over his desk and spoke in a hushed voice. "There are seven of us who know why the crime lab was out today. You are all trusted members of this department, and I don't want even a whisper of this in anyone else's ear until we know what in the hell happened. One day we got two suicides, the next day it looks like we got two murders. For godsakes, we don't need a bunch of reporters crawling down our necks, or the public to be in a panic." The sheriff's voice was quiet and forceful.

Twardy's color rose as he spoke. "Dawes, you're the lead on this one. I'll have a meeting with the other detectives and the rest of the brass, get 'em in the loop. Helluva time for Kenner to be on vacation."

Kenner, the chief deputy, was on a fishing trip somewhere in the Canadian wild.

The sheriff looked at me, then at Smoke. "Dawes, we need answers, and we need them yesterday."

Smoke raised his eyebrows. "With your approval, Sheriff, one of the deputies here can drive the evidence down to the BCA for analysis."

The sheriff shook his head. "No, I want you to do it. Call in some favors from your buddy—what's his name—at the bureau. I know DNA takes a while, but find out if there're latent prints on anything taken from either death scene, and who the hell they belong to. Get a handwriting expert to examine the suicide notes, see if they were written by the same person. And that powder residue, depending on what it is, could be a link between the deaths."

"Will do, but it's Friday, almost noon. It may be tough to—"

The sheriff slammed his fist on the desk, and we all startled in reaction. "I don't care if it's Christmas Day! Get somebody down there to put a rush on this! We have to know what we've got here—sooner rather than later." Yelling threw the sheriff into a coughing spasm.

The six of us left the office so the sheriff could recover in peace. Mason and Carlson went home, Weber and Zubinski headed to the mobile crime lab, and Smoke and I went to the evidence room for the dryer hose, razor blade, and suicide notes. The BCA already had the soda cans with the unknown traces of white residue.

Local jurisdictions collected evidence, and the BCA processed what the county and city agencies couldn't. The Winnebago County Crime Lab contained the equipment to collect, but not process, most evidence. Unfortunately, as the primary investigation unit for the state, the BCA's work was backlogged by weeks, sometimes months. We optimistically hoped the autopsy reports on Arthur Franz and Marshall Kelton had been completed and written.

Smoke drove his squad car into the sheriff's garage, and we loaded the evidence. "Wanna ride along?" Smoke asked me.

Both Weber and Zubinski looked disappointed they had not been chosen. Going to the Bureau of Criminal Apprehension was not part of a routine workday. I had only been there twice for training. "Sure," I said.

"Teacher's pet," Mandy Zubinski mouthed at me, her hazel eyes holding mine. She was jealous of the friendship Smoke and I shared and had started a rumor the previous year that we were having an affair. I heard Mandy had a crush on Smoke, but didn't know if that was true or not.

Smoke had told me people believed what they wanted to believe, and if Mandy's story bothered me, I needed thicker skin. He said he considered it a compliment anyone would think I would be interested in an old geezer like him. In any case, I hadn't gone out of my way to befriend Mandy Zubinski since then.

The rain had reduced to a sprinkle, making the fifty-mile drive easier. "So, who owes you a favor at the BCA, Smoke?" I asked.

"Oh, one of my buddies, Darin Henning. I think I've mentioned him." He glanced at me and I nodded. "He's the Forensic Science Supervisor in the Criminalistics Laboratory. But I owe him a lot more favors than he owes me by now. We were deputies together in Cook County. Darin went on for further training and worked his way up at the BCA. Which reminds me, I better call to see if he's even there today."

Smoke got Darin's machine and left a message. His cell phone rang about twenty minutes later.

"Hey, my friend. Busy down there?" Pause. "Figured as much. Say, we got a situation in Winnebago, and I need your help." Another pause. "Well, we sent you some evidence last week, and then some more this week, on a couple of deaths. We're on our way down there with a few more things, and I was wondering if you could meet us. I'll tell you about it when we get there." Pause. "Sergeant Corky Aleckson. . . . Yeah, you'll get to meet her, but she's too young for you. . . . Thanks, see you in about thirty."

Smoke clapped his phone shut. "Good. We don't have to go with a Plan B, whatever that might have been. Darin says he's so far behind another afternoon won't make any difference. Welcome to our world, huh?"

We checked in at the front reception desk at the Minnesota Bureau of Criminal Apprehension, each of us carrying a bag of what we hoped would help provide answers to the mysterious circumstances of Arthur's and Marshall's deaths. The young male attendant was seated in a bulletproof glass cage. Smoke gave him our names and told him Darin Henning was expecting us. The attendant phoned Henning, nodded, and handed us the sign-in sheet. He asked for our identification, looked through our bags then pushed a button to unlock the door, allowing us access into the secure area where Henning was waiting.

Smoke and Darin grasped hands in an enthusiastic shake. Darin slapped Smoke on the back then turned to me. I guessed him to be about forty, just under six feet, more cute than handsome. His light brown hair, thin on top, was trimmed short and neat, but he needed a shave. There was a sparkle in his blue eyes that made me wonder what he was thinking. He gripped my hand with almost as much vigor as he had shown Smoke.

"I am too old for her," Darin told Smoke, eyeing me up and down. "Elton says you're a sergeant. In what, the cookie patrol? You look like a teenager."

For some reason, I liked him immediately.

"Ponytail, no makeup—" I started.

"Good genes," Smoke finished. "And not the kind she's wearing," he added when Darin glanced at my legs.

We followed Darin to his office, and he motioned us to set the bags on a small conference table. "All right, tell me what you got here and what you need."

Smoke stepped forward and emptied the individually packaged items on the table. My bag contained only the dryer hose, which I set on a chair. Smoke gave Darin a rundown of what we needed and why. Darin took notes and attached them to the outside of the evidence bags.

"Okay, shouldn't take too long to take care of this, except for the DNA, of course. When the legislature decided to include all felons in the DNA database, it added to our load exponentially. We processed about fifteen hundred cases last year alone. At least, because of the convicted offender samples, we got a grant to outsource some of the caseload."

Darin held up the evidence bag with the cigarette butts and stared at it for a minute. "Our average turnaround on DNA is two months. Course, it doesn't much matter if a guy's incarcerated and not going anywhere, but for cases like yours, we do our best to be more timely. I'll speed it up as much as possible."

"We do appreciate this, Darin. I'll never get out of being in debt to you," Smoke said.

"I quit running a tab on you long ago." He waved his arm in the air. "Okay, we'll take the dryer hose and the questioned documents to the Criminalistics Lab. Biology will do the DNA on the cigarette butts and these aluminum cans. Drug Chemistry has the first soda cans with the powder residue. Hennepin do the autopsies?" Darin asked, referring to the Hennepin County Medical Examiner's Office.

"Yes," Smoke confirmed.

"They're quick, so we can possibly get the toxicology report on the first case faxed over here today, if we're lucky." He bopped his head from side to side, thinking. "The second one? Maybe some time next week."

Darin phoned the Hennepin County Medical Examiner's Office. They located the file on Arthur Franz's autopsy. It had been dictated, but not typed up. Darin requested they fax a copy to his office as soon as it was completed.

"Okay, grab the bags and let's get cracking."

The Minnesota BCA was state-of-the-art and mammoth in size and scope. The four laboratory divisions had twelve separate sections. I was familiar with the Breath Testing Section in the Toxicology Laboratory because I had taken the Intoxilyzer 5000 Course to run tests on intoxicated drivers. It was a small area compared with the other three sections we'd visited that day.

Drug Chemistry had literally thousands of pills in little clear drawers from floor to ceiling, lining the walls of the lab. I could not fathom how they had devised their system of organization for drug identification.

"Drug Chem can usually get results out in less than a month. Hopefully they'll have it done this afternoon on your cases," Darin said.

We headed to the Criminalistics Laboratory for the Latent Fingerprints and Questioned Documents sections. Darin signed the dryer hose and razor blade over to a woman about my age named Shelly, and the alleged suicide notes for comparison to an older gentleman named Harold.

Darin looked at his watch. "I haven't had lunch. Let's head to the cafeteria and give the experts some time to process the evidence."

We made our selections and sat at a table in the middle of the room. It was almost two o'clock. There were only a few others in the room. Surprisingly, my cheeseburger was juicy and flavorful, and I devoured it a little too fast.

"We've got the Automated Fingerprint Identification System, AFIS, which conducts latent searches of the FBI database —very efficient system—can get us info we didn't have easy access to before." Darin said and bit into his chicken salad sandwich.

"Smoke—" I started.

"Where?"

Darin craned his neck around at the same time Smoke said, "What?" and then looked at Darin. "She's talking to me. Smoke is my Oak Lea nickname."

"I have known you for—what—sixteen years, and didn't know you had an 'Oak Lea nickname.' How in the heck did you get the nickname 'Smoke'?"

"Long story, and there is a young lady present who doesn't need to hear all the particulars. Suffice it to say, when I was a junior in high school, I was in a fish house with a girl, and we weren't exactly fishing when I accidentally kicked over the lantern and started the place on fire."

Smoke looked at me for my reaction, but I managed to keep a straight face. I had figured as much. "She thought she was pretty clever. She went around telling everyone, 'where there's smoke there's fire, and "Smoke's" real name is Elton.' The name stuck." Smoke actually blushed recalling the memory. I didn't try to hide my silly grin from him.

Darin laughed for nearly a full minute. "You were an old dog even then, you son of a gun."

"Change of subject. Tell me what's new in your world," Smoke said, clearly uncomfortable with the attention the conversation had given him.

"Not a whole heck of a lot. I work, eat, sleep, not much time for play." Darin shrugged. "This crime solving business gets in your blood. Who needs a social life? I'd hate to ruin another woman's life by marrying her." He looked at me then explained. "I was married for six years back when I was a deputy with Elton—Smoke." He grinned at the last word. "And how about you, your social life still about as exciting as ever?"

"I had dinner with an old friend this week and," he looked at his watch, "if we get out of here early enough, we're going to do it again tonight."

The vision of Smoke and my mother kissing replayed in my mind. It bothered me that it bothered me so much and I didn't know why.

Darin's phone rang.

"It's Shelly," he said as he answered. "You're sure?" he said into the phone. "And the blade? . . . Okay, thanks." Darin hung up. "Are you ready for this? There are two partial prints on the razor blade, but not a single print on the dryer hose."

Smoke swallowed, drew his eyebrows together and asked, "Not one?"

"Nada," Darin confirmed.

"Damn. Well, Arthur wasn't wearing gloves, and we didn't find any at the scene, so I'd say that's proof positive he didn't rig the dryer hose."

"But not proof of who did. Good thing it's not your only piece of evidence."

As if on cue, Darin's phone rang again.

"Andy? . . . On both cans? . . . Okay, send them over to Shelly to check for latents. . . . Good work." Darin looked at Smoke, then me. "Ever hear of haloperidol?"

Smoke nodded and I shook my head.

"Psychotropic drug, used to level out people with severe personality disorders," Smoke explained.

Darin nodded. "There's an expression to describe the way people on haloperidol walk called the 'haloperidol shuffle.' The drug zones people out."

"And it was found on both cans?"

"Affirmative."

"How common is it?" Smoke asked.

Darin bopped his head back and forth again, a trait I had begun to recognize as his habit when he was considering, or estimating, something. "I'd say rare. It's a Schedule Two drug, high potential for abuse, severe restrictions on its use. Used mainly in hospitals where it can be regulated and controlled."

"So, if we're looking at people who are on the drug, they are probably hospitalized, or else we're looking at someone who has access to the drug at work?" I asked.

"Most likely," Darin said.

"Well, I'm glad it's a prescription drug. I was worried it was something like GHB, the date rape drug. Much harder to track that back to the source," Smoke observed.

Darin nodded. "Want dessert, or another cup of coffee?"

He seemed to have all the time in the world, though we all knew he was swamped with work. When Smoke and I declined, Darin said, "Then let's see how Harold is doing with the notes."

Harold set his magnifying glass down and stood when he saw the three of us. He walked to the end of the table where he was working and picked up the notes, one in each hand.

"Take a look." He waved us over with his head. "These notes were printed on the same printer using different font styles and sizes, probably to make them look like they were written by different people. There is a very slight wave three inches down, and if there were more printing, the pattern would show up every three inches, by my estimate. It was caused by slight damage to the roller, probably a paper jam and the person ripped the papers out without releasing the hold."

Harold studied the documents for a second. "The signatures were also made by the same person, and probably traced from the original signatures. The pen was held straight down, not at an angle, which virtually everyone does when writing." Harold demonstrated what he meant, and it looked like a very awkward way to hold a pen. "The deepest impressions are on the left and bottom of the letters." He traced the areas in question. "Same person signed both letters. There is no question in my mind."

"You are the man," Darin said as he picked up the bagged notes. "On to Latents."

Smoke and I followed our piper, thinking, not speaking.

Shelly was gently brushing fine white powder from a soda can, revealing many fingerprints, most of them smudged. There were two distinct prints Shelly captured with a piece of sticky adhesive. She taped them to glass slides for identification. "From the size and shape, it looks like the prints belong to one person. The other soda can, found at the scene with this one, are from the same person."

"So, it was one person who drank from both cans?" Smoke asked.

"Yes," Shelly confirmed.

She looked at the name on the glass slide. "On the can from the Arthur Franz case, I was able to get three clear prints, all from the same person. On the beer can . . ." she paused and looked at her notes ". . . the one from the Marshall Kelton case, I got a perfect set of left hand prints, like he picked the can up once, drank from it then set it down. There were also a right thumb and index finger prints at the top of the can, from the same person who made the left hand prints. They also match the partials I lifted from the razor blade."

Darin, Smoke, and I looked at the slides for a few minutes. I collected latent prints from time to time and admired how effortless Shelly made it look. It wasn't as easy for most of us to lift identifiable prints.

"Okay Shelly, bang-up job as always. I think we know the answer to the owners of the prints on the cans found with Arthur Franz and Marshall Kelton. Run 'em through the database. They should come back to the Winnebago attorneys. If you get a hit on the third set, the soda cans found in the field by Bebee Lake, call me right away," Darin instructed.

Darin, Smoke, and I walked back to Darin's office.

"Thanks for pulling strings, Darin. We'd hate to have waited two weeks, much less two months, for this," Smoke said with sincere gratitude.

Darin clapped his hands together. "Glad I could help. The eighty-seven counties in this state keep us hopping, that's for sure, but certain cases have to take priority over others."

Smoke nodded. "Can I use your phone? I better call the sheriff from a land line."

"Help yourself." Darin slid his phone across the desk to give Smoke better access.

While Smoke told the sheriff what the afternoon and the BCA had revealed, Darin pulled me aside. "So, you got yourselves a murder investigation, or I should say, two murder investigations?"

I nodded, wondering what was next. It was the first time I had been part of one.

"Well, you got a good guy in Elton. Calm, systematic, nobody's fool," Darin added.

"He's taught me a lot. He's my best friend in the department," I admitted.

"The one he had dinner with this week?" Darin raised his eyebrows.

I smiled. "No."

Darin frowned slightly, studying my face. "Not that it's any of my business, but how old are you? Seriously."

"Almost twenty-nine."

He grinned and nodded. "Then I'm not too old for you. I'm thirty-nine. You live in Oak Lea?" I nodded.

"No wedding ring?" he asked and I shook my head. "Seeing someone?"

"Yes."

Darin snapped his fingers and made a clicking sound. "My usual luck."

Something about him made me smile.

Darin's questions about my dating status reminded me I hadn't talked to Nick all day. "Excuse me for a minute." I pulled my phone out of my pocket, turned it on, and saw I had two

Christine Husom

missed calls, both from Nick. It was after five, so I tried him at home. "Hi, Nick."

"Corky, I was worried about you! Where are you?" Nick asked.

"The BCA."

He paused for a second. "The what?"

"The Minnesota Bureau of Criminal Apprehension in St. Paul. Smoke and I are here on business."

"On your day off?" he asked.

"Yeah, I ended up working. Anyway, I won't get home for a couple of hours."

"Do we still have a date?" Nick asked, concern in his voice.

"I want to see you, but I don't think I can concentrate on a movie. Would you mind coming to my house? We can order take out," I suggested.

"Sounds good to me. Call me when you get home."

"Will do."

Darin had obviously been eavesdropping. "A new boyfriend?" he asked.

"Why do you ask?"

"He doesn't know what the BCA is." Darin was an investigative diehard.

"Oh, well, not everyone does, I guess. Not that it's any of your business, but we met recently and have had a few dates. You can't really call him my boyfriend."

Darin smiled and nodded. "If it doesn't work out, will you keep me in mind? Elton has my numbers."

"All right, ready to face rush hour traffic, Corky?"

Smoke interrupted so I didn't have to answer Darin. What would I have said?

"You're driving."

Smoke checked his notes. "So we're waiting on the autopsy reports. Arthur's should be done soon?"

Darin nodded.

"Any idea on the DNA?" he asked Darin.

"We'll push for the first part of next week. Which reminds me, let me check with Shelly, see if she got a match on the prints." He picked up his phone and dialed. "Shell, what cha got? . . . Okay, later." He shook his head. "The third set of prints isn't on file. The attorneys, at least, were fingerprinted for their background checks when they got hired."

The double-edged sword of using fingerprints to identify good guys: you only needed them if something bad happened to them.

"Damn. If his prints aren't on file, chances are slim to none his DNA is either," Smoke said.

"I'll walk you out," Darin offered.

Traffic was lighter than Smoke had predicted. He merged onto a westbound lane of Interstate 94. Friday, especially during the summer months, was an early shove day. Many offices closed by noon, and a growing number of factories offered flexible work schedules to accommodate longer weekends.

"Smoke, any idea what the connection between Arthur and Marshall might be, who their mutual enemy is?"

"By connection, you mean aside from being lawyers?" he asked and I nodded. "You know we didn't find any obvious answers going through their offices. Professionally, they were on opposite sides of the courtroom, so it's probably not a client, unless someone had a reason to blame both sides. And what are the chances of that?"

Smoke pulled into the far left lane to get around a semi-truck going about forty-five miles an hour.

"The possible suspect's fingerprints are not on file, so the killer hasn't got a criminal history. When I called the sheriff from Darin's office, I could tell he's about ready to stroke out." Smoke paused. "He doesn't want to throw the people into a panic over this, but he's a little nervous we could have a serial killer on our hands—one with no known criminal history."

"No. Oh my gosh!"

"Exactly. Twardy's preparing a memo for sheriff's personnel and calling an emergency meeting for everyone in the county attorney's and public defender's offices tomorrow morning. Brass will be there. All deputies are invited, but not mandated."

Saturday morning. "Isn't Marshall's funeral tomorrow?"

Smoke nodded. "Meeting's at eight-thirty, funeral's at ten. Sheriff wants to brief the staff from the offices—but the lawyers, especially—to be on the lookout in case some psycho is out there gunning for 'em. We've never had anything even close to this before, so it's anybody's guess what we're up against. Marshall was killed on the same day as Arthur's service. Twardy doesn't want a repeat performance."

"I can't believe this is happening in Winnebago County."

My cell phone rang. The number was listed to Arthur Franz. "It's Marion McIllvery. She must have seen my number on Caller ID. I tried her last night."

"Okay. Tell her I want to talk to her."

"Sergeant Aleckson," I answered.

"Hi, it's Marion McIllvery. I got back from Duluth a little while ago and saw you called." She spoke quietly in a monotone, no emotion in her voice.

"I did. Thank you for calling me back. How are you doing with everything?" I asked.

"Not too good, but I'm hanging in there. Is that why you called, just to check?" she said.

I wished I was speaking to her face to face. "No, actually, I'm sorry. This is difficult for you, but, you heard about Marshall Kelton?"

"The public defender for Winnebago? Arthur's mentioned him, of course. What about him?"

Was it possible she hadn't heard Marshall had died? "You haven't heard the news?"

"I haven't listened to the news or read a newspaper since Arthur died. I couldn't stand what they were saying about him," Marion confessed, sadness gathering around her words.

I hadn't counted on that and tapped Smoke's arm. "Marion, I'm here with Detective Dawes, and he'd like to talk to you." As I handed the phone to Smoke, I whispered what Marion had told me.

"Hello, Marion, Dawes here. Sergeant Aleckson tells me you haven't heard what happened to Marshall Kelton. The only way to tell you is straight out. He's dead." Smoke paused to let the words sink in. "He died the same day as Arthur's memorial service. . . . I know. . . . We don't believe it is a coincidence. . . . There is no easy way to say this. Will you do me a favor and sit down? . . . Okay, . . . We believe both Arthur and Marshall Kelton were murdered. . . . Marion, are you there?" Smoke held my cell to his chest. "It sounds like she dropped the phone."

Smoke brought the phone back to his face. "Hello? Marion, are you there? . . . I know this is all a terrible shock."

Smoke relayed what had transpired since my discovery that morning. "I hate to ask you this right now, but it's important. Do you know of anything Arthur and Kelton may have been involved with that would have gotten them killed? . . . Nothing? . . . Well, take some time, think about it, we'll talk to you tomorrow. . . . Are you going to be all right? . . . Will you call your friends to come and stay with you? . . . Okay."

"What did she say?" I asked.

"'Thank you, I knew he didn't kill himself. Thank you.' Now we just gotta figure out who did."

"She didn't know of a connection between Arthur and Marshall?"

"Nope, not outside the courtroom, at least. Same story we've been getting everywhere."

Chapter 30

Alvie

Alvie sat in the library parking lot across from the sheriff's office at the courthouse. She faced the lake, with her back to the department, watching the comings and goings through her rearview mirror. When she first pulled in, she saw the little sergeant's classic car parked in the lot with the police cars. Then, about an hour later, an unmarked police car parked next to it. Who got out but that ace detective, Dawes, and the little sergeant?

She knew detectives didn't wear police outfits, but the sergeant had on a little tee shirt and a pair of jeans. Maybe there was something more going on between them they didn't want people to know about. Hanky panky, probably.

The little sergeant got in her car and drove away, out toward where she lived. Good, not heading to the probation officer's house like she did way too often, as far as Alvie was concerned. The detective went inside the sheriff's department for a little while. Then when he got back in his car, he drove west. Alvie followed him. Hopefully he was going to his house and not the little sergeant's. Dawes had to go home sometime, didn't he?

Alvie was glad there was a car between her and the detective, just in case he recognized her car from that one morning outside the public defender lawyer's house. Dawes and the little sergeant had sure stared at her long enough that day. What were they so interested in, anyway?

The green car in front of her slowed down more than the detective did going around a curve, and Alvie was afraid she'd lose him. Good, he was still in sight.

They went past the Beebe Lake road, and Alvie smiled at the fond memory of what had happened there. Then past the little sergeant's road and on about two more miles. She saw the detective's right turn signal flash, and all three cars slowed down as he turned north on a blacktopped driveway. Must be doing pretty well for himself if he could afford to blacktop a long driveway like that. Alvie couldn't see how long it was, exactly, because it went into a woods, but it looked pretty long. Maybe as long as hers.

Alvie kept driving. She'd find a hidden place to park someday soon, then hike back to the house and scope things out. As long as he didn't have a dog, she'd be fine. If he did have a dog, she'd figure that out, too. The green car ahead of her was still driving west when Alvie took a U-turn at the next crossroad and headed back to Oak Lea.

She cruised past the Speiss house, cursing out loud when she saw the curtains were closed, a sure sign Speiss was gone. That woman was impossible. Maybe she was at the little sergeant's house. No harm in checking. There was a field road down a ways from the little sergeant's driveway. The place in the cornfield where she had parked for the Bebee Lake death was too far away, plus then she had to fix the row of corn she'd driven through. Too much work. Besides, with all the extra exercise she had been getting, her clothes were getting a little baggy, and she didn't want to buy new ones.

It would soon be over. Another few weeks and three more people would have families wondering why they had killed themselves. When Alvie drove past the little sergeant's house, she saw a car in the driveway, but it wasn't the probation officer's. Now what? Okay, well, she knew where the detective lived, probably. She'd find out for sure in the next few days if that was really his place.

Alvie didn't know when that probation officer would get home, so the best thing to do was to drive to Rockwell to scope out Jason Browne's place. His note was patiently waiting in her trunk, so he could die anytime. *Is that okay with you, son, or does he have to be the last?*

Chapter 31

I was so happy to see Nick, I threw my arms around his neck and didn't let go until he said, "Do you want to talk about it?"

I looked into his very handsome face, smiled, and shook my head.

"Okay then, wanna fool around?" He pulled me closer for a kiss.

I was beginning to discover life could be so ironic. I had begun the first serious relationship of my personal life when the most serious set of events was occurring in my professional life. I was on emotional and intellectual overload and wished the world would stop just long enough for me to process what I thought and how I felt. Important, critical things were happening. They were issues of life and death, and I didn't want to make any mistakes.

I took Nick's hand in mine and led him into the living room. "Nice place," he said as he looked around the room done in navy and tan. "Couch looks comfy," he teased.

"It is." I gave his chest a little push. "The decorating is thanks to my mother. When I built my house, she made it her special project for two months, I swear. It seemed like every time the phone rang it was my mother asking me to meet her to check out colors, or fabrics, or fixtures."

Nick laughed, and I reveled in the sound of it. "Hey, I wish I had a mother who cooked and decorated for me. When do I get to meet her?" he asked.

"If you're up to it, my grandparents will be back from Nisswa next week, and my brother is coming from Colorado, so Mom is planning dinner. She'd love for you and Faith to come."

"Sounds fun. Speaking of dinner, what do we have planned for tonight?" He followed me to the kitchen.

"Speaking of Mother, when I got home I found this note on the kitchen counter." I handed it to him.

Nick read out loud, "'Hello, dear, I tried a new chicken fettuccini recipe and it's pretty good so I put a casserole in your fridge. I love you.' Mmm, sounds better than take out."

I scanned the contents of my refrigerator while the microwave heated the casserole. "I've got deli coleslaw or a bag of Caesar salad," I said.

"Coleslaw is good."

"Got it." I pushed aside bottles of dressing, mustard, and plastic containers of unknown foodstuffs to look for beverages. "And to drink, I've got one cola, three flavors of mineral water, apple juice, or beer."

"I'll have a beer."

I handed him the drink. "I suppose wine would be better with fettuccini, but I haven't got any on hand."

"Beer is fine, really."

I glanced at the microwave. "There's nine minutes left for the casserole, so let's sit on the patio."

We settled on the two lounge chairs my mother had found at a garage sale. "The air is sure fresh after that front moved through this morning and broke up the humidity," Nick commented as he stretched his legs and took a sip of beer. "Tell me about your day. Someone call in sick, is that why you worked?"

The past day's events were a movie running over and over in my mind, squeezing at my heart. It was possible word was leaking out about what we had discovered in the cornfield and by the lake that morning, but it wouldn't be from me. As much as I wanted to talk to Nick, to tell him what we'd found and everything I'd learned at the BCA, I couldn't. Not until the sheriff held his press conference.

I had to weigh my words carefully. "Some things happened in an investigation that I assisted with. I promise to tell you every detail as soon as I can."

Nick reached over and put his hand over mine. "You look so burdened, that's all. I wish I could help."

"Your being here is a huge help." The microwave beeped. "Let's eat."

The sheriff had arranged for a large conference room in the courthouse for the Saturday morning meeting. Everyone had orders to tell no one outside their offices about the gathering, and surprisingly, it seemed no one had. Smoke had worried reporters would be camped outside, trying to gain access to the closed meeting, but there were none.

I wasn't scheduled to work until the afternoon shift, but I dressed in my full uniform for Marshall Kelton's funeral. I walked into the conference room, amazed at the large number of people who filled the space to near capacity. Scanning the sea of faces, I saw Chief Bud Becker, Oak Lea police officers, most every staff member from both the public defender's and the county attorney's offices, plus nearly every deputy, detective, sergeant, lieutenant, captain and secretary in the sheriff's department.

What had the sheriff put in the memo to get such a turnout? I hadn't checked my e-mail. Smoke saw me in the back of the room and motioned for me to join him and the sheriff at the front table. The sheriff looked solemn, bordering on ill. He gave me a slight nod.

"Let's get started," Sheriff Twardy addressed the group. People around the room murmured, "shhh," "quiet down," "we're starting." Within seconds, the room was still.

"Thank you all for showing up on short notice. This has been a tough week for the county. We lost two very fine men, Arthur Franz and Marshall Kelton. We all tried to understand why in the hell they would kill themselves, and now we know they didn't." The sheriff got right to the point of the meeting.

Audible gasps were heard, along with whispers of "what?" The sheriff held up his hands to signal everyone to be quiet so he could go on. "Sergeant Aleckson is here to tell you what she found yesterday. Then she and Detective Dawes will fill in the gaps, and I'll take it from there."

The sheriff could have warned me. I wasn't prepared to speak. I hadn't even written my report. But every detail of the previous day's events had played so many times in my mind, I believed they would be in my memory until the day I died. I pulled out the memo pad with my notes to reference, in case speaking in front of the group got the better of me. Speech had not been my favorite subject in high school. When I started talking, the words spilled from my mouth, beginning with spotting the downed cornstalks and ending with the findings at the BCA. I heard a gasp, sharp little intakes of breath here and there, but no one chatted while I spoke.

Smoke held his comments until I finished. "Now you know why you're all here. Someone killed Arthur Franz and Marshall Kelton, and we need all the help we can get to find who that is. And because we don't know who it is, or what his motive might be, we don't know if anyone else is at risk."

"Oh my God!" Barbara from the public defender's office jumped up, stunned. "Are you saying someone will try to kill one of us?" Tears ran down her cheeks.

Sheriff Twardy raised his arms again, but people couldn't stop talking among themselves. "Listen up!" he called. "This is exactly what we don't need, to have you running around half-cocked, in a panic. You are all intelligent people or you wouldn't have the jobs you do."

"How can we help but be scared when you tell us something like this?" asked Julie Grimes—pale and tight-faced—from the county attorney's office.

The sheriff didn't answer for a moment. "It is natural to be concerned, of course. That's why I want all of you in the loop, so you will be more aware of unusual circumstances or suspicious people. We have no reason to believe any of you are in danger, but until we find this nut, I will rest easier knowing you aren't oblivious to the situation."

"So what can we do?" Ray Collinwood, assistant county attorney, asked, his belly straining against his shirt.

"Cover your backsides," Smoke said.

"What do you mean?" a fairly new public defender asked. I didn't know her name.

Smoke went on, "Normal safety rules—keep your doors locked, don't open up for strangers if you're alone, stay away from isolated areas, pay attention to people you don't know hanging around your neighborhoods . . ."

I didn't hear the rest of Smoke's words as panic gripped me. Sara! Someone had been in her home when she was away. And her neighbor had seen a stranger parked on her street earlier in the week. Was the same maniac who had killed Arthur and Marshall after one of my best friends, too? But why?

When I tuned back in, the sheriff was talking, ". . . and we need your help. If you can think of anyone who made a threat, real or implied, to Franz or Kelton, or if you know of anything they were involved with that would have gotten them killed, you aren't doing anybody any favors by keeping it to yourselves."

No one answered. We were still at square one.

Sheriff Twardy gave everyone a few more minutes to think, then said, "I'll be holding a press conference this afternoon, and any leaks before then will be grounds for immediate dismissal if you're in the sheriff's department. I can't order you folks in the other offices to do the same, but I'm asking you to keep this confidential 'til then. Show Marshall Kelton's family some respect and let them get through his service then I'll talk to them before we go public with this information."

The sheriff consulted his watch. "The service begins in twenty minutes, so this meeting is over. Remember what I said."

I didn't think anyone would be forgetting any time soon.

Chapter 32

Alvie

By the time she got to the traitor's house, the sun had set and it was dark in the house. There was one small light on in the living room, and it looked to Alvie like no one was home. The perfect set-up. She could have a good look around and make her plans.

Jason Browne lived in a rambler on a street with a bunch of other ramblers that looked about the same. Alvie had her man disguise on. She walked up to the front door and rang the doorbell, just in case someone really was home. No one answered, so she tried the door. Locked. She went around to the back door. Also locked. Okay, so it wasn't going to be quite as easy as she had hoped. Then she noticed the kitchen window was open a crack, and the screen came off from the outside. What luck, after all.

The window was about four feet by five feet, plenty big for her to crawl through with no problem. Once inside, Alvie looked around. Small, but a pretty nice place, better than the traitor Jason deserved, that's for damn sure. It was even neat and clean.

Alvie patted her pocket, double-checking to be sure her gun was there. She had to be prepared in case someone came home. She pulled her mini flashlight out of another pocket. She couldn't be turning on all the lights and let everyone know she was there. Alvie continued her exploration of the house and made an exciting discovery in the spare bedroom. There was a gun cabinet with seven long guns, shotguns or rifles. Alvie really didn't know the difference. The doors were locked, but the drawer underneath them wasn't, and what was inside but two old pistols? They looked like antiques, but they probably still worked. Where would the traitor keep the bullets?

Alvie nosed around and found a box filled with all kinds of shotgun shells and bullets under the bed in the master bedroom, of all places. A regular treasure trove, loaded with all she needed to take care of the traitor, and his wife too, if she got in the way. Alvie looked through the box and picked up the one she thought would fit in one of the revolvers. The damn thing spilled all over. Alvie had a heck of a time finding all the bullets in the thick carpet. Sometimes the latex gloves were real clumsy to work with.

She headed to the other room with the bullet and loaded it in the pistol. A perfect fit. Alvie figured the best thing to do would be to keep three or four of the bullets, so she would have them with her when she needed them. If she had to go fumbling around under the bed in the other room, it wouldn't work. She replaced the gun in the case. They'd probably notice if it was missing.

Alvie waited a long time, but the traitor and his wife didn't come home. Probably out having a high old time, something Nolan could never do. She decided it was better they were gone. It would give her a chance to better prepare for next time. Alvie packed the bullets next to the new murder-suicide note in the trunk of her car, ready for her next visit to the Browne household.

Suddenly, an all too familiar pain gripped her. Not that headache again! Why did she keep getting them lately? And, as if she didn't have enough to think about, she'd have to pick up Henry's prescription soon. Did she dare lift any more pills after the hoopla it had caused last time? It was not the kind of attention she needed at that particular time of her life.

Should she go back to the traitor's house or go to the funeral? She'd already had the satisfaction of seeing how broken up the public defender's family had looked when they saw how he died, so why go to another funeral if she didn't have to?

Chapter 33

I tried to pay attention to what the priest was saying about Marshall Kelton, but found it nearly impossible with all that had transpired since the previous morning. I looked at Stefany Kelton and her children, then at Brock Kelton and the rest of the family members, and wondered how they would react to the news that Marshall had been murdered. How would I feel?

After the service, I headed to the squad room in the sheriff's department and began my report on the cornfield and Beebe Lake investigation. A new deputy was running a criminal history check on a man he had just arrested. We made small talk for a few minutes. Sheriff Twardy planned to meet with the Keltons at one o'clock and wanted Smoke and me there, so I concentrated in earnest to finish my report before then.

At twelve-thirty, Smoke came in and set a plate of food next to me. "You didn't stay for the lunch, so I brought you some."

"Thanks."

The egg salad sandwiches, chips, and brownie hit the spot.

"How's the report coming?" Smoke asked.

My mouth was full, but I said, "Just need to proof for good grammar."

"I'll do that. You eat." He patted his breast pocket, located his glasses then spent the next ten minutes reading. "No mistakes that I can see. Good synopsis, complete."

Sheriff Twardy and Chief Bud Becker were in Stefany Kelton's living room when Smoke and I arrived. Arthur Franz's death had occurred outside of Oak Lea, but Marshall Kelton had died within city limits, so Becker's office would assist the sheriff's department in any way they could. The adults gathered from the

Kelton family included Stefany, Brock, his parents, and a sister. They sat quietly, shocked by the sheriff's update on the circumstances of Marshall's death.

"You know the Winnebago County Sheriff's Department will leave no stone unturned until we find out who is responsible for this horror. We don't know why Arthur Franz and Marshall were targeted, so if you can think of any connection, anything Marshall mentioned, even in passing, that he and Franz were involved with outside of work . . ." the sheriff said.

Brock spoke first. "I was very close to Marshall. He was my best friend. When he talked about Arthur Franz, and that wasn't often, it was in reference to work. He admired him professionally, but I don't think they even had lunch together."

Stefany shook her head. "No, I don't think they did. Once, when we had a party, Marshall invited a few people from the county attorney's office and included Arthur to be polite. But Marshall told me he knew Arthur wouldn't come because he never socialized with people out here. He lived in one of the metro suburbs, Maple Grove or Plymouth, I think. Marshall thought he might be gay and didn't want people out here to find out."

Neither Stefany or Brock had thought of any personal connection between Marshall Kelton and Arthur Franz since we had first asked the question the morning Kelton's body was discovered.

"We don't want to take up any more of your time. I'm sorry we had to meet like this right after the funeral, but . . ." Twardy looked at his watch ". . . I'm holding a press conference in an hour and wanted you to hear about it from me first."

Sheriff Twardy stood on the front lawn outside the courthouse, the carved black letters of "Winnebago County Sheriff's Department" visible over his head. His professional demeanor and interactions worked well with the public, and they showed their confidence in his administration by re-electing him every four years. Those who didn't know the sheriff well might mistake his heightened facial color for a little too much sun. The rest of us worried about his blood pressure numbers.

Four major television stations from Minneapolis, one from St. Cloud, and another from Willmar had cameras and crews awaiting Twardy's announcement. Several area radio stations were represented, including our local one. A man from Oak Lea's government cable access channel had the best spot—front and center. There were at least twelve reporters and photographers gathered. Paul Moore, our local paper's writer, was talking to Chief Bud Becker.

Vehicles passing by pulled over to see what was going on, and the courthouse lawn began to fill with people who detoured from wherever they were going to be part of the action.

Chief Becker and Smoke joined the two deputies who flanked the sheriff. From where I stood, Sheriff Twardy was barely visible behind the many microphones and cameras.

The sheriff began. "This will be brief. As you know, in the past ten days, two prominent attorneys in this county have died: Arthur Franz, Winnebago County Attorney, and Marshall Kelton, Chief Public Defender for the Tenth Judicial District. The initial belief in both cases was that they committed suicide. However, new evidence has emerged which leads us to believe they did not. We now consider both deaths as open homicide investigations . . ."

Electricity sparked through the air, igniting chatter so loud we could no longer hear the sheriff's voice over the din.

Sheriff Twardy waited while the two guard-duty deputies stepped forward and held their hands up to demand quiet. After a minute, people quieted enough to hear the rest of the story.

"We have no suspect, or suspects, at this time and cannot begin to speculate why these men were killed. We have no reason to believe anyone else is at risk, but you should all be aware of this

221

situation. If anyone has information on either death, please contact us. We will follow any and every lead to solve these heinous crimes as soon as we possibly can. Thank you. I'll take a few questions." The sheriff pointed to a gray- haired reporter from an area radio station.

"David Graham, KLLK Radio, Little Mountain. Sheriff Twardy, what evidence came forward that changed the two deaths from suicides to homicides?" he asked.

"I am not at liberty to give that information, as it could compromise the investigations. I will say we are in contact with the Minnesota Bureau of Criminal Apprehension, which is working to process the evidence we do have."

"Sir? Oh, Patricia Bolan, KARE-11 News. Sir, since both men killed were lawyers, do you have reason to believe other lawyers may be targeted as well?"

"We have no reason to believe that, no. But we cannot rule it out, either."

"Sheriff Twardy, Paul Moore, *Oak Lea Daily News*. Then do you believe the suspect may be a serial killer?"

The sheriff's face was beet red by then. "We cannot rule that out at this time."

The crowd went wild with the realization there might be a serial killer in their own community. There hadn't been a single murder in the county for three years, then there were two in ten days. Looking at the people clutching each other, animated in their distress, and reacting to sudden uncertainty, I felt a momentary helplessness.

It was my job to help keep these people safe from those who wanted to hurt them. But on that afternoon, standing with them on the courthouse lawn, it seemed like a formidable task, a challenge to the oath I had taken to protect and serve.

Chief Becker touched Sheriff Twardy on the shoulder, and the sheriff took a step back. Becker spoke into the microphone. "There is no reason to panic, folks, but keep your antennas up.

This is my town, and by gum, we'll work around the clock with the sheriff's department to solve these cases." He whispered something to the sheriff, and Twardy shook his head. Becker concluded, "That's all for today. We'll give you updates as soon as we can. Thank you."

The two bodyguard deputies hustled the sheriff through the department door. Becker stayed behind, and people pushed in to talk to him, needing assurance, wanting more answers. Smoke caught my eyes and leaned his head slightly to the left. I followed him to his car.

"I'm going to have court administration do a search of all the court cases Franz and Kelton have had together," he said.

"That could be in the thousands," I said.

He shrugged. "We have to start somewhere."

"But if the suspect doesn't have a criminal history—" I started to argue.

"It could be a friend working in cohort with a criminal," Smoke countered. "I found out Arthur Franz started here as an assistant county attorney eleven years ago, this month in fact. Kelton was here a few years before that. We'll start with the most recent cases and work backward. Could be someone who was recently released from prison. Could be someone in for life who hired a killer."

The scope of the investigation was spreading like a fire sweeping across a dry hay field.

I could almost see Smoke's mental gears turning. "I'll have the jail run a check to see if any of their inmates were on haloperidol while in custody, see where that leads. If we have to, we'll get a search warrant for records from the area pharmacies."

"What do you want me to do?" I asked.

His eyes leveled on mine. "Do your job. And pray."

"I've been doing a lot of that already."

Chapter 34

Alvie

Alvie parked two blocks away from Browne's house. Not much happening in his neighborhood on a Saturday morning in July. She lifted a toolbox from the passenger seat and made her way to Jason's back window. The box was empty, but she wanted to look official, in case any snoops happened to see her and wondered who she was. Alvie figured she looked like a regular fix-it guy with her coveralls, ball cap, and toolbox.

Her gun sat in her right hip pocket, ready for action, if she couldn't get to Browne's pistol on time.

The kitchen window was just like she had left it the past night. She put her ear to the crack and listened. Not a stir in the house. The Brownes could be sleeping, even though it was after nine. Alvie crawled in, closed the window behind her to keep any loud noises inside, and crept to the bedroom, gun in hand. She had seen on a show once where someone had shot through a pillow to cover the sound. That's what she'd do.

Nobody home. *Damn.* She couldn't keep showing up there. Someone was bound to see her one of the times. And Rebecca couldn't stay at her friend's house every night. She would start to wonder why her grandmother suddenly wanted her away so much, and what would Rebecca's friend think?

No, Alvie couldn't go back there until the next weekend. She'd have to work on the detective and probation officer in the coming week. One of them would pan out. She could sneak out during the night when Rebecca was sleeping if she had to. That was probably the only time she would find either one of those characters home.

Alvie drove about a half mile past the ace detective's driveway and turned north on an unmarked, unpaved county road. She pulled over, her vehicle parked at an angle, half in a ditch. She crawled uphill to get out the driver's side, then realized it would have been easier to slide out the passenger door.

The woods of mostly maple trees might have been a pasture at one time. The floor had since filled with sapling trees, ferns, and burning nettles. Alvie knew if the nettles touched her bare skin, she would go nearly crazy with the burning, itching, and scratching. No need to crawl through the stuff. She could walk that leg of the journey to the detective's house.

Alvie reached a clearing and spotted a log home all by itself, isolated from the rest of the world. It was sitting practically on top of a little lake, not much smaller than the one the county attorney had died at, but bigger than the pond the judge had died in.

Drowning. Another drowning. All the lakes and ponds in Minnesota were good for something. Alvie hadn't known the detective would provide his own lake, complete with a dock he could fall off.

A big black dog Alvie figured was a lab came bounding around the house, in hot pursuit of a squirrel. The squirrel gave him chase for a minute, then scampered up a tree, yelling chatters to the dog below. The lab took several leaps around the base of the tree, answering the squirrel with barking threats, but the squirrel wouldn't come down. The dog finally gave up and plopped down in the shade, his nose high in the air, sniffing.

Alvie's heart pounded in her chest as she peered around a mature maple. A dog. Damn. Must not have picked up her scent, what with the little critters to keep it busy. She'd probably have to shoot the thing. But not then. There was no sign of the detective, anyway. Where was everybody? No Jason Browne, no Sara Speiss, no Detective Dawes.

One more try at the Speiss house, and if that didn't work out, she'd take her headache and head home. *No need to get so impatient, right, Nolan? It's still over a month until your birthday. We can take a little extra time if we have to. Do things right.*

Alvie hiked back to her car, stepping around the burning nettles. She decided to wait on Speiss. She didn't even want to know if Speiss was home, so she stripped off her man disguise and stowed it in the hidden safety of her trunk. She would go home and clear her mind of all her problems and frustrations. She and Rebecca would play board games and forget the rest of the world was even out there.

Chapter 35

"**T**his came in about twenty minutes ago. Communications assigned it to you." Sergeant Chip Roth handed me the paper citing a burglary complaint report from an Ann Browne in Rockwell.

Rockwell. "I handled a home burglary complaint there a couple of weeks ago. Same deal—party returns home from vacation and discovers someone has broken in. Rockwell hasn't had a problem with that for a long time. Hope it's not a trend."

"Neighbors just gotta watch out for each other," Roth said.

"Easier said than done. Anything else?" I asked as I scanned the burglary complaint.

Roth handed me some long narrow envelopes, each containing a warrant on someone wanted for something. "Here. Warrants left the usual stack. Not that you're going to have any time to track down warrants with all the extra calls we've gotten the last thirty minutes since the sheriff held the press conference. Oh, and guess what? I managed to track down Keith Gilles, believe it or not. Got him locked up. Again."

"Good job. Where'd you find him?"

"His mother's place. I think she was sick of covering for him. When she opened the door for me, she called for Keith to come into the living room." Roth huffed out a little laugh.

I shook my head. "How long has he been hiding out since he jumped bail?"

"Six weeks, seven weeks."

"Oak Lea Bail Bonds will be happy they won't have to hire a bounty hunter to find him." I gathered my briefcase and gear bag. "Okay, well, enjoy the rest of the day."

"Yeah, if I turn off my home and cell phones and don't answer the door." Roth rocked his head back and forth and rolled his eyes.

I let out a loud exhale. "I know. I haven't even checked my home messages yet. After the news broke, my mother, who never calls my cell, was the first to call me on it. Then she called my grandparents in Nisswa and my brother in Colorado, so they all called me. And the man I've been seeing left me two messages when I was taking the other calls. I finally got back to him just before I went on duty." I paused, then asked, "And you know Sara Speiss?"

"Yeah, sure."

"Well, she called me from Brainerd, and like just about every other county employee, is pulling her hair out trying to figure out who had it in for both Arthur Franz and Marshall Kelton."

Roth rubbed his hand across his midnight shadow of a beard. "The whole county is goin' nuts. Just to let you know how bad it is, I think since the sheriff gave his press conference, communications has gotten over forty calls from people reporting suspicious persons. Communications had to call in two more officers to field phone calls. Nine-one-oners can hardly get through."

"Unbelievable. We have to get to the bottom of all this—stop this madman, whoever he is," I determined.

"We will. With the BCA involved, and everybody and their brother calling in to report their theories, something will pop."

On the drive to Rockwell, I laid my memo pad on the seat next to me and paged through it, keeping one eye on the road. There was a notation to ask Marion McIllvery whether Arthur Franz had kept an appointment calendar.

No time like the moment.

Marion picked up on the third ring. "How are you, Sergeant?" She sounded more rested than the last time we had spoken.

"I'm doing pretty fine, thanks for asking."

"I was watching the Twin Cities Triathlon, and the little scroll on the bottom of the screen said Sheriff Twardy of Winnebago County had held a press conference to address the murders of two prominent attorneys. It will be on the five o'clock news."

Poor communications. They would have to call in still more back-up. "It doesn't seem real all this is happening here, but I guess that's what everybody says when it happens to them," I said.

Marion's voice gained volume. "And what did Artie, or Marshall, for that matter, ever do to anyone? Nothing personal, surely, nothing to deserve this. What kind of a sicko kills someone, two someones, and makes it look like suicides?"

"Someone who doesn't want it to look like murder, so there won't be an investigation. At least that's what Detective Dawes thinks." I was in Rockwell, so I pulled my squad car over in front of a hardware store to finish our conversation.

"Marion, did Arthur keep an appointment book or daily planner?"

"Why, yes. I gave him a Palm Pilot for Christmas last year. Why?"

"We didn't find one among his things, and we thought there might be some answers in it. You know, maybe someone he met with recently. So you don't have it there?" I asked.

She was silent for a moment. "No. I didn't even think of it until you mentioned it just now. Artie always kept it with him. But you said you didn't find it?" she questioned.

"Not in his office or car."

"And it's not here. Like I said, he always kept it with him. That is strange."

Smoke's phone was busy, so I left him a message to call me. I found the Browne residence in a fairly new development near the elementary school. A short, slightly chubby woman with brown hair, about my age, opened the door a second after I rang the bell.

I extended my hand. "Hi, I'm Sergeant Aleckson, Winnebago County—"

Before I could finish, the woman took my hand and guided me into the house. "Come in, Sergeant. This is so upsetting." I glanced around the simply furnished, not very creatively decorated, but neatly kept, living room.

"Just for the record, are you Ann Browne?" I asked.

"Yes." She dropped my hand but kept walking, so I followed her down a short hall into a bedroom. "We just got home from an eight-day vacation. We were going to come home tomorrow, but decided to spend our last day off at home instead."

She walked into the bedroom then continued, "Anyway, we got home about an hour ago, and when we carried our suitcases in the bedroom, we saw someone had been in here."

I looked around, but the only things I could spot out of place were the two suitcases.

"We called nine-one-one right away, and the first thing they said was, 'Is this an emergency?' and I said, 'Someone was in our house when we were on vacation' and they said, 'Okay,' and then they asked me my name, address, and all that."

Ann Browne looked around as if she had suddenly remembered something. "I don't know where my husband is. Oh, probably still unloading the car." She spoke her thoughts out loud.

"Mrs. Browne—"

She waved her hand to correct me. "Ann."

I nodded. "So tell me how you know someone was here." I retrieved my memo pad from my pocket, ready to take notes.

"Hello, Corky." I wheeled around to face the male owner of the voice. Jason Browne, tall, lanky Jason Browne. Another ghost from my past. "I heard you became a deputy," he said. I hadn't seen Jason for over ten years, and he acted a little embarrassed to see me.

I held out my hand, which he took. "Good to see you again, Jason. I didn't realize this was your house. So Ann is your wife?" I asked.

"She is," Jason said and smiled.

I nodded. "She was about to tell me what happened."

Jason walked over to the bed and pointed to the carpet. "There are two bullets here on the carpet. I have a stash under my bed—I inherited my dad's guns and ammo when he died. We keep the guns in a case in the spare room, and the ammo under the bed here." He picked up an old box of bullets and handed it to me. "This box was full, and when I saw the bullets on the floor there, I checked. And besides the two on the carpet, there are three others missing from the box."

"And the pistol they go with?" I wondered.

"Still in the case. It seems like it was moved, but I couldn't swear to it." We headed into the other bedroom. Like the rest of the house, it was clean, but sparsely furnished. There were no pictures on the walls or other personal touches lying around.

Jason started to open the cabinet that held several guns, but I stopped him before he got the door opened. "Are any of those guns loaded?" I asked.

"No," Jason answered, looking a little surprised. "None of them have been loaded since I've had them. I've never actually shot any gun. I mean, I'm not a convicted felon. My case was pled down to a gross misdemeanor, but . . ." Jason looked at his hands then stuck them in his pocket.

"He just feels so bad about what he did when he was a kid and is a little afraid something awful might happen if he goes hunting, or target shooting, you know." Ann Browne finished for Jason. I had a feeling she did that a lot.

"I understand. Which gun belongs with the bullets?" I asked, peering at two pistols.

"The Browning," he said.

I slipped on a pair of latex gloves, removed the nine millimeter pistol from the case, and examined it closely. It was clean and unloaded.

"How did the burglar get in?" I asked.

Jason and Ann looked at each other and she answered. "We don't know. The doors were locked."

"Anyone besides you two have a key?"

Ann nodded. "Jason's sister. She's been watching the house for us. She stops in every day after work, just to check. You know, does a walk-through. I called her right away, even before I called nine-one-one, and she said she was here yesterday and didn't notice anything out of place. But she did say she might not have seen two little bullets lying on the carpet, you know. Anyway, she said she double checked the back door when she left and it was definitely locked."

"Okay, I'll have a look around, take some photos of the bullets, and dust the gun and bullets for prints. Then I'll get the rest of the information from you that I'll need for my report." They both nodded.

The Brownes followed me as I explored the house, looking for signs of the burglar's entry.

"Did you open this window when you got home?" I asked. The kitchen window next to the back door was open a crack.

"No, we leave it that way, you know, in case of tornados," Ann explained.

It was a common belief in Minnesota that having a window open a crack would help reduce the pressure of the strong winds blowing against an airtight house, and perhaps save it from blowing down during a violent storm.

I stepped outside for a closer look. "Your screens come off from the outside, and a person could easily fit through this window. If it was me, I'd take my chances with the tornado and keep my house secure, especially with guns in the house."

Ann looked especially sheepish and put her hand on Jason's bicep. "You were right, honey. We'll keep the windows locked when we're gone from now on."

When I had taken the needed photos and collected the latent prints from the Browning—there were none on either bullet—I sat at the kitchen table with Ann and Jason to verify the information they had given.

"So you can't think of anyone who would know you stored that ammunition under your bed?" I asked.

"Not one person. Just Annie and I," Jason answered.

"Since nothing was taken, except for three bullets, my best guess is someone found your stash, got spooked, spilled some, grabbed what he could, and fled. Maybe it was when your sister came, or maybe it was someone ringing the doorbell. Obviously, those are only theories."

I paused, then went on, "My advice is, get a safe, or some kind of lock system for your guns and ammunition. Someone out there has been here once, and could come back now that he knows what you've got. Keep your weapons secure."

"**S**ix-oh-eight, Winnebago County."

"Go ahead, Six-oh-eight," Robin answered for communications.

"I'm clear the burglary complaint. Anything pending?"

"Sergeant, phone communications."

My heart thumped against my protective vest as I punched in the number. Of late, every time I was advised to call in, a major tragedy had occurred. "It's Corky. What's up?"

Robin sounded frazzled. "Oh my God! We are swamped with suspicious person calls, and we have to check them out. Sheriff is putting eight more deputies on the road to handle them. He said when you were clear Rockwell, you should head back to his office for a strategic planning meeting. Oh, and Detective Dawes is crashing on a cot in the juvenile holdover for an hour, in case you're trying to reach him. He didn't get any sleep last night."

"Thanks, Robin."

By the time I got to the Winnebago Sheriff's Department, the place was swimming in a sea of brown uniforms. Eight deputies who had a coveted weekend off had been called in for extra duty. There was a little grumbling, but with two unsolved murders on the books, everyone in the department was committed to finding out who was responsible.

I stopped by Sheriff Twardy's office and found a note taped to his door stating, "Meeting in Squad Room," so I made my way there. The sheriff assigned the eight extra deputies to be rovers, responding to calls wherever they were needed in the county. The seven deputies already on duty patrolling their scheduled areas were relieved to have the needed assistance.

". . . So, report to Sergeant Aleckson. She'll report to Detective Dawes. Dawes isn't the investigator on call this weekend, but since he's been working the Franz and Kelton cases, he's offered to help work any leads you get."

I spotted Smoke in the group. Short nap.

"Any questions?" Sheriff Twardy asked as he looked around the room.

A few deputies shook their heads, but no one answered.

"Okay, you're dismissed. Communications has stacks of reports to follow up on. Divide 'em up and get to work. Oh, and thanks for pulling extra duty."

Smoke held back to talk to me. "I got your message just before the meeting. What's up?"

"I talked to Marion McIllvery to see if Arthur had a day planner. She said he had a Palm Pilot that should have been with him."

"Hmm. Since it wasn't, are you thinking it may contain some information that would be incriminating to the killer?" he asked, thumbing his nose.

"What do you think, Detective?"

"I'd say could be. Oh, by the way, Captain Palmer is in the jail office, running the medical records of the inmates, including those still in custody. He's checking on all psychotropic drugs, not only haloperidol. Our guy may have been on a different one prior, and on haloperidol now."

"That was smart."

"Yeah, wish I could say I thought of it, but it was Palmer's idea," Smoke said.

"Does he have any idea how many inmates we're talking about?" I wondered.

"No. Haloperidol isn't very common, but there's usually someone in custody on a schedule two narcotic of some sort, not necessarily psychotropic."

"Like you said, we gotta start somewhere."

Smoke nodded and blinked his eyes. "Hopefully, it will help narrow the search when court admin runs the cases Franz and Kelton shared."

"They'll start that Monday?"

"I talked to Sandy Kress."

Sandy was the court administrator and had guarded the records there for at least twenty years. Smoke went on, "She's got some family deal going today, but she'll go in tomorrow and start the computer on its search. She has no idea how many hours it might take and doesn't want to bog down the system during business hours."

I rolled my eyes. "You mean we're not the only ones with dinosaurs for computers?"

"Guess not."

It was a long evening keeping up with fifteen deputies who were keeping up with all the calls for service. Nick phoned after ten o'clock to invite me over for a drink after work. I was afraid I'd be tempted to have one too many drinks, so I headed home instead.

My house was quiet, like usual. That night it seemed downright lonesome. I thought about calling my mom. To be honest, I was surprised she hadn't called me again, with the murders all over the news. It was late and I was planning to go to church with her in the morning, so I decided not to call.

I paced. I soaked in a bath of lavender salts. I sipped on milk warmed in the microwave. Finally, I grabbed the book from my nightstand I had started reading at least fifty times, only to fall asleep before getting very far. I was wide awake, but not absorbing much anyway. The author's words waited, inviting on the page, but I couldn't concentrate. I was too restless. On edge.

A sense of foreboding was growing inside of me, tightening my muscles and bringing tears to my eyes. How were we going to solve these heinous crimes?

Chapter 36

Alvie

Alvie had to take the day off from her mission. Since Speiss and Browne had both been away from home the day before, chances were they'd be gone for the whole weekend. Probably be coming home sometime that night. Half the people at work spent weekends at their cabins. The whole project was just getting so complicated. Alvie had made a decision. If she could get away easily later that night, she'd make a try for one of them. If not, it meant the next day would be better. Most people were home on Monday nights anyway.

She and Rebecca had the day to spend together. Alvie would make it Rebecca's day and do whatever she wanted. The world out there could take care of its own problems. Alvie could wait one more day to take care of hers.

Chapter 37

I rolled out of bed feeling as if I had been run over by a bulldozer, but there was no point trying to sleep. It was Sunday morning, and my mother had been nagging me forever to go to church with her. If there was ever a time in my life when I needed spiritual comfort and help, it was then. My professional life was in turmoil, with the entire county in a panic over the murders of Arthur Franz and Marshall Kelton. It was extremely upsetting for all of us—the families, friends, co-workers, sheriff's personnel, and the citizens in general. The people were looking to the sheriff's department to solve the terrible crimes as soon as possible, increasing the pressure we already felt.

I drove to my mother's house to see if she wanted a ride to church. When I pulled into her driveway, I was surprised to see Smoke's personal SUV parked there. I was even more surprised to find him standing in my mother's kitchen, pouring coffee into a mug, wearing nothing but boxer shorts.

"Smoke?" I said.

He looked like he hadn't slept for days and regarded me for a minute before speaking. "Corky. I never see you in a dress. You look very pretty."

"And you look . . . not dressed," I countered, trying not to stare, but his body was beautiful.

I had seen many naked, and near naked, men performing my duties as an officer of the law, and had come to expect any one over the age of forty to be at least a little flabby. But not Smoke. He was long, lean, defined muscle, with abs that would be the envy of anyone, at any age.

"Yeah, well, it's not what it looks like. Coffee?"

He handed the mug to me, turned his back, grabbed his jeans from the back of a kitchen chair, and slipped them on. I watched, scrutinizing his movements and body. I spotted a faded, two-inch scar on his right shoulder blade, the only noticeable flaw on him.

Smoke turned back to me as he retrieved his tee shirt. He slid it over his head and arms, then pulled it over his waistline. I couldn't stop gawking. He studied my face a second and frowned slightly. If we hadn't known each other so well, it would have been an even more awkward moment.

"Your mother was nearly a basket case last night and didn't want to be alone. You were working, so I spent the night. On the couch," Smoke said.

"Where is she?"

"Still sleeping, I'm sure. She practically wore out the carpets walking around most of the night. I think she finally passed out from sheer exhaustion a couple of hours ago."

"What was wrong? Did something happen?" I asked.

"You know her better than I do. She's worried—about you, and about everybody else who lives in, or works for, the county." A lot of people.

"Poor Mom. She can be her own worst enemy sometimes." The coffee Smoke had brewed was good, almost espresso.

"She went through a lot when she was young, with your dad and all." He appeared lost in thought as he sipped his coffee. "Why are you up so early, all dressed up?"

"Church. I was going to see if Mom wanted a ride."

"Yeah, I'd let her sleep. I'll stay here 'til she wakes up. Later this afternoon, I'm going to the courthouse to check on the data from court admin. Palmer called a little while ago—that's what woke me up—to tell me he has the list of inmates from the last twelve years who were on psychotropic drugs. He put it on my desk. We can start cross referencing with the court cases when they're ready."

"That seems like a huge job," I said.

239

He scratched his arm then shrugged. "Well, we'll find out. What are you gonna do? I don't think I can bill the county for all the O.T. I'm working."

"You're earning it. But when are you going to catch up on your sleep? I don't want you getting sick on top of everything else, and I know you haven't slept much lately."

Smoke grinned above the rim of his coffee mug. "You don't think three hours total for two nights is enough for an old guy like me?"

"No."

I talked to my mother before I went on duty for the evening shift. She was planning to spend the day, and maybe the night, with Gramps, so I didn't have to worry. I wandered through the sheriff's department and found Smoke at his desk thumbing through pages, poring over the list from the jail administrator.

"Corinne," he said when I slid a chair next to him.

"Elton," I countered. "Got anything?" I plopped onto the chair.

His face crinkled in a grin, then sobered. "I don't know. A lot of familiar names. I was going to cross off the ones I know are dead, or spending their days in a state hospital or prison, but at this point we can't rule out anyone. Whoever left his fingerprints on the soda cans is not on file, so that means it could be a friend, or loony family member, of one of these guys."

Smoke pulled off his glasses and pinched the area between his eyes. "I'm still waiting on court admin. Sheriff is home today, hopefully resting. I think all the events of the last two days have taken another year or two off his life." He shook his head.

I needed to clear the air and changed the subject. "Smoke, I'm sorry if I was rude this morning."

"Not a problem. I shouldn't have been wandering around in my skivvies. I wasn't really awake."

"I was just a little shocked. I mean, not that it's really my business, but thinking of you and my mom, together . . ."

"We're not."

"Smoke, I stopped by my mother's the other night and saw you kissing . . . 'where there's "Smoke" there's fire.'"

"I let you in on that, and you're going to throw it in my face the rest of my life?"

"Maybe," I teased.

He smiled despite himself. "I'm actually a little embarrassed you saw that. I admit, we did get caught up in the moment, but what you saw is all there was." He picked up my hand and held it. "I have known your mother most of my life, and been friends with her for almost that long. I thought we could take it to the next level, but . . . I don't think Kristen wants that, and I'm not so sure I do either." He squeezed my hand, dropped it gently, then stretched back in his chair.

"John Carl thinks she still believes my father will come back," I said.

"John Carl may have hit the nail right on the head. And how do you compete with a ghost?"

I shook my head. "I don't know, Smoke. John Carl and I have lived with our father's ghost all of our lives. I guess we just grew up accepting that he was part of the family. We couldn't see him, but we knew he was there."

Sergeant Chip Roth gave me the rundown of the day shift. The suspicious person calls were down to a more manageable rate, thank goodness. The sheriff had assigned two extra deputies to the shift to act as rovers, as needed.

My personal cell rang a little after seven p.m. "Hi, Corky, I'm home."

"Sara. How was your weekend?"

"Good for the few minutes here and there I could put Winnebago County out of my mind. But I did spend a lot of time playing with my new niece. She is the cutest baby I have ever seen. So, you still busy with calls?" she asked.

I pulled in behind a car doing thirty-eight miles an hour in a thirty-mile-an-hour speed zone. The driver must have seen me and immediately slowed to twenty-eight miles an hour. "Not like yesterday, but they're still keeping us hopping. Are you unpacked?"

"Working on it right now. That's a funny question for you to ask."

"Don't think I'm paranoid, but I want you to stay at my house tonight," I told her.

"Paranoid about what?"

"Until we find Arthur and Marshall's killer, it would just make me feel better."

"They were lawyers—I'm not a lawyer," she argued.

"No, but someone was in your home last week, and someone got Marshall in his home."

"Corky! You're scaring me."

"I'm scaring *me*. Sara, you have the key to my house, so make yourself comfortable and I'll see you when my shift ends." End of discussion.

"Can I bring my laundry?"

"Of course. And food might be a good idea."

"Kristen didn't fill your fridge this weekend?" she teased.

"Not before I went to work, but you never know, by now there may be a four course meal waiting for us," I said, then let out a little "huh!"

"In my dreams. It's bad you and I practically survive on deli food and frozen dinners."

"Thank God for the occasional treat of my mother's cooking," I added. "Later."

Smoke phoned me at nine-fifteen to tell me Sandy Kress had gone back to the courthouse to check the report on the court cases

Arthur Franz and Marshall Kelton had shared. The report had finished running and produced a list of 1,463 cases. Some of the plaintiffs appeared more than once, and Sandy estimated there was somewhere in the neighborhood of 1,100 individuals to choose from.

I returned to the sheriff's department shortly after ten-thirty to complete and file my evening reports. When I opened my briefcase, the first paper I pulled out was the goofy, unexplained note I had received the day of Judge Fenneman's funeral. "WHAT MAKES SUICIDE AN ACCIDENT?" Just one more thing to ponder in the midst of a lot of other things.

I stared at the sheet for a moment then heard myself yell, "Oh my God!"

I couldn't believe I hadn't noticed it before. I ran to the evidence room and retrieved the photos from the scenes of Arthur's and Marshall's deaths. I couldn't wait to get back to the squad room. I removed the photos—first Arthur's, then Marshall's. "Oh my God!" I repeated.

Smoke answered on the second ring, sounding groggy. "You're never going to believe this. I think Judge Fenneman was murdered by the same guy that killed Arthur and Marshall."

"Who is this?" he croaked.

"Very funny."

Smoke cleared his throat. "Okay, tell me."

"You know that note I got? The one that said, 'What makes suicide an accident?'"

"Yeah."

"I'm ninety-nine point nine percent sure it was printed on the same printer as the alleged suicide notes of Arthur and Marshall."

"No shit?"

"No shit."

"Shit."

"Now what?" I asked.

"I'll fax a copy of the note to the BCA first thing tomorrow and have Questioned Documents do a comparison for us. Leave me a copy on my desk. I'll call Twardy, let him know what you think."

"You're going to call him tonight?" Better him than me.

"He'd be mad if we waited until morning. He is the chief law enforcement officer for the department."

Sara gave me a hug, more than happy to see me. "Corky, your house is kinda scary at night. I'm used to being surrounded by neighbors and the lights from their houses. Out here the only lights are the stars."

I glanced out my picture window. "One of the things I love about being away from the lights of town—you can see the stars."

"Fill me in on the latest news. Any leads?"

Sara followed me around as I pulled off my duty belt, watching my nightly ritual of checking my Glock and putting it in my bed stand. I took off my uniform and laid it on a side chair, then slipped into my pajamas, relaying the events of the weekend in detail.

I plopped down on the bed, and Sara did the same. "But the kicker—you're not going to believe this—I think the same guy that killed Arthur and Marshall also killed Judge Fenneman."

"No way!" Sara's eyes blinked, then grew large with surprise.

"Way," I answered.

"But Judge Fenneman's death was ruled accidental. What did they call it?"

"Sundowning," I said, and she mouthed, "Oh, yeah."

"And Arthur's and Marshall's deaths were ruled suicides. And what did that note say, the anonymous one I got? Here." I pulled my copy of the note from my briefcase, handed it to Sara and pointed to the words. "Now the note makes a little more sense. If the person who killed Fenneman wanted it to look like a suicide, but the death was ruled accidental, I'm guessing he figured his note would inspire further investigation, and the cause of death would be changed to suicide. Who knows?"

Sara shook her head. "That doesn't make sense."

"Not to you and me, but I don't think the killer's elevator goes to the top floor, which makes him even scarier. Who knows what he'll do? That is really a bold act to get a patient out of his hospital bed, not to mention following Arthur to his lunch site and killing him by a public landing where anyone might show up. And how about Marshall? Killing him in his home on a Sunday afternoon? His brother could have come in right in the middle of it."

"This is so freaky." Sara shivered, then rubbed her arms. "I'll never be able to get to sleep tonight. Let's talk about something else. Tell me about your love life. How is Nick?"

Nick. "Gosh, I haven't seen him for a few days. I've hardly talked to him, even. With all this going down, there hasn't been a lot of time."

"You have to make time," Sara reminded me.

"I know. Working evenings and weekends doesn't help." I paused, then confessed. "Sara, there's something wrong with me."

"What do you mean?"

"I feel stupid telling you."

"We're best friends. You know you can tell me anything. It must be juicy. I didn't think anything embarrassed you."

"Okay, you are going to think I am totally screwed up. You know, I really thought I was falling for Nick, and then yesterday morning I went to my mother's house and Smoke was standing in the kitchen in his boxer shorts."

"*Your* mother's?" She raised her eyebrows in surprise.

"Yes. Now get this. After I got over my initial shock of seeing Smoke almost naked, I realized I'm attracted to him." I let the words sink into Sara's mind for a moment. "And, the worse part, I felt a little jealous of my mother."

Sara patted the bed and moved closer. "Okay, let me get this straight. Smoke sleeps with your mother, then the morning after, you see him in her kitchen, find him attractive, and feel jealous of your mother?"

It sounded worse out loud.

"He did stay over, but he didn't sleep with her," I explained. "He stayed because she was scared. You and I both know Smoke has been interested in my mother for years—it's not exactly a secret. And now, just lately, they've had dinner a couple of times. But my mother's still in love with my father."

"Who was a good friend of Smoke," Sara added.

I gave myself a slight bop on my forehead with my fist. "Yes. Just tell me I'm totally screwed up. I already know I am."

Sara reached over and squeezed my hand. "Who isn't when it comes to love? It would be great if everything was black and white, but in matters of the heart, things can get pretty muddled. You know the three words that describe why I haven't gotten married: Jeff, Kyle and Barry."

I smiled at Sara. "Yeah, I guess. But why Smoke all of a sudden? He has been one of my best friends for a long time. And he's a lot older."

"And very attractive. And smart. And kind. Maybe it's because he's a good friend. You know him, you trust him." She paused. "But what about Nick?"

"I just don't know. Maybe I'm just scared how I fell for Nick so easily, and we've only spent a few evenings together. You know what he asked me when I told him I've never had a serious relationship?"

Sara raised her eyebrows. "What?"

"He asked if the reason I haven't dated much is because I'm afraid I'll fall in love, then the guy will die and leave me alone. Like my father's death left my mother alone."

"That's kinda heavy—what'd you say to that?"

"I guess I didn't answer." I picked up a pillow and hugged it to my chest.

"Well, what do you think?"

"I don't know. He could be right, I guess. I have never seriously wondered about it before."

"Okay, to take it a step further—do you think you are looking for a father figure in Smoke, you know, a substitute for the father you never had?"

"Geez, Sara, are you my psychoanalyst all of a sudden?"

"You brought it up, wondering if you're 'screwed up.'"

I made a face at her, crossing my eyes, sticking out my tongue. "I don't know what to say. I don't even know how I should feel. But when I really think about it, I guess I didn't know what I was missing not having a father—a live one, that is. My two grandpas were always there for John Carl and me. They did more than enough trying to make up for the dad we lost. So am I looking for a substitute father in Smoke? Maybe, maybe not. Am I avoiding a commitment with Nick because I'm afraid I'll lose him? Maybe, maybe not."

Sara gave me a sympathetic smile and a look that said, "What can I say?" I tossed the pillow at her.

Chapter 38

The sheriff called me in at nine o'clock Monday morning for a meeting with Smoke and the five other Winnebago County investigators to review the cases on Arthur Franz, Marshall Kelton, and Judge Fenneman. It was a toss-up as to who looked more haggard, Sheriff Twardy or Smoke.

"Okay, Dawes, tell us what you got," the sheriff directed at Smoke.

"I faxed a copy of that anonymous note Sergeant Aleckson received to the BCA this morning, and her hunch was correct. Questioned Documents confirmed all three documents, the two 'suicide notes' and that one-liner note, were all printed on the same printer. That gives a positive link to the three deaths, and it narrows the search on the court cases to ones the three of them shared."

Smoke swallowed a sip of coffee. "Court admin will run that computer search tonight, after court shuts down for the day. I started checking on all the former inmates who were prescribed psychotropic meds, comparing that against the list of court cases, but now I'll wait until I have the shorter list on the cases all three of them had together."

"What about the pharmacies?" I asked. "Are you still planning to get a warrant for those records?"

Smoke nodded. "If need be. We'll see what shows up when we compare the court cases and the inmate med records from the jail," he said.

Sheriff Twardy pointed at two of the investigators. "Okay, Harrison and Conley, this case is priority one, so help Dawes with whatever he needs. And Aleckson, good job recognizing the connection between the three notes. You work until seventeen hundred then take the rest of the evening off."

A kudo and an evening off. "Thank you, sir."

"Okay, back to work, everyone. I'm going to sit on this latest discovery, that Fenneman was likely murdered . . ." His voiced cracked and tears gathered in his eyes. "I'm not going public with the latest info for a day or so. I'll talk to Clarice Moy, but keep it from the public until we have a little more to go on. Everybody okay with that?"

We all nodded then filed out of the sheriff's office in silence, wondering what we were up against. None of us had suspected Judge Fenneman had been killed until the previous night. The day before we'd had two murders; now another made three. Would our killer strike again, or was he done? Solving the three murders would take cooperative hard work from everyone in the department, and lots and lots of luck.

Chapter 39

Alvie

Alvie was working the day shift, nine-thirty a.m. to six p.m. Her least favorite time to be at the nursing home. The administrator and her secretary, chaplain, maintenance guys, program director and staff, human services, and director of nursing were there, in addition to all the other workers. It was too many people and gave Alvie claustrophobia. She was glad to escape to the break room by herself a little after one o'clock. She picked up the Sunday edition of the *Star Tribune* metro section and almost stopped breathing. The top headline read, *Winnebago Attorneys' Deaths Investigated as Murders.*

Alvie's head began to pound again, and she had to concentrate to keep the newsprint in focus. *Sergeant Corinne Aleckson of the Winnebago County Sheriff's Department found evidence which opened an investigation into the deaths of Winnebago County Attorney Arthur Franz and Public Defender Marshall Kelton. Arthur Franz was found dead in his vehicle July 22. Marshall Kelton was found dead at his home on July 26. Both deaths were initially listed as suicides, but the newfound evidence has led authorities to believe both men were murdered. Sheriff Dennis Twardy held a press conference yesterday—"*

Sweat gathered under Alvie's arms and beaded on her forehead. Why hadn't she killed the little sergeant and her friend, that probation officer bitch, when she had the chance? In fact, she'd had more than one chance. Now look what letting down her guard for the sergeant had done. It had gotten her in trouble. Well, the little sergeant would have to be stopped, and soon. That very night, in fact. No matter how late Alvie had to wait for her, she would.

The probation officer, the detective, and the traitor all had to die in less than a month. She couldn't take a chance on what the sergeant would stumble onto next time. There wouldn't be a next time.

And what evidence? Alvie had left no fingerprints, and there were the suicide notes she had so carefully typed and traced. She hadn't left anything personal in the prosecutor's car or the defender's house. Alvie searched her memory bank, but came up with next to nothing. She had drunk soda in the field across the lake and might have left her cans there, but so what? Kids did that stuff all the time. They couldn't get her on soda cans. Besides, it had been raining so much that summer they were probably buried in mud.

It was a game the sheriff's department was playing, Alvie was sure of that. Like all the games the system had played with Nolan's life. They had played and played until it killed him. Well, it was about to stop. She'd see to that.

Chapter 40

I phoned Nick during a morning break. After our greetings I asked, "How was the science museum yesterday?"

"It was really something. I think I enjoyed the program more than the girls did, but they had fun too. The twins have been a great addition to Faith's life. How is your extended tour of duty going?" he asked.

A loaded question. "Okay. Just. A lot is going down, so we're putting in overtime trying to find our bad guy."

"I finally read the Sunday paper late last night. Quite a splash in the metro section. Any new leads?"

"Some, but we're still checking them out." I looked at the stack of papers on the table in front of me. "I'm actually working now, so I'll be off at five. You have dinner plans?"

Nick groaned. "Worse. I have a hospital board meeting at seven. But how about lunch?"

"Sorry, I'm taking Mom out. She's a little distraught with this whole business, and my chosen profession in general," I explained.

"She's your mother—she's bound to worry about her little girl. We could get together later, maybe watch a movie? I should be home by nine," Nick said.

"Sure, give me a call after your meeting. Sara is staying over for a few nights, but she often has things going on."

"Why is she staying at your house?" Nick wondered.

When I explained, he was kind enough not to tell me I was silly being concerned Sara might be in danger from the killer.

Lunch with Mother turned out to be a good thing for both of us. She needed reassurance everything would be okay, and for some reason, being with me always helped to calm her down when she was distressed. I think it was the part of me that reminded her of Carl. She had told me many times that she'd always felt safe when he was around. She had drawn strength from him somehow.

When my mother felt more relaxed, she started making plans. "Why don't you and Sara come over for dinner at Gramps' tonight? I'm doing a fish fry with those last fish you two caught. They've been in the freezer long enough, and Gramps has been after me to make them."

My favorite meal. "I can't speak for Sara, but I'd love to. What time?"

"We'll eat about seven. I have to do inventory this afternoon and probably won't finish until six."

I poked my head in Smoke's cubicle before I went off duty. "How are you doing?"

Smoke's drawn look had eased. "I am feeling downright human again. That four-hour nap was just what the doctor ordered." He smiled.

"Good. So court admin will be running that report about now?"

Smoke consulted his watch. "Sandy should be on that right about now."

"How late will you be here?" I wondered.

"Not real late—maybe eight, nine."

"Call me if you find something, or if you need me."

Smoke waved at me. "Will do. See you tomorrow."

Sara wasn't at my house when I got there. I listened to my phone messages, got out of uniform, and took a quick shower. My Grandpa Brandt didn't use his air conditioner, and his house was usually too warm for my comfort. I slipped into shorts and a tee shirt and stepped into my Haflinger sandals.

"Are you home?" Sara called out from the kitchen.

"Just coming down," I answered and headed down the steps.

Sara came out of the kitchen. "I bought a bottle of wine and set it on ice in the freezer to cool. I'm going to change then we'll have a glass before we go to dinner, okay?" Sara asked.

"More than okay," I said.

I sat on the couch and closed my eyes to relax and meditate for a few minutes, but images of Judge Fenneman, Arthur Franz, and Marshall Kelton filled my mind. They played like a video collection, jumping from one scene to the next and back again. Public servants, all dead by some sicko's hand. Why? What had they done? And was that same person after Sara? Arthur and Marshall had had over 1,400 cases together. And those two had shared umpteen cases with Judge Fenneman. Should Sara's probation clients be figured in the mix?

"Are you too tired for a glass of wine?" Sara's words shifted my thoughts.

I opened my eyes and focused on my friend. "No. I'm fine."

"Okay, you sit there and I'll get it." She returned minutes later with the drinks and settled on the overstuffed chair opposite me. "To good friends," Sara said and held up her glass in a toast.

"To good friends," I repeated and took a sip of wine. "Mmm, it's really good."

"I owe Arthur for all the wine advice he gave me over the years," Sara said, her voice cracking, tears gathering in her eyes.

"To Arthur." I held up my glass.

Sara smiled and raised her glass. "To Arthur."

"Sara, when we talked last night, did I mention I met another ghost from my past on Saturday?"

She drew her feet under. "No, who's that?"

"Jason Browne."

Sara thought for a second. "Wasn't that Nolan Eisner's partner in crime?"

"One and the same. You weren't his probation officer, too?" I asked.

Sara shook her head. "No, he wasn't one of mine. I think he was Carrie's, or maybe Dorothy's. I can't remember now. So where'd you see him?"

"Burglary complaint. Someone got in his house and stole a few bullets."

"Bullets?"

"I know, weird. I figured they got scared off in the middle of the theft and didn't get far."

"I have learned that nothing that happens in this business is too weird." She stood up. "Well, I have to go potty, and then I'm going to get a little more wine. How about you?"

"No, I'm good."

"He wasn't one of mine," but Nolan Eisner was! *Nolan Eisner, the common denominator.*

Nolan's criminal complaint jumped out of my memory bank from the day Smoke and I had searched Marshall Kelton's office. Judge Fenneman, Arthur Franz, Marshall Kelton, Elton Dawes, Sara Speiss: all involved with the arrest, conviction and prison sentence of Nolan Eisner. And Jason Browne was the one who had turned him in to the authorities. And who was in the hospital the night Judge Fenneman died? Rebecca Eisner. Alvie Eisner, her grandmother and Nolan's mother, could certainly have the motive to want those people dead.

I jumped up, unclipped my cell phone from the waistband of my shorts, and hit Smoke's number. Before I could lift the phone to my ear, I heard a low, haunting, emotionless voice behind me command, "Turn around."

Alvie Eisner stood in the entrance of the living room with one large arm wrapped around Sara, her hand clapped over Sara's mouth. The other hand held a gun, which she slowly waved between Sara's head and me.

Sara's green eyes were circles filled with raw terror on a face drained of color. Her chest was rising and falling rapidly beneath Eisner's arm. I was so shocked I thought I was imagining things for a second. Then reality reached my brain, and I knew what I saw was real. My vision tunneled, blurring around the edges, focusing on my friend and the monster holding her captive in the sanctuary of my living room.

I remembered my phone and prayed the call had gone through to Smoke and not to his voicemail. I couldn't hear him with my ear so far from the phone, but determined the one chance Sara and I had for survival was if Smoke heard us. I carefully tipped the receiver slightly upward and toward where Eisner and Sara stood, hoping Eisner wouldn't notice.

"Alvie Eisner. What are you doing in my home?" I asked loudly. She stared at me with a hate that forced prickles of fear through my entire body. Somehow, it felt both hot and cold at the same time. My bowels loosened and my limbs twitched. I gripped the phone so it wouldn't fall from my numbed hand. Despair threatened to suck me in, to consume me, when I realized Sara and I were about to die.

"Put the gun down. It will only make things worse," I commanded, my voice more steady than I felt.

Alvie Eisner looked disgusted. "Worse for you. Not for me. Not for Nolan."

"What about Rebecca?" I shot at her.

Alvie Eisner's nostrils flared a little and her eyes narrowed. "I'm doing this for Rebecca. Now, shut up. It will be over soon."

I prayed for more time. "Before I die, tell me. Did you kill Judge Fenneman, Arthur Franz, and Marshall Kelton?"

She didn't hesitate to answer. "Yes."

Alvie Eisner had nothing more to lose by killing Sara and me. When she was caught for the other murders, she would be going away for life. What were two more victims?

Stall. As long as possible.

"One last thing. Why are you doing this? And why us, Sara and me?" I asked.

Emotion formed around Eisner's words. "Because they killed my son. You shouldn't have gotten in the middle of this, but you did, so now you have to die along with the killers."

I met Sara's eyes and blinked my own toward my cell phone. I nodded my head, ever so slightly, in an attempt to signal her I wouldn't let us die without a fight. Words from my training, "I will survive!" spurred me on and gave me inner fortitude.

Alvie Eisner towered over my small friend. I mentally practiced throwing my phone at her head and then, with all my strength, hurled it. The phone hit its target, just behind Eisner's left temple, setting her off balance and staggering to the right. Her gun fired in my direction. If I was hit, I didn't feel it. I saw the gun fly toward my computer cabinet, the same direction Eisner was headed, trying to regain her footing.

"Run!" I screamed at Sara and she did. "Call nine-one-one."

I don't know how I got to the gun before Eisner, but I must have dived for it. I found myself on top of it, working my hand under me to get a firing grip. Suddenly, her crushing weight was on top of me. I worked both arms under my chest and squirmed to get my knees up under my stomach, then lifted my butt and bucked Eisner off my back. She rolled with a thud, but grabbed my leg before I could scramble away.

I aimed the gun at her chest and pulled the trigger. It didn't fire. I pulled again—damn! I didn't dare take my eyes off Eisner for the split second it would take to find the safety button to see if it was on. I was accustomed to my Glock, which had no safety.

Dear God! Eisner was strong, made even stronger by her blinding hatred. My right leg was pinned to the ground, my ankle held in a vice-grip—first by Eisner's right hand, then her knee as she lunged for her gun. I pulled the trigger again, hoping the gun had momentarily jammed when I had tried to fire before. No luck. I moved the gun as far as I could from Eisner as she reached for it, then threw it across the room with as much power as I could muster.

When the gun left my hand, she slapped me across the face before I could block her blow. I was stunned for a second, close to seeing stars then saw both her hands seemingly aimed for my throat. I delivered a karate chop to her windpipe, and she exhaled a choking "gghhh" sound.

I moved enough to get a little distance and delivered a forceful blow to Eisner's ribs with my free leg. She howled in pain, and when she retched, I broke free. I rolled away, jumped to my feet, and retrieved the gun I had pitched.

"Lie face down on the ground with your hands on your back!" I heard the loud order behind me. I felt a little shaky, but held my position with Eisner's gun aimed at her head. I glanced quickly to locate the safety and slid it off. I was ready to shoot her if it came to that.

Deputy Brian Carlson stormed in, followed by Mandy Zubinski and Todd Mason. All had their guns drawn and pointed at Eisner. She looked at them, then at me, a stunned expression of disbelief on her face. We would not hesitate to shoot her if she tried anything, and Eisner knew it. She put her face in the carpet and stretched her hands to her back. Carlson moved in cautiously, kneeled on her shoulder, and handcuffed her.

Mason and Zubinski got on either side of Eisner and guided her to her feet and out the door. I noticed Sara leaning against the wall, arms clutched around herself, tears streaming down her cheeks, her face blotched with red. Carlson reached his hand out to Sara, led her to the couch and held her, petting her face and speaking softly.

I didn't see Smoke until he was standing inches in front of me, his eyes wet with unshed tears. He lifted me into his arms and I rested against him, drawing from his warmth and strength.

Smoke's voice was quivering. "I have never had five more panic-filled minutes in my life. If anything had happened to you . . ." He pulled away slightly, his hands on my shoulders. "Let me look at you. God, you're bleeding."

"I am? Where?" I looked down.

He touched the areas as he said them. "The left side of your face is all red. Your right cheekbone. Looks like rug rash. The side of your neck—scratch marks. Your knees. Again, rug rash. You have to fight that ox?" he asked.

"A little."

"She fought like a little banshee. I've never seen anything like it," Sara offered from the couch.

"That's my girl."

Smoke held my head, stroking my jawbone with his thumbs. He bent down and kissed my forehead, my nose, then brushed my lips with his. His kisses were soft and warm, and very familiar somehow. I was both touched and surprised. Smoke had never been intimate with me before that moment. Understandably so.

Smoke slid his arm around my waist and led me to the armchair across from the couch. It was the same one Sara had sat in ten minutes earlier, casually sipping wine. I found that almost impossible to comprehend. Smoke swung his leg over the arm of the chair and sat down close to me, facing Sara and Carlson. He rested one hand on my shoulder. I noticed both Sara and Brian had interested, questioning looks on their faces. Thank God it wasn't Mandy Zubinski sitting there. More fodder for her rumor mill.

"All things considered, now that the two of you are safe, I can say thanks for cracking the case, as awful as that must have been. Tell me what happened," Smoke said.

I looked at Sara and nodded for her to speak. "Well, we were having a glass of wine then I left to use the bathroom and get a refill. When I came out of the half bath off the kitchen, Alvie Eisner was standing there, pointing a gun at me. Before I could yell, she grabbed me and dragged me into the living room."

Sara shook her head, trying to absorb her own words. "Smoke, Brian said you heard the conversation between Corky and Eisner and had communications get the closest squads here. How?"

"Thanks to Corky's fast thinking." Smoke tucked a finger under my chin. "How did you manage to dial my number with a gun pointed at you?" he asked me.

"I didn't. I dialed just before. When Sara was in the other room, all of a sudden it occurred to me that Alvie Eisner was a likely suspect. I was going to tell you, but before I could talk, she was here. In the flesh. With Sara in a death grip. At first, I actually thought I was hallucinating." I turned to face him. "You know how I've been having all those strange feelings and intuitions since this whole nightmare began with Judge Fenneman's death? But back to the phone call. I prayed you could hear what was going on, Smoke. Thank you." I squeezed his hand.

My mother came rushing in and scooped me in her arms. "What on earth happened? I looked out my window and saw two squad cars drive by, toward town, so I went to the bedroom, and there were two more squad cars here. You're all messed up, dear. What on earth happened?"

She would not like the story one little bit.

"I'm all right. I'll tell you all about it, Mom, but can we talk about it later?"

Sheriff Twardy, three investigators, plus a host of deputies, made their way through my doors in the next twenty minutes. The sheriff ordered me to take the next three days off, which, added to my scheduled days off, meant that except for writing my report, I wouldn't have to be at work for a week. Time for some debriefing, refocusing.

Twardy fussed over me for a while, then asked, "Are you sure you don't want to get checked out at the hospital?"

"I'm sure. I may be a little stiff tomorrow, but I'll be fine." I was grateful my karate training, ballet lessons, and physical conditioning had prevented any real injury.

"How about I bring dinner over here tonight instead of you and Sara coming over to Gramps'?" Mother asked.

Food? "Mom, thanks, but I really don't have any appetite."

Mother took charge of my house the rest of the evening, making coffee for my fellow officers, tidying the living room, attending to Sara and me. When Nick phoned, Mother told him the story, and he hurried over to be sure I was still in one piece. He stayed for a long time, holding me, telling me to consider a career change. Eventually, everyone left except Sara and my mother, and I didn't argue when they insisted on spending the night.

It was after midnight, and I lay in bed staring at the thin stream of light creeping in from the hallway, spanning my bedroom ceiling. My mother was next to me, her protective arm across my stomach, puffing little breaths of sleep. Tears rolled from my eyes and dropped to the pillow supporting my head. I was overcome with the raw emotion of gratitude for being alive. Alvie Eisner had been determined to send me to my death, but I wasn't ready to go. There was so much more in the world I wanted to do, see, touch, hear, taste, smell, and experience.

And there were many unanswered questions to settle. What would happen at Alvie Eisner's trial? Would she be ruled competent even to stand trial? What would become of sweet little Rebecca? Could we locate another family member to take care of her, to love her? How would she ever understand it all?

And, on a personal level, what would happen in my relationship with Nick? With Smoke? Would our professional relationship remain the same constant it had been for six years?

It was almost too much to ponder, especially in light of all the emotions I had felt as I fought for my life, and in the moments after. I put my hand over my mother's, closed my eyes, and said my prayers.

Epilogue

Questioning Alvie Eisner was a painful process for Smoke and the other detectives. Every answer had to be prodded, slowly squeezed out of her. Eventually, they pieced together a cursory summary of her life. Alvie's mother had left when she and her brother Henry were children. She didn't know where her mother was, or if she was still alive.

Alvie hinted at, but wouldn't elaborate on, the abuse she and her brother had suffered at the hands of the uncle who lived with them. Her brother lived in a local group home and had multiple mental problems. Alvie said Rebecca and Henry were the only living family she knew about. She would not name Nolan's father, but said he was dead.

We worked hard to locate Rebecca's mother, without success. There was no family to assume Rebecca's care, so Winnebago County Human Services placed her in foster care while continuing to search for her mother. I longed to visit Rebecca, but given my involvement in her grandmother's criminal case, I was advised to stay away for the time being.

It didn't take investigators long to discover where Alvie had gotten the haloperidol to drug Arthur Franz and Marshall Kelton. Butler Drug was relieved they had not made such a grave error in Henry Eisner's prescription refill. Analysis of Judge Fenneman's IV tubing revealed traces of haloperidol, also.

DNA testing confirmed Alvie Eisner was the one who had smoked the cigarettes and drank the soda in the cornfield by Beebe Lake. It also proved she had licked the stamp and the seal on the envelope of the note she'd sent me. It was her straight, gray strand of hair that had caught in the hinge of Judge Fenneman's eyeglasses on the night he died.

When we searched the Eisner farm, we found more supporting evidence to build an airtight case against Alvie, with or without her confession. Her size ten Propet work shoes were a perfect fit in the footprint cast collected from the cornfield. We found a man's jumpsuit and a mustache in the trunk of her old Chevy. Smoke and I had seen the same vehicle on Marshall's street the morning his body was found. We had thought it was a man behind the wheel, but it was Alvie Eisner. When I showed the picture of the automobile to Mrs. Sanford, Sara's neighbor, she said it looked just like the car that was parked on her street. She was sure of it when she saw it again.

We located the three bullets taken from the Browne's home, Arthur Franz's Palm Pilot, and a personal calendar belonging to Marshall Kelton. We found two murder-suicide notes, one allegedly written by Jason Browne and the other by Sara Speiss, printed on the same printer as all the other notes, the same printer connected to the computer in Alvie's living room.

There was a box under Alvie's bed containing the papers from Nolan's criminal case, and evidence someone had practiced tracing over the officials' signatures. We found a scratch paper containing a series of numbers. The hospital confirmed it was the code to disarm the emergency exit door. We talked to the nurse who had smoked a cigarette with Alvie Eisner outside that exit.

We discovered five pieces of paper that had been torn from one larger sheet of paper, each containing a name and description: Jason Browne, double-crosser; Marshall Kelton, useless public defender; Sara Speiss, spineless probation officer; Arthur Franz, merciless county attorney; Detective Dawes, heartless cop. Holding the pieces of paper in my hands sent chills though me, grateful for the living, mournful over the dead.

The most shocking, unexpected discovery in our search of the Eisner property was made in Alvie's spare bedroom. A bullet was lodged in a piece of woodwork surrounding the window, making the investigators curious. On closer look, they noticed a dark stain on the wood floor under a throw rug and used a Luma Lite to confirm the stain was blood. In addition to the large pool on the floor, many lavender splatters appeared on the walls and floor, consistent with the blood spray from a close range shooting.

During questioning, Alvie broke down and actually wept as she relayed how she had killed her uncle—whom she finally named as Nolan's father—when she caught him sexually abusing Nolan. The uncle was not employed and apparently had no friends, since a search of the records revealed no one had reported his disappearance. If Alvie had reported her uncle's abuse all those years before, things might have turned out differently, but that was a big "if."

Alvie's life and perceptions had spiraled downward, leading her to justify and embrace acts of murder. Whether she was found competent to stand trial or not, in my mind she was a madwoman who had robbed three precious people of their lives. Judge Fenneman, Arthur Franz, and Marshall Kelton had died because Alvie Eisner's warped mind decided they deserved to. It would be up to the courts to determine her punishment. What she had done to her uncle was between her and God, as far as I was concerned.

There were still times in the weeks that followed when I was jolted from sleep, terrified because I was being choked by Alvie Eisner in a nightmare, her piercing stare as cold as her hands. My heart pounded when I awoke—threatening to explode in my chest, my bed drenched with sweat, chilling me to the bone. *She is in the Winnebago County Jail*, I would remind myself, speaking the words out loud, over and over. One night I called the jail to be certain the words were true.

Yes, Alvie Eisner was still locked up in jail awaiting trial, stopped before she could hurt or kill more people. And, as horrendous as it was, the experience with Eisner renewed my dedication to stay vigilant in the career I sometimes hated, but mostly, truly loved.

Also by Christine Husom

Buried in Wolf Lake A family's Golden Retriever brings home the dismembered leg of a young woman and the Winnebago County Sheriff's Department launches an investigation unlike any other. Who does the leg belong to, and where is the rest of her body? Sergeant Corinne Aleckson and Detective Elton Dawes soon discover they are up against an unidentified psychopath who targets women with specific physical features. Are there other victims, and will they learn the killer's identity in time to prevent another brutal murder?

An Altar By the River A man phones the Winnebago County Sheriff's Department, frantically reporting his brother is armed with a large dagger and on his way to the county to sacrifice himself. Sergeant Corinne Aleckson takes the call, learning the alarming reasons behind the young man's death wish. When the department investigates, they plunge into the alleged criminal activities of a hidden cult and disturbing cover-up of an old closed-case shooting death. The cult members have everything to lose and will do whatever it takes to prevent the truth coming to light. But will they find the altar by the river in time to save the young man's life?

The Noding Field Mystery When a man's naked body is found staked out in a farmer's soybean field Sergeant Corinne Aleckson and Detective Elton Dawes are called to the scene. The cause of death is not apparent, and the significance of why he was placed there is a mystery. As Aleckson, Dawes, and the rest of their Winnebago Sheriff's

Department team gather evidence, and look for suspects and motive, they hit one dead end after another. Then an old nemesis escapes from jail and plays in the shocking end.

A Death in Lionel's Woods When a woman's emaciated body is found in a hunter's woods, Sergeant Corinne Aleckson is coaxed back into the field to assist Detective Smoke Dawes on the case. It seems the only hope for identifying the woman lies in a photo which was buried with bags of money under her body. Aleckson and Dawes plunge into the investigation that takes them into the world of human smugglers and traffickers, unexpectedly close to home. All the while, they are working to uncover the identity of someone who is leaving Corky anonymous messages and pulling pranks at her house. A Death in Lionel's Woods is a unpredictable roller coaster ride to the electrifying end.

Secret in Whitetail Lake Christine Husom has once again captured the essence of a rural Minnesota mystery as she draws readers into the Secret in Whitetail Lake. When the Winnebago County Sheriff's Department stumbles upon a car at the bottom of Whitetail Lake, what appears to be a probable accident from three decades earlier, turns into something far more sinister that makes this story a page turner.